JINXED

JINXED

A DOWN & OUT IN BEVERLY HEELS NOVEL

KATHRYN LEIGH SCOTT

Cumberland Press
New York

Chair image by Nicholas Evans
Interior design by Caitlin Alexander

Also available in e-book

TRADE PAPERBACK ISBN: 978-0-9862459-5-4

LIBRARY OF CONGRESS CONTROL NUMBER: 2015901010
CUMBERLAND PRESS, NEW YORK, NEW YORK

For author contact and press inquiries, or to order signed copies, please visit www.kathrynleighscott.com.

Books by Kathryn Leigh Scott

FICTION

Down and Out in Beverly Heels

Jinxed

Dark Passages

September Girl

NONFICTION

Last Dance at the Savoy

The Happy Hours

Now With You, Now Without

A Welcome Respite

The Bunny Years

Dark Shadows: Return to Collinwood

Dark Shadows Memories

Dark Shadows Almanac

Dark Shadows Companion

Lobby Cards: The Classic Films

Lobby Cards: The Classic Comedies

For Geoff, always and forever

1

"I'll ask you again," he says, his voice low. "Your husband's kidnapping was a hoax. You helped him disappear, right? Where is he?"

The FBI agent, his blinding white shirt open at the neck, leans in so close I can smell the warm raisin scent of his body. The question echoes in my mind with a dizzying sense of déjà vu. Why can't I remember anything?

He glances at the pages in his hand, then back to me, a sly gleam in his eye. "C'mon, you should know this, Meg."

Then it comes to me and I blurt, "No! You've got it all wrong. I had nothing to do with his disappearance. You have to believe me!" I really do have nothing to hide, but the truth sounds strained even to my ears, especially with a pair of caramel-brown eyes looking intently into mine.

"I know you were in on it, sweetheart, but that's okay." His voice is husky as he pulls me close and whispers, "Because it's you I'm after, not him."

I give him a quick punch in the shoulder and burst into laughter. "I'm reporting you to the Bureau, buster. You're not getting away with this!"

Jack drops the script in my lap and grins. "Try me."

"Later." I swing my legs up on the couch and bury my toes under his knees, wriggling them against the soft sun-bleached denim of his blue jeans. "Come on, you're supposed to run lines with me, not make them up." I toss the script back in his lap.

"What've you signed on for, anyway?"

"It's a webisode, an Internet series. You can watch it on a smartphone. An iPad. Maybe even your fancy Dick Tracy two-way wristwatch."

Jack makes a face as he shoves the script onto the coffee table.

"Hey, don't look at me like that. These days the phone rings and I say, 'Yes, where? What time?' I've gone from the silver screen to an LED screen the size of a Snickers bar."

Jack laughs and gets up, leaning over to give me a kiss. "How about a glass of wine? I want to hear more about this."

"You're out to make fun of me," I tease, my eyes following him appreciatively as he pads barefoot toward the kitchen.

His six-foot frame moves easily, a slim torso attesting to vigorous handball workouts and daily jogs—and, I would imagine, the rigors of his FBI job, though he doesn't talk much about it. Jack lives in a clearly defined Guy Pad, a one-bedroom condo overlooking the marshy Ballona wetlands, a coastal freshwater expanse just south of Los Angeles International Airport that was once owned by billionaire eccentric Howard Hughes. The musky smell of marshland and distant cawing of birds skimming over the grassy inlet drifts through the open balcony doors.

"No, seriously, tell me." Jack pulls a bottle from the wine cooler and opens it with a corkscrew mounted on the quartz countertop. He glances up. "Who's directing this mini extravaganza?"

"Cornelius Shaw, a sixteen-year-old kid who goes by the name Corky." I join him, perching on a stool at the counter. "He's into film noir and obsessed with Ida Lupino. How could I resist?"

Jack pours pinot grigio into two chilled glasses, hands me one and touches his glass to mine. "Sounds like a Turner Classic Movies geek. How did he find you?"

"Not through my agent, believe me. But these days you can track down anyone, especially if you're as resourceful as Corky. He's been making movies since he was twelve. Now his folks have given him a choice between auto insurance and a film budget, which gives you some idea of what I'm getting paid. His mom drives him everywhere. I bring my own lunch."

"Wait a minute, that scene we were reading takes place in some so-called FBI headquarters. That's a pretty elaborate location setup. Don't tell me he's going to try to sneak you into the Federal Building?"

"If he could, he would, believe me. Instead he does it all with CGI, or what passes for computer-generated imagery when you've got a vivid imagination and no money. It gives a whole new meaning to fixing it in post-production. You've heard of garage bands?

This is a garage film studio with the walls lined in blue cloth. At night, his dad parks the family Honda in there."

"And the upside?"

"Lots of close-ups?"

Jack laughs. "That's it?"

"What the hell, it's fun! I'm looking at blue bed sheets and imagining I'm in a city park or a jail cell. He fills in the background later on his computer. Everything feels primitive, yet it's all high-tech. And it's so collaborative, like the way it must have felt making two-reelers with Charlie Chaplin a hundred years ago, and—"

Jack leans in to give me a kiss. "And?"

"The kid is sweet and trying hard and maybe he's a young Orson Welles or Steven Spielberg . . . and, let's face it, he had me on Ida Lupino."

Jack smiles. "But you know he's riffing on what really happened to you, right?"

I swallow hard. Wine runs down my throat in a chilly river. I cough, stalling for time, then meet Jack's eyes. "Yeah. I figured he might have read a few news stories about me."

"You think?"

"Well, the title *Conman and His Lady* was a tip-off. Now he's calling it *Forsaken*. But I thought, why not? The story he's written is different from what really happened to me. The husband is caught and the money returned. I'm cleared. Life goes on."

"The way you wish it had happened."

I nod. Left unsaid is that in Corky's perfect film-noir world I wouldn't have lost everything I own, including my home, and ended up living on the streets in my "Ritz-Volvo." It's hard to get past the fact that the man I loved and married swindled so many other people besides me, destroying their lives, too.

"But what about you, Jack? Don't you wish things had gone differently on your end?"

Corky's teenage sensibilities don't run to nuance and his script is not subtle. While he couldn't know what was actually said during my interrogation, his tough-talking FBI agent pretty much lays it on the line.

"I don't have to do any intense memory work to prepare for that scene, you know?" I say to fill his silence. "I remember what it feels like to be grilled like that. I was truly scared and probably looked guilty as hell. C'mon, Jack, you were the one grilling me! You remember as well as I do."

My cheeks burn. If I'd just kept my mouth shut, by now he'd be unbuttoning the blinding white shirt and unzipping his sun-bleached jeans, and I'd be tearing off my own shirt and jeans. His face, so close to mine, with a shadow of stubble hollowing his cheeks, his close-cropped gray-flecked hair curling like goose down behind his ears, sends a wave of longing rocking through me—so why am I pursuing this?

I should be way past this by now, yet residual anger grips me. A year ago, FBI Agent Jack Mitchell was in charge of inves-tigating my fugitive husband and suspected me of being in on the scam. Does he still wonder what I knew and when I knew it?

I wonder the same thing: How much did Jack know? When did he know it? Had he given me an inkling of the FBI's history with the man I knew as Paul Stevens, I could have protected my-self. Burned into my brain is the sense that I was treated as noth-ing more than collateral damage.

If it's true that love doesn't care who owns it, I bought it at a terrific price with my second marriage. Paul made loving him easy, but that was his agenda, with a big payoff for him in the end. With Jack, love runs deeper, but trust still comes hard.

Perched on a stool, wine glass in hand, I look around Jack's sleek kitchen, seeing my future life as I could live it. The cup-boards are already equipped with two of everything, not just ser-vice for one, and there are pegs for two robes in the bathroom. What could be better than to live here with Jack in security and comfort, our past issues resolved and behind us? But it's not the case—yet. I'm not prepared to enter a relationship that's not on an equal footing. If trust is one challenge to overcome, the need to redeem myself is another.

Jack slides the base of his wine glass around in a slippery puddle on the countertop. "It's my job," he says quietly. "If I could undo the harm, I would."

I nod and sip my wine, preparing for my own admission. "You asked if I was aware this kid was exploiting my own ripped-from-the-headlines story, and I am. It was a clumsy way of letting you know I'm still picking at the scab. I wish I could stop."

"I think I knew that," he says, tapping my glass gently with his. "It takes time. For both of us." He slips his arm around my shoulder. "How about some fresh air?"

He tops up our wine glasses, and on our way to the balcony, I look around the familiar apartment, imagining myself nesting here permanently, not just roosting a night or two at a time. Jack, a widower, has created his own private space, a peaceful haven close to nature and ocean tides, where everything visible is rooted in the present. Not only is there no clutter, but there are no mementos from a past life. His slate appears wiped clean; the skills of his trade evident in that he's left no revealing clues for me to find. It's his choice, his own way of dealing with the death of his wife and the restrictions of his job.

I envy Jack for making peace with his loss and moving on. The night air is balmy, ruffling my hair as I lean back against the brushed steel railing. I catch a glimpse of the two of us in the inky reflection of the sliding glass doors, both of us barefoot, wine glasses in hand. I'm leaning into Jack, my bobbed ginger hair grazing his shoulder. We look like a carefree couple pictured in a cruise brochure, celebrating their happy, prosperous life together. I smile at the masquerade. *Who are these people?*

Jack, channeling an image of his own, says, "I'm off to Seattle in the morning. Maybe when I get back we could drive out to the desert for the weekend. How about staying at Two Bunch Palms?"

"I'd love it." I'm more than ready to embrace the present. I wrap my arms around him, hugging the warmth of his body as we kiss. Then we look at each other, both startled as we feel my hipbone vibrating against his. My hand dives into my pocket to retrieve my cellphone.

"It was good for me," Jack laughs. "You?"

I give him a lingering kiss, barely registering the caller's name before answering.

A female voice asks for Meg Barnes. "Yes, that's me. What? Yes, of course. Where? What time?"

In less than a minute, the call is over and I'm gaping at Jack in disbelief. "That was *The Today Show*. They want to do an interview with me to celebrate the twentieth anniversary of *Holiday*. I can't believe it's been that long since I played Jinx!"

"That's wonderful. I'll catch the show in Seattle. When do you leave?"

"I'm flying to New York the day after tomorrow. But I'll be back before the weekend, I promise."

"What about your film noir?"

"After tomorrow, it looks like Corky's dad gets to park the Honda in the garage for a day or two."

"I'm glad we're still on for Two Bunch Palms." Jack puts his arm around my shoulders and looks up at the star-filled sky. "It's nice out here tonight."

I turn into his embrace and murmur, "I had an even nicer place in mind inside."

"Funny," he says, smiling. "I was just thinking the same thing."

Even with water gushing in the sink, I'm able to hear the CNN reporter in Seattle announce, " . . . body of a teenage girl found early yesterday morning has been identified as a Ukrainian student missing for two months. Homeland Security and FBI agents investigating the case say . . . "

At the mention of the FBI, I stop cold, my toothbrush wedged in my mouth, listening for Agent Jack Mitchell's name. He's still in Seattle and chances are he's part of the field operation investigating the teenager's death. It wouldn't be the first time I've seen him on television speaking about a breaking case he hadn't yet mentioned to me. I peer into the half-gloom of my hotel room, my eyes on the screen in case the camera cuts to him.

But the broadcast moves on to images of raging wildfires in the parched Southwest and I resume brushing my teeth. I'm only hours away from my own television interview, in which I'm meant to be bright and engaging at a time of morning one can barely call day.

An appearance on *The Today Show* is a welcome taste of my former life, but at least I'm not expected to don the famous swallowtail jacket and satin shorts Jinx once wore. As the thought pops into my head, grim suspicion prickles my scalp. They wouldn't! It's absurd. Yet it occurs to me to ring Pat, my agent, to find out if anyone from *The Today Show* called to ask for my measurements. I stop myself from grabbing my cellphone, figuring Pat wouldn't appreciate being awakened in her Santa Monica bedroom at 2:47 in the morning.

Thank God I have a cool pair of skinny black pants and a terrific-looking fitted jacket in my garment bag in case someone in production has brainstormed surprising me with the signature Jinx ensemble. At my age, I don't do shorts. Period.

Not that I've porked up and let myself get flabby. I'm toned enough to wear a tank top, but that doesn't mean I'm willing to let an audience of several million viewers (mostly women) make unwelcome physical comparisons between the current me and the Jinx of yesteryear. Would Diana Rigg willingly climb into her Emma Peel *Avengers* outfit? Nope. Maybe Michelle Pfeiffer would wear her *Batman Returns* leather to nice effect, but I hold the line. There are standards to maintain.

In the lobby of the hotel, the doorman smiles and takes my garment bag. The limo driver nods and opens the door. Never mind that the temperature is reaching the century mark and it's barely six thirty a.m. Forget that the street smells like hot tar and humidity is sticking my tank top to my skin. It's July in the Big Apple, and whatever the weather, it's good to be home again.

The fact that I live in LA and haven't resided in New York for several decades doesn't mean I don't think of Manhattan as home. Any actor who's spent time encamped in a roach-infested railroad flat in Hell's Kitchen, sweating it out as a waitress or bartender while awaiting that elusive career break, gets it. Actors struggle in Hollywood, too, but there's a gritty exhilaration that comes from surviving grimy, late-night subway rides and a five-floor walkup to a spooky apartment with a door that boasts three deadbolts and a security bar.

Soon after I moved to New York, I was heading to just such an apartment, a sublet I shared with two other aspiring actresses, when a skinny guy on a bike grabbed my handbag—and I wouldn't let go. I screamed and held on, clutching the bag with both hands as I ran alongside his rickety two-wheeler. Then I tripped on a manhole cover and sprawled onto the pavement, skinning my knees, hands and chin, with the thief and his bicycle tumbling on top of me. My dress was ruined, my shoes badly scuffed, and I had a bloody nose, but my cheap plastic handbag containing three bucks and change was still in my possession, a triumph! The thief was back on his feet and cycling up the street before I could pry myself off the pavement. Who doesn't have a war story like that to tell about living in the Big Apple? It's a rite of passage.

That experience and a few others less notable for bruises and bloodshed were enough to establish a lifetime bond with New York. When I arrived I was a virgin (not for long) and still had chipmunk cheeks (not for long, either) left over from a corn-fed

Nebraska girlhood. I did Off-Off-Broadway (so far-far off we were barely in the same borough), a few trade shows, some commercials, a stint on a soap opera and a national bus tour of *Barefoot in the Park* (where I met Dirck Heyward, my first husband) before signing on as a studio contract player in palm-tree-laden La La Land. Now, gliding the streets of Manhattan toward Rockefeller Plaza in leather-lined, air-conditioned comfort, memories of those long-ago days rush back in a flood.

The limo driver waves his cellphone at me, interrupting my reverie. "Excuse me, Ms. Barnes, I have the production assistant on the line—"

"She wants to speak with me?"

"I think she just wants to make sure you remembered the hat."

"Tell her it's here on my lap." I look down at the thin cardboard box bound with grosgrain ribbon, not bothering to mention I almost did forget it back at the hotel.

"Ms. Barnes has it," he says into the phone, then laughs and catches my eye in the rearview mirror. Affecting a haughty Colonel Blimp accent, he says, "Gwen told me to tell you, 'Awfully good of you, my dear.'"

My molars clamp as I hear him utter the popular catchphrase that, thanks to a TV series I starred in, became a national fad for a while. I manage a smile, knowing what's expected of me. "Just tell her, 'All in a day's work,'" just as my character, Jinx, would have responded to her boss, known only as the Magician.

The driver flashes me another look in the rearview mirror and winks knowingly. "I bet you get this all the time."

"Jinxed again!" I sigh, with the practiced weariness that always gets another chuckle.

The *Holiday* specials were two-hour television movies, part of a rotating wheel of detective shows that aired once a month for several seasons. Each production was geared toward a holiday: Valentine's Day, Halloween, Mother's Day, even Groundhog Day. Winston Sykes, faking a British accent and sporting a monocle, played a magician; I was his assistant, Jinx. Winnie and I solved crimes, all of them holiday themed. My costume, a swallowtail jacket with satin shorts and a top hat, was a Marlene Dietrich rip-off (*Morocco, The Blue Angel*), but a younger generation will always associate that sexy getup with me.

"All in a day's work" has become a lifetime's work, and why would I complain? It's the whole reason I'm appearing on *The Today Show*. My mother in Nebraska has been alerted. My sister-in-law in Milwaukee has sent out an all-points bulletin to nieces and nephews, who surely have better things to do than watch Auntie Meg teach Savannah Guthrie how to fling the famous top hat around like Oddjob slinging his metal bowler at James Bond.

Speaking of special agents . . . I wrap my fingers around the cellphone in my pocket, tempted to send Jack a text. Something funny and a bit naughty like: *Thinking of u, hoping it was good for u 2*. I hesitate and decide against it. If indeed he's in the throes of investigating the death of the Ukrainian teenager, it's not the distraction he needs right now.

I leave my phone in my pocket and instead drum my fingers on the thin cardboard box that holds Jinx's top hat. My friend Donna, a fan and inveterate collector of showbiz memorabilia, acquired it at a church charity auction. If I lose the hat, I'm done for. Not only would I sacrifice a friendship, I'd be forced to give up Donna's generous room and board in her Holmby Hills estate. Without Donna's largesse, I'd be living in my car, the redoubtable Ritz-Volvo.

With a roof over my head that doesn't come with four wheels and a dashboard, I'm managing to get back on my feet. My agent is helping me find enough acting work to keep me literally off the streets, even if it means sucking it up to do television commercials for decrepit, diseased and leaking body parts. As Pat points out, "All the gals are on TV selling something, honey, and some of 'em have Academy Awards on their mantels."

She's right. Spokeswomen of my generation are hawking adult diapers, not tampons. Denture fixative, not Doublemint gum. I think Pat takes a certain pleasure in sending me out on commercial calls for acid reflux, hair loss, brittle bones and retirement communities. But who, other than someone with Oscar-caliber talent, can spew streams of dense copy with caveats about side effects that result in death and still make you want to buy the stuff? One does long to do a nice hair-color ad that only claims to cover the gray.

In my case, I'm happily collecting residuals on a commercial for a sleep aid (in which I spend most of the spot tucked into bed with my eyes closed) that's keeping my Volvo tanked up and insured. The subject of getting a place of my own hasn't come up yet. Donna seems to like my company, and I'm not cut out to live like a hermit. If I'd found it that much fun rattling around on my own, I wouldn't have leapt so eagerly into the disastrous second marriage that eventually left me without a home. I could kick myself, but why add injury to insult?

But this is no time to dwell on the past, especially on a morning blazing with sunshine and the fun of an appearance on *The Today Show*. With that thought in mind, I pull my cellphone from my pocket and tap out: *Thinking of u, hoping it was good for u 2*.

The town car turns onto 48th Street, Rockefeller Plaza nearby. "Not too much commotion here this morning," the driver says. "At least Justin Bieber isn't doing the show today. These teenyboppers camp out around here for days. Not me, not in this heat I wouldn't." He looks into the rearview mirror and winks. "Well, maybe for you, I would. I gotta tell ya, as a kid I had a poster of you on my bedroom wall."

"Really," I murmur. No need to say more. The look in his eye tells me what his adolescent fantasies were. I'd just as soon he kept them to himself. Besides—and this is happening to me more and more lately—I could've sworn that the driver, trim and sporting a dapper cookie-duster mustache, was close to my age.

"You kidding me? Every guy at school had one of those posters," he says, pulling up at a side entrance. "You musta made millions."

"In my dreams! Farrah Fawcett had a better manager than me."

He laughs. "Well, you were hot stuff, lemme tell you. I mean—hey, sorry, you still are—know what I mean?"

I know what he means. "Well, I hope you kept the poster. I hear there's quite a market for them on eBay."

He laughs uncomfortably and I know in a flash that he had one of those mothers who threw away every adolescent treasure the moment he left home. That's why there's eBay.

The driver pulls over and stops. "Lemme get your garment bag for you," he says, sliding out and opening my door. Hot, soggy air envelops me as I step onto the pavement. The driver hands me the garment bag, toasty warm from the trunk. "Have a good show, Miss Barnes. And listen, hope you didn't mind—"

"I'm flattered. And thanks. I'm glad you have such good memories of *Holiday*."

"You're the best. Sorry I won't be driving you back, but it was great meeting you."

A young woman with choppy blond hair and a chirpy voice scurries up to me. "I'm Gwen," she says, reaching for the garment bag. "Let me give you a hand with that." She flashes me a smile and stands back, holding the side door to the lobby. I tighten my grip on the box containing Jinx's top hat and hurry inside the building.

"We'll check you in first, then drop your stuff off. We usually go straight to the green room, but we've set aside a dressing room for you," Gwen says, striding ahead, her short skirt flipping saucily with each step. "Anything you need, just let me know."

"Thanks. Some water would be great."

"No problem. There should be some in your room."

I sign in with an NBC page at the security desk, then follow Gwen down stairs and through a labyrinth of corridors. Near the end of a hallway, she ushers me into a small dressing room. I drop my bag on the dressing table next to a plate of fruit and two bottles of water.

Gwen hooks the garment bag on a rack and flicks on lights encircling a mirror attached to a wall above the dressing table. "Settle in and I'll be back in a minute." She's about to leave, then turns back. "You want to see if anything needs a touch-up?"

"Good idea." I unzip the bag and shake out a black lightweight linen jacket that I'll wear over my tank top. "It looks fine. Why don't I go into makeup if they're ready for me."

"Hey, you're easy!" Her smile is bright, her voice chummy. "My God, I was just a kid when I used to watch you on television. I'm just so thrilled to meet you. I can't wait to see you do your famous hat tricks. Everyone's excited!" She laughs again. "Let me check with makeup and I'll be right back."

"Great. Ready when you are." She bounds out the door. I close it after her, then tuck my hands in my armpits to warm them. I'm freezing. I suspect it's due more to nerves than the Klondike chill in the room. Gwen has managed to gush all the right things to make me tense up about performing the hat tricks. A little practice warm-up wouldn't hurt.

I untie the ribbons on the box and slide out the flat satin disk. With a flourish, I snap the mechanism and the top hat pops open. To television audiences, Jinx's hat is as iconic as Columbo's beat-up raincoat or Barnabas Collins' wolf-head cane. Maybe someday Donna will bequeath the top hat to the Smithsonian, like Archie Bunker's rocking chair.

I put on the linen jacket before practicing my routine, praying that I haven't lost my touch. Fortunately, like riding a bicycle, it all comes back. When I first got the role, I trained with an old vaudeville showgirl who was living out her years at a Hollywood retirement home. The fact that her name was Roxie only added to the charm of the peroxide blonde, who still had terrific legs and a tiny waist at seventy-plus years of age. She'd worked with bubbles, fans, flags, feathers and veils of every description, but hat tricks were her specialty. She was only too happy to show me the moves I needed to play a magician's assistant.

I snap my heels together and extend my hand, hoping I can still manage to roll the hat down my arm onto my fingertips. On the third attempt, I get it right—then try again and again until I can do it with ease. I twirl the hat in my fingers, snap it, toss it, catch it and fling it in the air just right so it will fall on my head, cocked perfectly. I concentrate so completely on my rehearsal that I'm unaware Gwen has entered my dressing room until she claps her hands.

"Wow! Terrific!" she says. "I'd love to watch more, but I gotta get you into makeup. You ready?"

"All yours," I huff, trying to catch my breath. "Let's go."

We wind through a maze of corridors to the green room and an adjacent brightly lit makeup room. A plump young woman wearing bib overalls and a tee shirt gives me a sunny smile as she introduces herself as Lydia. I greet her, sliding into a makeup chair still warm from the last occupant.

"Any allergies? Contact lenses? Something I should know about?"

"No, just careful around the nose. It's prosthetic."

She laughs and I settle back in the chair. It takes me a while to figure out that the glint in her mouth is a metal knob piercing her tongue. I've already taken in the studs and rings adorning her ears, nose and eyebrow. I won't let myself think about what's going on under the overalls.

For the next half hour or more, while Lydia dabs at my face, I stare into the middle distance, trying to keep my eyes off the glittering tongue stud. Every filling in my mouth cries out, my glands empathetically secreting metallic-tasting saliva. I can't imagine what happens when Lydia eats something cold like ice cream, or drinks hot coffee. Or chews gum. Maybe, like dentures, she stores the hardware in a glass of water by her bedside at night. Try as I might, I can't halt my brain's morbid speculations.

I'm grateful when Gwen arrives to shepherd me into the green room to wait for my segment. Fortunately, the sweet rolls, bagels and cream cheese are thoroughly picked over and I don't indulge. I watch the monitor, feeling my hands grow icy with anticipation. Savannah is sitting on the couch chatting amiably with an author about—what? My ears have shut down. I'm not listening to the interview so much as watching Savannah's lively girlish gestures. Anxiety mounts. What am I doing here, anyway? I've been prepped in advance during a long telephone interview with a producer, but my mind is blank, my fingers icy as Popsicles.

During the commercial break, I'm led, freshly fluffed and powdered, to the stage area. I perch on a stool, glancing over my shoulder at the crowd gathered outside in sweltering Rockefeller Plaza watching a segment with Al Roker, Matt Lauer, Natalie Morales and Savannah. A camera swings into place for a close-up of me as Savannah announces our upcoming interview. "It's just so neat," she says to Matt. "Who can forget Jinx and that hat!"

"And I hear you're getting a lesson from the pro," Matt teases. "Have you been getting some coaching on the side?"

"If only! I feel like butterfingers already."

My three seconds on camera trying not to look overly exuberant or just plain silly feels like an eternity. The red light flicks off before I do something dumb like wave at the camera. I catch a glimpse of Savannah trotting into the studio, at least two feet taller and ten pounds slimmer than I had imagined. She stands crane-like on one foot, sifting through a handful of pages, then glances over at me, fanning her fingers in greeting. A moment later, she slides onto the other stool, hooks the heel of one shoe on a rung and grins at me with a twelve-year-old child's wide-eyed wonderment.

"I've just been dying to meet you. What fun! But I'm so nervous I'll do it all wrong."

"Don't be. I'm nervous enough for both of us." She laughs and I sit up straighter, stretching one leg to the floor in a pose I hope makes me look a little slimmer and taller.

"You working on anything now?" she asks.

"Yes, a little independent project called *Forsaken*."

"Great! Want me to mention it?"

"Better not," I say quickly. "It's still in production." *What am I thinking? It's a webisode with a two-buck budget!*

The floor manager gives a countdown and I hear the first few notes of the *Holiday* theme music, an easy jazz riff that washes over me in a wave of nostalgia.

My eyes fasten on the teleprompter and I read along with Savannah as she says, "Growing up I loved this show . . . *Holiday* was so bright and sparkly, just like Jinx, the adorable magician's assistant played by Meg Barnes. Welcome, Meg."

"Thanks, Savannah. I'm glad to be here."

"Sorry, but I keep wanting to call you Jinx."

"Go ahead. Lots of people do. I only wish Winston Sykes could join us."

"You were quite a team. And full disclosure, everyone, I was one of those little girls out in the backyard trying to do all those hat tricks. Really, I was one of your biggest fans. What do you think made the show so popular?"

That's my cue. I talk about the first *Holiday* show, a Christmas special that was such a ratings hit it spawned a series. Savannah asks me about Winston Sykes, the Magician with the monocle and posh English accent. I remind her he was actually Canadian and has now retired to live north of the border.

"You know, I think it was the chemistry between Winnie and me, like *Moonlighting* in the eighties, with Bruce Willis and Cybill Shepherd. The key to the show is that teasing, bickering, opposites-attract relationship. And the stories were fun, sort of whimsical."

"And now it's back. That famous Fourth of July episode with the great chase sequence inside the Statue of Liberty is airing Saturday night . . . Can't wait to see it again! And the whole series is coming out now on Blu-ray for the twentieth anniversary of the show."

"You know, I haven't seen it since it aired . . . "

"Well, I hope you haven't forgotten the signature moves."

I hand her the collapsed hat that's been nestling in my lap. Savannah squeals with pleasure. "Thanks, Jinx!" She holds the satin disk up to the camera and then hands it back to me. "Go on—pop it!"

"All in a day's work." With a flourish, I snap the brim and Jinx's magician's hat pops open.

"Okay, now show me how it works. I'll stand over here."

I collapse the hat again, then sail it toward her. She reaches for the whirling disk, but gets whacked on the elbow instead.

"Whew! That thing's lethal!" she yelps.

"That's the whole idea. It's how Jinx knocked out the bad guys."

Savannah Frisbees the hat back to me, but the disk nosedives to the floor. "Whoa, what's wrong with me?"

I show off a few of Jinx's best moves, even managing to twirl and do a fancy backhand throw. There was a time when I could sling the disk while managing a one-handed cartwheel, too. But that was then. Today I'd land in the ER. For a finale, I snap the hat open and flip it onto my head, cocked over one eye, and wink. "Jinxed again."

"Oh, wow! Thank you so much for being on the show today. I'm so glad *Holiday* is coming back as a new series!"

The segment ends with a commercial break. My mouth falls open, her words buzzing in my ears. "What? A new series?"

"That's what I hear. It's on our network. Hey, you were terrific!" Savannah gives my arm a quick tap and hurries off to prepare for another segment.

"She's right. Terrific!" Gwen says, handing me my shoulder bag. I fall into step behind her as she leads me back to my dressing room. "You were the highlight of the show today. By the way, your phone was vibrating. I think you've got some admirers ringing."

I fish my cellphone out of my bag and check the voicemail. The first message is from Donna, of course, tuning in from Los Angeles, where she's caught the network feed online. I sling the bag onto my shoulder and call her back. "So what'd you think?"

"For an old duffer, you still have the chops, Meg. You were spectacular!"

"Thanks. I can't believe it, but I was actually a bit nervous. It's been a while since I've done one of these interview things."

"Well, it didn't show. And what's this about the series coming back?"

"That's what I'd like to know. I'm a bit long in the tooth for Jinx, but—"

"Fingers crossed, Meg. That would be great."

I rotate the top hat in my hand, imagining myself back on the lot shooting a series again. "Listen, Donna. Let me call you back when we can talk, okay?"

"Sure, I'm here. And I mean it, you were terrific!"

"Thanks. I'll catch up with you later."

What could be better than a return to *Holiday*? My mind reels at the thought of starring in a series again. Following Gwen down the corridor to my dressing room, I feel almost dizzy imagining myself back playing Jinx—a role I love!

Gwen steps aside as I enter my dressing room. "You okay? Take your time. We have a car ready to take you wherever you want to go. Let me know when you're ready."

"Great. I'll just be a minute." I close the door, toss my bag on the dressing table and stare at myself in the mirror. Fully made up, I don't look bad. I'm still slim, my face holding up nicely. I'd have to work out, get back in tip-top shape to play Jinx, but I could do it. I pop the hat, give it a twirl and flip it onto my head, cocked over one eye.

Yeah, looking good. I could do it. I grab a half-empty water bottle off the dressing table and chug the remains. *No doubt about it!*

My cellphone vibrates in my pocket. I pull it out and glance at the screen. It's Pat, my agent. "Hey, there!"

"Hey, there, yourself. You sure make me proud, kiddo. You were magic."

"Thanks! So what's all this about a new *Holiday* series?"

"That's what I'm calling about. Just got word that it's a go. You believe it? They're thinking mid-season replacement."

"Fabulous! I'm thrilled. Can't wait to see a script. But what about Winston? You think he'd come out of retirement to do it?"

"Winston? No—wait a minute, cookie. This'll be a whole new cast, you know?"

My mouth goes dry. "A new Jinx? Another actress?"

Even as the words slip from my mouth, I glimpse myself in the mirror as I am—looking okay, especially for someone who hasn't been nipped, tucked, lipo'd or Botoxed, but I'm not a kid. I'm not immune from sags, bags and crow's feet. What was I thinking? Me? In shorts, flouncing around, bantering with Winnie the way we did some twenty years ago? *What was I thinking?*

"Of course, Pat," I murmur. "A new Jinx. I figured that. But, I mean—didn't you say they called you?"

"Yeah, yeah, they've already hired a young gal and they'd like you to give her some coaching. You up for that? They really liked what they just saw of you on *The Today Show*. Of course, I'm pushing for a recurring role for you. You know—make you a part of the series—but in the meantime, hey, I figure it's some dough in your pocket, right?"

I hear Pat fumbling, and she doesn't normally fumble. She deals it straight and knows damn well I went skittering off the tracks, momentarily delusional that I would be cast as Jinx. "Sure, I'm up for it, Pat. You never know—I mean, sure, I'll coach her. Why not?"

"Great. The gal's name is Chelsea Horne. And by the way, they changed the name of the new series. Instead of *Holiday*, it'll be called *Jinx*."

"*Jinx*?"

"Yeah, it's all about her, not the Magician. We'll talk when you get back. Call me."

Mercifully, she hangs up.

I take the top hat off my head and snap it closed. Someone else playing Jinx? Sure, why not? A countless number of actors have played Hamlet. How many gals have played Blanche DuBois in *A Streetcar Named Desire*? Okay, maybe Jinx isn't quite in that category, but it's a good role, one I created. She's mine! *Was* mine.

I glance in the mirror and see sad, hurt eyes looking back at me, eyes that I mustn't let anyone else see—not ever. Nor can I say out loud what I'm feeling—that no other actress is going to get Jinx right.

I slide the hat back into its scuffed box, tying the fraying grosgrain ribbons. Whoever plays Jinx is going to have to get her own damn hat. This one is mine. Or, rather, it's Donna's. Some things are sacred. *Damn!*

I hate myself for feeling this way, but I can't help it. I wonder if all the Catwomen feel this way about seeing another actress suit up in the ears and leathers?

My cellphone dings. I flip it over and see a text message from Jack.

Virtually the best, but better in person . . . soon!

3

I didn't plan it this way. Chelsea Horne, America's newly minted Jinx, was supposed to meet me in Holmby Park at three o'clock, forty-five minutes ago. And counting. I arrived early, of course, because I always do. For some time (nineteen minutes, to be exact) I stood near the entrance to the bowling green on the south side of the park, where we'd agreed to meet, alternately watching thickset Russian immigrants playing chess on wobbly card tables and joggers speeding by on the walking paths.

I'd already filled Jack in on my new assignment, reaching him in Seattle shortly before I boarded my flight back from New York. I'd made teaching Chelsea my hat tricks sound like a lark and he'd laughed, making me feel even better about taking on the job.

Any remaining misgivings I'd had about training my replacement vanished when Pat told me the fee she'd negotiated.

I ambled to the north end of the park, past the putting greens, restrooms and picnic area, to the playground, glancing back to make sure I hadn't missed her arrival. I didn't. It's a small park. I would have seen her.

Meeting in Holmby Park, a charming oasis of trees, meandering streams and a pond, had been my idea, arrived at after a series of text messages exchanged with Chelsea. I thought it would be a better place than Starbucks to get acquainted with my young replacement. We could stroll along the paths, chat a bit, and then find a quiet, grassy area to work out in with the hat.

What I've been able to glean about Chelsea Horne on the Internet is thin but impressive: five foot seven, slim, pretty, with reddish brown hair, a description that matched my own at age twenty-one. But judging from a range of photographs available online, she's in a class of her own. With an angular face, prominent cheekbones and intense eyes under thick brows, she has a quirky beauty that's exceptional. She'd be hard to miss.

Taking a path that crosses a narrow stream in the middle of the park, I spot a chunky young man with curly hair who I instantly recognize as Corky Shaw, the teenage director of *Forsaken*. I'm about to call out his name when I realize that he's hunched over, camera in hand, filming something. I watch him slowly circle a middle-aged man wearing a pin-striped suit and an old-fashioned fedora, who is sitting on a bench holding a newspaper. I wait until Corky puts his camera down and the man removes his hat to fan himself.

"Hey, there! Corky!" I wave as he turns and sees me walking toward him. "What's up? I thought you'd wrapped the film already."

"Meg! Wow, hey, hi!" He grins, rocking from one foot to the other in a boyish display of awkward exuberance. "Just doing some, you know, pickup shots. Hey, this is my Uncle Joe. He's playing the bookie."

"Joseph Shaw. Please call me Joe," the man says, standing up and extending his hand. "You're the Meg Barnes he keeps raving about? So I meet you, finally."

He's tall and stocky, with thinning hair and a faint chalky pallor that could just be Corky's attempt at applying some makeup. Joe smiles affably, but there's a guarded look in his pale brown eyes. I sense he's sizing me up, which only spurs me into displaying my most genial side.

"Good to meet you, too, Joe. I'm playing Gloria, the 'wronged woman' in Corky's film. I'm sorry we don't have any scenes together."

"No, no, please. I'm not an actor. I only agreed to do this today if I didn't have any lines." He sets the fedora on his head. "But I think it was the hat that got me the job. It belonged to my father." In fact, the hat suits him and plays into his old-world courtliness.

"Meg's great, Uncle Joe. I can't believe I got her to play Gloria! I mean, I wrote the script with her in mind."

"Yes, so I understand," he says, with a charming bow to me. "It's very kind of you to help my nephew out with his hobby."

"Not at all. I've loved working with Corky and I think this is far more than just a hobby for him. He has real talent. I can't wait to see the finished work."

"Yeah, neat. Thanks! I'll have a trailer together pretty soon," Corky says, bobbing from one foot to the other. "I just have some more exteriors to shoot. There's a house up the street that's perfect for Gloria's mansion."

"Then we better get a move on, Corky." Joe looks at his watch, then turns to me. "Corky's mother is working this afternoon and he needed a driver. Do you live around here?"

"Close by." I gesture vaguely toward a gated entrance across the street from the bowling green. "I'm actually meeting someone here."

"Nice neighborhood. You're very lucky."

"I know. It's lovely." I glance around and spot a lanky young woman climbing out of a red sports car. "Actually, that might be her over there."

Joe and Corky turn to look just as the coltish beauty, wearing jeans, a tee shirt and a baseball cap, leans into the open window of the sports car. The three of us watch, transfixed, as she wiggles her bottom, raises a leg bent at the knee and kicks it back a few times while talking animatedly to the driver. Eventually she thrusts her head and torso through the window and wiggles her bottom again like a frisky puppy. I glance at Corky and see that he's filming her energetic mating dance.

"Hey, buddy," I whisper. "I'm betting that gal's a member of the Screen Actors Guild."

"If she's not, she should be," he mumbles, not taking his eye off the camera.

The girl's bottom stops wiggling, but she leans farther into the car. Moments later, she stands up and waves as the car peels away from the curb. Still unaware that the three of us are gawking at her, she takes her time checking her cellphone before turning around. When she does, I wave.

"Meg?" She takes in the three of us, her look wary as she approaches. "I thought it was just going to be us."

"It is. But I ran into some friends. Corky and Joe Shaw, this is Chelsea Horne."

"Wow, hi," Corky says, looking at her through a camera lens. "I can't believe I'm, like, really meeting you in person."

"Yeah, hi," she says, eyeing the camera. "Hey, could you put that down, please? It's a little pervy."

"Hey, yeah, sorry," he says, flashing her a nervous smile. He clutches the camera behind his back and stares at her, enraptured. "I, like, forget sometimes, you know? I saw you in *Winner Take All*. Awesome. Really awesome."

"Yeah?" She stares at him blankly. "Thanks."

"Nice to meet you," Joe says. "We have to go. Ready, Corky?"

"Yeah, sure. Nice to meet you, Chelsea." He turns beseeching eyes on me.

"Actually, Cornelius Shaw is a filmmaker," I say brightly, picking up on his desperate cue. "Corky's just wrapped a project called *Forsaken*."

"Awesome," Chelsea says, her delivery modulated a tone above boredom to mild indifference. "Cool."

"Yeah," he nods, his dark curly hair bouncing around his pale, cherubic face. "Cool."

Chelsea looks at her cellphone again as Corky rocks back and forth on his heels. Joe prods his arm, then takes his elbow and pulls him away.

"Bye, Corky. Say hi to your mom and dad," I call out as the two head up the footpath. "Nice to meet you, Joe."

While waiting for Chelsea to finish checking her messages, I reflect on how much she and Corky managed to express to each other in a handful of syllables. *Hang in there, ET, there's still hope for intergalactic communication.*

Meanwhile, with time on my hands, I take stock of the millennial generation's version of Jinx. She's thin, not quite anorexic. Her face is sculpted alabaster with full lips, large hazel eyes and thick brows, all familiar from the online photos, but in person there's a bonus—a rich, throaty voice that gives her an unexpected dimension. I'm intrigued. She is her voice, I realize; mysterious and mesmerizing.

When she finally looks up from her cellphone, I ask, "So, what happened? I thought we were meeting at three."

"Yeah. Am I late? Sorry. You know, costume fittings. My manager, something or other . . . Anyway, I'm here now. Hi."

"Hi."

I could have done with a bit more of an apology, but I'm not in the mood to scold. Nor am I in a rush to speak. I'd sooner let her set the tone for this meeting. She, apparently, is in no hurry to do so. I wait. I have no idea what she thinks of me, but her hazel eyes are sizing me up.

"Hey, I'll bet you don't think much of having someone else play Jinx."

"You just better be good." I smile.

She smiles, her eyes appraising. "With your help."

Okay, that's a start. I realize that I've lowered my voice a register and thrown in a little huskiness that doesn't come naturally. I hope she doesn't notice. I point my feet toward the path through the center of the park and she follows. "I hear you have a table read coming up and start shooting a week from Monday. That's not a lot of time to prepare."

"It's what I've got." She reaches into her shoulder bag. "Show me your hat, I'll show you mine."

I take the box with the grosgrain ribbon from my own shoulder bag and pull the ties. "It doesn't belong to me, you know. I have to be careful with it."

"Sure, it's an antique. I get it." Her cat's grin sets my teeth on edge.

"Yeah, yeah, and yours probably has lasers and GPS. Besides, let's be honest about this, you screw up and post-production fixes it. I had to get it right, first take."

"No computer-generated imagery, Meg. I'm not going to be flying and walking up walls thanks to CGI." She drops her voice even lower and purrs, "Not that I couldn't do it on my own, of course."

I smile. I'm beginning to like her. "Where did you study?"

"Acting? Same as you." She gives me a sly look, letting me know she's done as much research on me as I've done on her. "New York, of course. Did some Off-Off Broadway, a couple of commercials, a few months on a soap before it got cancelled, then some episodic and a small role in an independent feature. That's what got me out here. Did you see *Winner Take All*? Played at Sundance."

"No, but I heard about it. Good for you. Who did you study with?"

"George DiCenzo. Harry Mastrogeorge. Dirck Heyward."

"Good, all good. I knew George. Studied with Harry. And you probably know already that I was once Mrs. Heyward."

"Oh, yeah. He said that he taught you all you know about acting."

"Dirck?" I whoop with laughter; can't help it. "Let's just say I learned a lot from Dirck. Acting might've been some of it."

"He thinks the world of you, you know. He mentions you in class all the time."

"Well, we spent a lot of years together." What else can I say? We married. We divorced. I have no idea what he may be saying about me and, frankly, it's not something I want to talk about with someone I barely know. However, I am impressed that Chelsea bothered to check me out on IMDb. The Internet Movie Database sometimes gets things wrong (I'm not about to correct the birth date, as it's in my favor!), but it's otherwise fairly complete.

We sit across from each other at a picnic table and I get an even better look at Chelsea. She's more relaxed than when we first met but there's still a guarded look. Something tells me she's the real thing, with natural instincts. She knows to let her voice do the work, without embellishments. There's no need for her to pump up sincerity, concern, vitality; her warm, supple voice signals it all whether she means it or not. I've known other actors with great voices—deep, husky, velvety, raspy or whisky-soaked with a burr—who lay it on and become tiresome. But however seductive her voice, I'm not sure I trust the girl. And her face has a disturbing familiarity.

"So, let's see your hat."

She plops a shiny polyester-sheathed disk on the redwood table, then bangs the rim and the hat pops open. I watch it wobble on the table, not unaware that it sounds like a spinning penny. "Nice. Probably lightweight, too."

"So, let's see yours."

I hold my black satin disk lightly between two index fingers and delicately tap a concealed mechanism with the little finger of my right hand. Magically, the hat pops open, and I set it gently on the picnic table, where it assumes an elegant, yet cocky pose.

"There you are, a thing of beauty in all its grandeur."

"I'll bet it could talk if it wanted to," Chelsea says. I know she's kidding, but my hat has enough personality to beg the question.

The two hats sit side by side, one still wobbling. Chelsea is going to have her challenges with this synthetic knockoff. "Yours lacks heft, that's the problem. Even if you land it on your head perfectly, without the weight it could fly off again. It's just not a real magician's hat and I don't think the prop master understands that. It looks more like a party favor, you know? A disposable New Year's Eve kind of thing."

"Got it, Meg. It's a piece of trash, okay? Meanwhile, the clock is ticking. I've gotta nail this before filming starts." She looks around. "Any chance we could go somewhere else to work on this?"

"Sure." While her charm isn't as abundant as I would like, that's no reason to forfeit the coaching job. "C'mon, I live nearby."

"Can we walk? I don't have a car."

Her words resonate. "No car?"

She shrugs. "A friend dropped me off."

"Really." I know it's true because I saw the guy in the fancy red sports car, yet my stomach flip-flops. How many stories have I told about being "dropped off"? Until Donna offered me a spare room in her house, I lived in my Volvo, parked curbside at this very park. I washed up in the public facility. Holmby Park was "home" to me. Now it's just my backyard. "Okay, let's walk."

Nobody walks in Holmby Hills, although there's no shortage of tour buses scouting the neighborhood for movie stars out checking their mailboxes. In addition to Aaron Spelling's former 56,500-square-foot chateau ("the Manor") and Hef's Tudor-style Playboy Mansion, Holmby Hills has also been home to Judy Garland, Elvis Presley and Frank Sinatra, among others.

"Blond Bombshell" Jean Harlow, who died at the age of twenty-six, lived in one of the most magnificent homes in the area, a brick house, originally painted brilliant white, built on a generous slice of prime real estate. Donna's grandfather, a Belgian immigrant and maker of the popular hand-milled Savoir beauty bar, became a close friend of Harlow's when she built her home in 1932, not far from his. One of Donna's prize mementos is a sepia photograph of her grandparents drinking highballs with Harlow in her hidden speakeasy just off the kitchen. During Prohibition, a speakeasy concealed behind sliding walls was as common as a butler's pantry in these luxurious homes.

Most of the mansions are protected from view behind electronic gates and masses of trees and shrubs. Fortunately I have a key to Donna's door and the security code for the gate. I tap in the numbers on the keypad and hear the soft grind of machinery as the heavy iron gates with the swirly Savoir soap S logo click open and glide apart. Without waiting for me, Chelsea bounds through the gates and walks up the curving driveway.

I'm about to follow her when I hear my name shouted. I turn around to see a blue Honda cruising slowly down the street with Uncle Joe behind the wheel and Corky hanging out the window filming me.

Flipping my top hat onto my head, I strike a showgirl's pose and wave as the car passes by, turns the corner and accelerates up the street.

By the time I catch up to Chelsea, she's standing near the orchid pavilion at the top of the driveway. "This is where you live? You must've made a mint off *Holiday!*"

"Don't get your hopes up. Jinx didn't buy this house. The place belongs to a friend."

"Some friend." She pivots slowly, taking in the tennis courts, greenhouse, kitchen garden and sweeping lawns. "How long have you been staying here?"

"Not long." In fact, I've lived here close to nine months, but it's not a subject I care to go into with Chelsea. "I've been looking for a place of my own."

"Why?" She gazes at the Olympic-size pool with its Jacuzzi, individual cabanas and outdoor cooking area. "Why would anyone leave here?"

I've asked myself the same question and I'm not about to answer it now. "That little two-story structure with the veranda just beyond the pool was Donna's playhouse as a child. She also had a pony."

"Of course. Who didn't?"

Actually, my brother and I had a pony on our farm in Nebraska, but picking up the edge in Chelsea's voice, I decide not to mention it. "Donna had the stables torn down some years ago to build her orchid pavilion here."

"Nice."

We walk across the stone-paved forecourt encircling a fountain banked with ferns and lilies. Rose bushes thick with white blooms line the walkway up to the main house, which has an old-fashioned storybook charm. Wisteria clings to the gables and vines climb around mullioned windows. Wide stone steps lead up to a carved front door fitted with a gated, wrought-iron peephole. Unwarranted pride of ownership washes over me as Chelsea looks around.

"I have to say, my little rented house would fit in her garage."

Donna's 1972 baby-blue Mercedes sedan is parked next to my Volvo, the only two vehicles sheltered in a massive garage that could house a Jiffy Lube without feeling cramped.

"Great, Donna's home. You'll get to meet her."

"Is she old?"

"Not unless you think I'm old."

There's no immediate response, which makes that affirmative. It also strikes me that in our hike from Holmby Park to Donna's house, Chelsea hasn't once mentioned watching any *Holiday* shows. Generally people gush a bit when they meet me. The series is often mentioned in the hushed tones reserved for shows like ours and *The Prisoner*. I can't say I mind. In fact, I like it. "So what's your favorite *Holiday* episode?"

"I just saw my first one last week. They gave me a couple of screeners, including a Fourth of July show with the Statue of Liberty. It was okay. But seriously, it seemed kind of pokey. Not much action." She looks at me warily, then shifts her gaze back to the house. "Hope you don't mind me saying that, but I wasn't born when the show went off the air, you know?"

"I figured. Well, that's okay." I'm sorry I brought it up, especially since I won an Emmy for that particular little "pokey" episode!

"Besides, I need to make the role my own. I mean, I see Jinx as this whole other person entirely. You know, more real." She plants a foot on the stone steps, crosses her arms and looks at me. "But, hey, that doesn't mean I don't need to learn how to do the hat stuff."

More real? I'd like to slug her, then stomp on her half-assed plastic hat, but should probably wait until after I get paid. "Sure. Just the hat tricks. Nothing more."

"Right, because I've already got an acting coach."

"That's cool."

I realize I'm standing with my palms up like I'm surrendering, which infuriates me. I clamp my errant hands to my thighs and wipe any expression from my face. Have I managed to conceal the dreaded thought that Dirck will be on hand out here coaching her—in my role?

A new game plan is called for. Clearly I will not become Chelsea's new best pal, certainly not the role model she'll forever praise for unstinting wisdom and guidance. Roxie, my beloved showgirl-mentor, taught me to stuff lamb's wool between the soles of my feet and the fishnet stockings to keep the coarse threads from cutting my skin. She told me to roll Mitchum's antiperspirant on my face before performing so sweat wouldn't run in rivers down my cheeks. She cautioned me never to use bunched-up plastic bags to fill out a bra ("You'll perspire and lose what ya got"). Roxie, who shared every trick of the trade, would have flattened me with a roundhouse wallop if I'd shown so little respect—and I would have deserved it! She didn't take guff from anyone.

What begins to feel like a Mexican standoff is broken by the sound of a door opening. We both look across the portico.

Donna, wearing a floor-length caftan that would be a tunic on me, waves and greets us with a sunny smile. "C'mon in. I saw the two of you walking up the driveway."

"Thank you, Donna. Listen, I hope it's okay with you if we have a practice session here. This is Chelsea Horne. She's going to play Jinx. Chelsea, this is Donna Bendix."

"Pleased to meet you, Chelsea. I saw *Winner Take All* on the Sundance channel. Great work! I love your voice."

"Really? Thanks so much. Kids used to tease me about the voice."

"Not anymore, I'll bet. Congratulations on getting the role of Jinx. Come in, come in, I'll give you the big nickel tour."

Instead of her comfy Dearfoams, Donna is wearing platform mules that add at least an inch to her height, but she's still diminutive next to Chelsea. She's also run a comb through her springy hair and dabbed on some lipstick, an indication she's spruced up to meet her drop-in guest.

Chelsea is pitch perfect, just the right amount of deference and enthusiasm. Is this because Donna watched *Winner Take All*? Commented on her voice? It's the conversation perhaps I should have had with Chelsea. Maybe I should have gushed a bit, too. Or at least complimented her on getting the role. What's wrong with me? Why is this young woman making me feel like something stuck to the sole of a shoe?

I turn to look across the portico at the eucalyptus, native oak and olive trees that conceal the property from the street. Breathing in the sweet scents of jasmine and rose, I'm trying to come to terms with this sudden bout of insecurity when, behind me, I hear the door slam closed. I've been locked out—inadvertently, I assume. I yank my key from my shoulder bag and jam it into the lock. Resigned, and more than a little irritated, I push the door back open.

Inside, Donna and Chelsea stand on the landing, looking up from the massive stone fireplace to the balcony above the two-story living room. The densely furnished interior, with its eclectic mix of Craftsman, Art Nouveau and Jazz Moderne, has the feel of a 1930s film set. I've taken my own "big nickel tour" a few times and still find the place amazing. I hear Chelsea asking the same questions I did, with Donna responding in her hushed museum-docent's voice.

"You see that hat with all the ribbons on the piano? It belonged to Mary Pickford. Those spectacles on the coffee table were Harold Lloyd's. This ice bucket was Charlie Chaplin's. My grandparents knew a lot of film people, but most of this stuff came from estate sales, including Judy Garland's black patent tap shoes. Too bad they aren't the ruby red ones." She plucks a gray fedora off a hat stand near the stairway. "It's Fred Astaire's, and the crystal in that cabinet was a wedding gift to Joan Crawford and Douglas Fairbanks Jr. The silver tap shoes on the bookcase belonged to Crawford, too."

"Um, Crawford?"

"Joan?" The two women stare at each other as though speaking alien tongues. They are, in fact, speaking across a century of film lore. Donna gives her a doubtful look. "You do know who the other actors I mentioned are, right?"

"Sort of. Judy Garland, I've heard of. I think."

This isn't going well. Donna's face sags a bit, but she's not giving up. "Well, let me take you upstairs to see my doll collection. A couple of them belonged to Deanna Durbin."

I clap my hand on my mouth before I can say anything. Donna's display of antique dolls, numbering in the hundreds, each an exquisite work of art, is her pride and joy, a collection she inherited from her mother and grandmother. Yet, I don't think it's a must-see for Chelsea. Maybe Justin Bieber's sneakers or Johnny Depp's fedora might do the trick, but a doll that once belonged to a teenage singer in 1938 isn't going to cut it with a gal who doesn't know who Charlie Chaplin is.

"Maybe another time," Chelsea says. "Could I use your bathroom?"

"Just down the hall there," I tell her. "Then maybe we should get to work on the hat tricks."

"Good idea. Back in a minute."

Donna and I don't say a word until we hear the click of the bathroom door. "Don't take it to heart, Donna. She loves your house."

"It's a bit of a museum." She looks around as though sizing it up through Chelsea's eyes. She shrugs. "Should I invite her for dinner?"

"Maybe another time. Let me see how it goes."

In fact, it goes well and Chelsea is all business. I leave my hat on the hall table and we work with hers, starting out with some flat-disk Frisbee on the lawn. The slick polyester is tricky, sailing faster but not as accurately as my vintage silk hat. But Chelsea is quick and moves well, treating our practice session as more than just an exercise in slinging the hat back and forth. There's a sense of purpose, some motivation behind each toss, as though she's intent on using the hat strategically as a weapon.

Inside the pool house, we move the Ping-Pong table aside to give us more room to work on the showier tricks, beginning with some crown rolls. I demonstrate by extending my arm horizontally, holding the top hat with my fingers inside the crown, the opening facing forward. Then I flick the hat with my fingers so the side of the crown rolls along my arm and I catch it at the top of my shoulder. I toss the hat to Chelsea and she gives it a try. Again and again, it tumbles to the floor.

"Relax. It takes practice, lots of it. And lock your elbow."

We move on to some end-over-end rolls. "Hold the hat with your fingers inside the crown opening, with your thumb on top of the brim and the opening facing downward. Keep your arm horizontal and completely straight... that's it, the same direction your head is facing. Now, use your fingers to flick the hat so that it rolls end over end. Keep your face pointing toward the floor and the hat will roll to a stop perfectly on your head."

"Yeah, right," Chelsea says, as the hat skitters onto the floor. But she's game and tries it again.

"Keep your thumb out of the way. You almost have it."

We finish up with some throws from hand to head, always my favorite. I ended almost every episode with a double-spin throw, the hat landing on my head, cocked over my right brow. "Jinxed again," I'd say, and wink. I doubt Chelsea's grittier, "more real" interpretation of Jinx will allow for this, but I show it off anyway.

"Cute," she says.

"Give it a try. Remember, it's your head that's catching the hat, not the hat finding your head."

It's not until long shadows creep through the French doors and darken the parquet floor that I look at my watch. Almost two hours have passed and my arms are starting to feel heavy. "How are you doing for time?"

"Omigod, I've gotta leave. Sorry, but can we wrap it up?"

"Sure. It's all practice now. You should be fine. We can work out some more whenever you like. Just call me."

"Great. I've got your number. I'll be in touch."

"By the way, Donna invited you for dinner. Sure you can't stay?"

"Thanks, but I've really got to run." She's silent for a moment, her thumbs jabbing her smartphone with a degree of dexterity I'll never master. "I've got a friend picking me up at the park." She slings her bag over her shoulder, ready to bolt. "Do you mind if I find my own way out?"

"Not at all. I'll lock up here."

Halfway out the door, she turns back. "Hey, thanks. I really appreciate this."

"You'll do great. Just ask the prop master at the studio to find you a better hat, or go online. It'll make the tricks easier."

"Thanks. I will."

She leaves the door open to the cool evening air and lopes across the lawn in long, easy strides. I don't know what to make of her, but I like the way she works. She has tenacity and a willingness to learn. Chelsea enters the main house through the side door to the den and I lose sight of her. I shove the Ping-Pong table back in place, fluff some pillows on the divan and lock the door behind me.

I've trained my nose to Donna's cooking and know as soon as I enter the house that we're having roast lamb for dinner. She comes out of the kitchen with two glasses of wine and hands one to me. "Is Chelsea joining us?"

"She's already left. Didn't she say goodbye to you?"

"No, but I was in the kitchen. How did you get on with her?"
"Okay."

"That's it? Just okay? She's a good actress, you know."

"I'm sure she is." I sip my wine and go to the front door to turn the lock. On my way, I pass the hall table. "What'd you do with my hat? I mean, your hat."

"Nothing. You had it." Donna heads back to the kitchen. "Dinner's ready whenever you are."

I look at the polished mahogany table, envisioning the pasteboard box with black grosgrain ribbons that should be there. It's not. Anger sears my brain with the sure knowledge that Chelsea's found herself a better hat—my hat!

I set my wine glass on the table, yank the door open and hurtle down the front steps to the driveway.

There's no sign of Chelsea, but the gates are just beginning to close. Fueled by a potent mix of adrenalin spiked with rage, I leap across the cobblestones to the grassy knoll, the most direct route to the gate, but catch my foot on the paving trim. I fall, skinning my knees and hands, and slither across damp grass, my body rolling over and over down the hill until I crash into a thick hedge.

I lie there, winded, watching the filigreed metal gates close with a sharp click. There's no way I can hobble down to the street and catch up with Chelsea now. Nor would I want to account for my grass-stained, disheveled appearance.

Taking stock of the damage I've done to my body, I'm grateful nothing feels broken. My face and hands sting, my knee throbs, and I have a sore hip that will probably turn purple and green before morning, but I'll survive. Slowly I roll over and sit up, shaken and feeling foolish.

Just as the last of the twilight fades into darkness, a timer switches on a Disneyland of twinkling lights, illuminating the trees and walkway. I sit for a few minutes, listening to the muffled sound of traffic whooshing down the boulevard on the other side of the hedge.

I'm mystified that Chelsea, knowing we're going to work together again, would steal Jinx's hat. Slowly, I get to my feet, wincing at the stiffness in my joints. How in the world am I going to explain the missing hat to Donna?

4

There are few things more startling than waking up to find your ex-husband grinning at you. I'd barely pushed myself up in bed and dragged my laptop onto my belly before I found myself staring into Dirck's gleeful face. Without thinking twice, I'd answered a call on Skype. Only my mother in Nebraska ever rings first thing in the morning. But Dirck, three hours away in New York, called bright and early.

"Gotcha! Hey, there, how's my girl?"

"Girl just woke up." I disable the video icon without hesitation. Not that Dirck hasn't seen me with bedhead or sleep-swollen eyes before, but I don't care to explain why my face is marred with scratches and bruises. Besides, his face, close up and leering, sporting Don Johnson stubble and a whiter-than-white toothpaste smile, is way more than I can handle at this hour. Worse, I can tell that his home Skype environment, with its manly-man props and artful backdrop, is professionally lit. *Who does that?*

"Hey, what happened? You disappeared."

"Why are you calling?"

"Wanted to catch up."

"I'm not up for a personal appearance. How's the family?"

"Pru's good. Priscilla just started walking. I gotta tell you, there's nothing like a kid to turn your life around. Amazing, huh?"

"Totally. And work?"

"Work's good. Voice-overs. Teaching a coupla classes, which leads me to—"

"Chelsea Horne."

"Yeah, you believe this? Like déjà vu all over again. I hear you're on board to teach your old hat tricks. Can't hurt, but I told her martial arts was the way to go."

"Thanks for the endorsement."

"Hey, no offense, but you gotta stay ahead of the pack. A little hat twirling is fine, but Jinx is combating crime, you know? Karate. Kickboxing. That's where the action is these days."

"Dirck, I haven't had my coffee yet, much less my Wheaties. Where's this conversation going?"

"I'm just saying, you know? That dainty, prancing-around stuff with cute winks isn't going to work. Jinx can't strut. Badass attitude and new technology, that's where it's at. Jinx has gotta be cutting edge. Lethal. Sexy."

"I'm going to hang up now, Dirck."

"Wait—"

I don't wait. I embrace new technology and badass attitude. Without prancing around, I disconnect with an easy tap of my finger. If only shutting up a noisome, preening, irritating, brainless, narcissistic former husband could always be so easy. But it never is. I'm about to set aside my laptop when the Skype ringtone sounds again. Why so persistent? I haven't seen or heard from Dirck in almost a year. I answer with another tap of my finger, curious to hear what he's really calling about.

"Hey, there, a little touchy this morning? Sorry about that. No offense, okay? You had your day in the sun—no one did it better than you, Megsie!—but now you just gotta let it go, know what I mean? New day, new play."

Got it. I should have known. Chelsea's assertion that she would portray Jinx entirely differently from me—grittier, more real—has come straight from Dirck's playbook. Of course Chelsea has to make the role her own, but is there any need to be so combative about it? Why is it necessary to denigrate the original, the role I originated—for which, I never tire of mentioning, I was awarded an Emmy?

As though hearing my thoughts, Dirck says, "No one can take that Emmy away from you, Meg. You deserved it. But that was a very, very long time ago. Times change. Gotta mooooove on."

I climb out of bed and dump the laptop on my pillow. The MacBook rocks slightly, but there's no alteration in the rolling, rich tones of Dirck's superb announcer's voice, for which he earns a hefty session fee, plus residuals. He's at his best selling trucks and trust, the latter category including insurance, pharmaceuticals and financial planning.

Perhaps his greatest pleasure is hearing the sound of his own voice, so I leave him to it while I go about my morning routine.

His deep, sonorous voice reaches me above the gush of water splashing in the sink and the buzz of my electric toothbrush. The sound cuts out as I close the shower door. I'm not surprised when, minutes later, I step out of the stall, wrap myself in a towel and hear him still blathering on about what it takes for an actor to make the grade these days.

"Competition is tough," he says in Jeep Wrangler mode. Then, putting a smile in his voice, he purrs, "But this gal's got the stuff. I knew it the moment I heard her."

"Where was that?" I sing out, while applying antiperspirant.

"Weren't you listening? What're you doing, anyway? I told you, I met her at a voice-over session. Man, she's something else. Didn't have much dough, so I told her she could audit my class for a couple of weeks. I don't usually do that, but I could see the potential."

A low rumble creeps into Dirck's voice, the kind he deploys for the taglines of "you owe it to your family" insurance commercials. "It's what I live for, Meg. Giving back." He repeats the line softly to himself a few times, dropping "Meg" and sounding more reflective, with a faraway lilt in his voice. Who is he trying to sell?

I exhale several times to keep from screaming, then ask, "So where is she from?"

"Who?"

"Chelsea."

"Wisconsin, maybe? Could be Indiana. One of those places out there, but without the twang and that terrible O sound. She's a natural."

"So you're through coaching her, then?"

"No! You kidding me? This is Big Time. She needs all the help she can get. I've got a Skype session with her later this morning. I just thought that you and I should be clear on parameters. Just stick to showing her the hat tricks and I'll take care of the rest, okay?"

"You're the boss." I exhale a few more times, although it's beginning to feel a lot like hyperventilating. "Listen, I gotta run."

"Wait, hang on. I was calling to let you know I'll be flying out on a red-eye to work with Chelsea in person. You know, before she goes on set."

"Great. Weather's fine."

"What I mean is, could you put me up? Just for a night or two."

"No!" My yelp is so vehement I lose my grip on the hairbrush. It clatters into the sink, overturning a water glass on its descent, sending shards flying. "I mean, no. No. I couldn't do that. Sorry, no."

"Oh. Right." His voice is dull, heavy with meaning. "Can't move on, can you? You're living in this big, fancy house and you can't find room for me?"

"You don't understand, okay? This isn't my place."

"So you can't ask to have a friend stay there? You're something else, you know that, Meg? I've got a wife. A kid. You and me? That's over. Long over. I don't need you. And you know something else? Life's been good to me. I like to pass it on. Give back. But that's just me, you know?"

The call ends in Skype's mechanical gulp. I'm left to stare at a decades-old headshot of Dirck on my computer screen, one from a biker movie, with tough-guy smoldering eyes and pouty lips. Ringing in my ears is not his winning voice-over voice, but the downtrodden marital voice I'd like to forget—the "everyone gets a break but me" whine.

In Dirck's estimation, life has not been at all good to him. Somebody else always got the breakout role, the big-bucks contract and all the Emmys and Oscars at the end of the rainbow. He was geared for Big Things, but all poor Dirck got was a wife who worked more than he did, earned more than he did and stole the limelight from him. In his equation, had it not been for me, he would have been a star. Excuse me, a STAR! I somehow held him back even as I paid his bills. Go figure.

Nerves jangling, I scrape up glass shards in wads of toilet tissue and wonder how Dirck knows where I'm living. The thought is barely a question before I have the answer: Chelsea. She must have called him last night after our work session. Fair enough; she was probably just checking in with him, confirming their Skype call this morning.

Still. Did she have to give Dirck a floor plan? Did she lay it on with the pool, tennis court and orchid pavilion? That would've been red meat to Dirck, who's still living in our old New York Westside walkup with a wife and toddler. The fact that I actually own nothing more than a Volvo with four decent tires and a capacious trunk would be meaningless to a guy who still dreams of champagne on a beer budget.

I whip my hair into a frenzied cyclone with the blow-dryer and imagine Pru negotiating three flights of stairs with a stroller and a squalling child. Yet, it's the life I imagined for myself in that very apartment.

I pull on a tee shirt and jeans, the unhip kind I bought on an outing to Costco with Donna. Now, she's someone who really passes it on! As I walk down the hallway, I hear a mewling sound that tells me Donna is still in her boudoir, not flipping gourmet crepes or whatever she's got on tap for breakfast. With a passing nod to discretion, I knock once on her door before entering a suite of rooms cast in twilight by heavy drapes at the windows. The dusky, high-ceilinged room, illuminated by low-wattage track lighting, smells of lavender moth repellant.

"There you are," she says, turning over two AARP-vintage baby dolls, both of them making that distinctive *whaaaa* sound of newborns. "I was going to ask you to give me a hand with these, but then I heard you talking to someone on the phone." There's a lingering pause I realize I'm slow to fill. Donna gives me a questioning look. "I didn't want to interrupt. Everything okay?"

"Fine. Just business."

I open a cabinet and pick up a fashionably dressed French bisque *poupée*, with an all-wooden articulated body, that's drooping on its perch. I gently tip a veiled, satin-ruched hat in place atop a finely coiffed painted head, then tether the doll securely to its Plexiglas stand. I'm only too happy to pitch in. But as I brush my finger across the ermine collar of a miniature velvet coat, I feel Donna's eyes assessing me. At least I didn't lie and tell her my mother called, but I'm not about to mention I had a half-hour Skype chat with my ex-husband.

"You spoke to Chelsea?"

"Just her acting coach."

"Funny she hasn't called to tell us what she did with the hat. You haven't been in touch?"

"No. I'd rather see what she does."

"How're you feeling this morning? I hope the Bengay eased the muscle aches."

"I'm fine, thanks. Just a little stiff. The scratches are already healing."

"Thank God. You looked like you'd been in a barroom brawl. I kind of wish you'd caught up with her."

"Just as well I didn't."

I carefully remove a flaxen-haired *bébé Bru* from a showcase. She's wearing a straw boater and sailor suit, a miniature tin pail and shovel attached to her porcelain hand. Like old folks, underneath their lace, ribbons and fancy bloomers, their skin—in this case, finely stitched kid leather—shows age. Glassy blue paperweight eyes meet mine, unseeing and fathomless. I could read anything into the empty doll-stare.

What was Chelsea thinking? She had to know I'd realize immediately that she'd stolen the hat. She knew I valued it. She knew it belonged to Donna. "I don't get," I mutter aloud. "Why would she take it without asking?"

"Maybe she misunderstood. Did you tell her she could practice with it?"

"No, of course not!"

"Okay, okay. How about some breakfast? I can finish this up later."

"Sorry, Donna. I didn't mean to snap. I'm just—I don't know, irritated? I can't figure her out. Why would she do a dumb thing like steal a hat?"

"Doesn't make sense. But if you want me to call her, I will. After all—"

"I know. It's your hat. Your house. You have every right—" A quick look at Donna's startled face tells me to make amends fast. "Sorry! I really didn't mean it to sound like that."

I sink onto the edge of the bed, holding the doll with the inscrutable stare. Feeling slightly unhinged, I turn the glassy-eyed *bébé* to face her sisters still in the cabinet. "What I mean is, it's my responsibility. I have to deal with it. She had no business walking off with your hat. But I just don't understand what this is about."

"Let's go downstairs and have some coffee." She opens a cabinet door and adjusts a baby doll with a carved wooden face inside its miniature antique crib. "Frankly, I'm sick of this. I just don't want to do it anymore, you know?"

"Huh?" I gasp, feeling walloped in the chest. I squeeze out words in a strangled rush. "Sick of what? Me? Sorry, I know I'm probably getting on your nerves. I've way overstayed my welcome and I'm sorry, but—"

Donna turns and stares at me. "I didn't mean you."

"Sure. Chelsea, I know, and I shouldn't have brought her here like that. It was very presumptuous and I'm sorry. If you want me to leave—"

"Stop, already! It's the dolls I'm sick of." Her arm swoops in an arc encompassing three walls of handcrafted mahogany cabinets brimming with antique dolls of every description. "Just sick and tired of it all!"

Stunned by her vehemence, I pivot to take in the full extent of Donna's collection. Any one of a number of these miniature life-like creatures, all dressed in custom-crafted finery, is worth the price of a luxury sedan. I glance back at Donna, surprised that she would disparage what I thought was a cherished family possession. She looks stricken, her hand clamped to her mouth.

"Donna, are you okay?"

"Shhhh, we'll talk outside," she whispers, as if hundreds of tiny porcelain ears are listening to us.

She takes the sailor doll from me, tenderly places it back in the cabinet and quickly closes the door. The room is hushed, but one can almost hear expressions of hurt and indignation behind the glass panes. I fear Donna's rash words will not soon be forgotten in these quarters.

I need coffee more than ever. I wait in the hallway, feeling vaguely uneasy, until Donna pulls the door closed.

"It gets to me sometimes," she says, still whispering. "They're just so demanding. Someone always needs fixing or doing. A ruffle here, a frayed arm there, it never ends." She sighs. "And I didn't collect them. It was all Mama and Granny's doing, but I'm the one left to take care of these little narcissists!"

If Donna is a little nuts, who am I to judge? "I'm sorry, Donna. I'll try to help out more."

"How about some coffee?" Back to full voice, she heads down the hallway with me at her heels, hoping breakfast will be forthcoming and hearty. She stops abruptly on the landing and peers over the balcony railing. "I mean, look at this!"

I follow her lead and look down at the vast living room and entryway, a space that could accommodate the film set for *Philadelphia Story* if it weren't cluttered with props from *Philadelphia Story* and a few dozen other vintage MGM, RKO, Paramount and Warner Brothers films. Donna's grandfather, an inveterate collector of movie ephemera, hobnobbed with studio moguls, set designers and prop masters to ensure he got the choice bits and pieces hot off the soundstages.

One reason Donna doesn't employ much household help is that she can't risk breakage; therefore, she takes on most of the upkeep herself. Living with Humphrey Bogart's fedora from *The Maltese Falcon* and Dooley Wilson's piano from *Casablanca* is somewhat thrilling; keeping everything tidy is not. Besides, Donna doesn't entertain on the grand scale her grandparents did, and these collectibles beg to be shown off.

The few guests she regularly invites for lunch or holiday dinners already know the answers to her "gotcha" questions. Sample: Who actually played "As Time Goes By" on the piano for Dooley Wilson? Whoever answers "Elliot Carpenter" takes home the jackpot.

Donna sighs. "I'm sick of dusting and polishing. Who needs to live like this? I just need a change."

"I don't blame you. It's hard work." After serving as resident houseguest for nine months, I can sympathize. After a while, a constant stream of trivia questions wears thin. I just want to pour water into a glass that didn't once belong to Jimmy Stewart. But then a terrible thought comes to mind. "Wait, what kind of change? Are you thinking of moving?" *Say it ain't so!*

Donna's give-me-a-break look is sufficient to quell my panic. "I'm not selling up, okay? And you're not leaving. You can't afford it. I'm not talking about that. I just need more spice in my life. And less clutter." She heads for the stairs and I follow. "Do cinnamon-apple griddlecakes sound good to you?"

"Great! And listen, whatever you decide to do about the house, let me give you a hand, okay?"

"Sure. I've got a couple of ideas."

"Anything you want to share?"

"Hmmm, maybe later."

Unspoken is a plea to give me some notice before she does something irrevocable. I've had a belly full of change and I'm not certain my system could tolerate anything too abrupt. It occurs to me that Donna and I demonstrate the yin-yang of copacetic living: one has too much, the other too little.

Twenty-five minutes later, Donna barely swallows the last bite of her griddlecake before she's on her feet, running her syrupy plate under the faucet. "You mind clearing up? I've got a couple of things I want to look into."

"That's fine. I was going to offer anyway. What else can I do? Laundry? Water plants? Fluff Greta Garbo's divan?"

"Very funny. Actually, thanks, the plants need watering." She dries her hands on a dishtowel and heads for the door. "See you later."

"Don't do anything too rash."

My words are spoken a beat too late. Donna, who is as impulsive as anyone I know, has streaked out of the kitchen at warp speed. The dolls have reason to worry. I envision the closing frames of *Citizen Kane*, with Donna's living room becoming a storehouse jammed with packing crates and dustsheets—and there's no reason not to think a few props from the Orson Welles film might actually be on hand.

Aside from washing up breakfast dishes and watering plants, my day is unencumbered until Chelsea decides to call. Technically speaking, I'm on the studio's clock. Thanks to Pat, my stint as hat-trick consultant pays handsomely. I'm on call not only to coach Chelsea but to choreograph fancy hat maneuvers whenever required. My marching orders are supposed to come through the production office, but Chelsea knows how to reach me, too.

I check my cellphone once again. No text messages light up the screen. For a moment, my finger hovers over the miniature keyboard. Should I text Chelsea? *How r u doing? Where's my hat?* I think not.

With the weather Southern California perfect, I head out for a brisk walk, phone in hand. At the bottom of the drive, I decide to take a swing around Holmby Park, although I doubt I'll find Chelsea practicing hat tricks near the bowling green.

The very thought of it brings back memories of my practice sessions with Roxie. She was a stickler for form. It wasn't enough that I got the hat to behave and land on my head properly, I had to do everything with—Roxie's term—flair. "Give it some ritz!" she'd trill in her put-on swanky voice that didn't quite mask its Bronx origins. "Must see some flair, darling!"

After exiting the park at the north end, I head into the maze of residential streets, knowing as I do so that my memories of *Holiday* have triggered thoughts of Dougie Halliburton, who directed most of the episodes. I first met him the day of my camera test for the role of Jinx. I was so in awe of him I could barely speak, but the thought of working with him made me want the role more than anything.

Jinx, the Magician's assistant, was a fabulous character, and thanks to Dougie taking a chance on a newcomer, I got the role of my career. He was a legend at the studio, a features director with a deft hand for comedy and a reputation for working exceptionally well with women. More than one actress won top acting awards for work she did with Dougie. He engendered confidence and always managed to say the thing that made you want to take a different tack, push the boundaries of what was expected.

I've taken to checking in on Doug regularly since his wife, Edie, died. He doesn't mind a drop-in visitor. I round the corner and spot him sitting in a rocker on the veranda, newspapers spread on a side table. Ridley, his Irish setter, lies in a heap at his feet. In dog years, I'd guess Ridley to be the senior member of the duo.

Dougie spots me, too, but doesn't bother to get to his feet. Neither does Ridley. Both watch me turn up the drive and mount the stairs to the wide, shaded veranda. Dougie is wearing his trademark safari jacket and blue jeans, his hair a tangle of gray curls.

"You walk here?"

"Yup, and didn't get arrested."

"Looks like you got mugged instead. What happened to your face?"

"I just tangled with some bushes in the garden. Bushes won." I tap my finger against a scrape on my chin that still stings when touched. "I didn't think it showed. I dabbed some concealer on it. Anyway, how're you doing?"

"Not so bad. A bit of gout is all." He scratches the stubble on his chin and glares at his right foot, which is nestled on a pillow atop a wicker footstool. "It's the curse of kings. Or, in my case, revenge on a country boy's love of biscuits and gravy. Helluva thing, growing old." He gives me a sidelong look, his rheumy eyes lighting up. "Hasn't stopped me, though. My nephew in Chattanooga sent me a Smithfield ham. Want to fix us up a coupla biscuits?"

"No," I laugh. "You're bad, and I'm not going to be your enabler."

"Shucks. Well, put the pot on before you settle in. I could go for some coffee. Strong."

"Right. Black, lots of sugar. Be right back."

I know Dougie's kitchen better than Donna's, where I'm barely permitted to make my own cup of tea. When Dougie means strong, he's talking coffee boiled with chicory in an old tin pot, some sort of odd Southern delicacy that could strip paint.

I cook his dose of poison while brewing a cup of Earl Grey for myself, all the while registering the sure signs of a widower living alone. Uncapped medicine bottles line the windowsill. Biscuits sit on tinfoil in the toaster oven, a sprung Pillsbury vacuum pack on the counter providing evidence of their origin. If I looked, I'm sure I'd find a side of ham and a saucepan of leftover gravy in the fridge. While waiting for Dougie's coffee to boil, I fish a skillet and a week's worth of plates and forks out of murky dishwater that looks like a swamp in August.

After cleaning the kitchen counter, I pick up my cup of tea and Dougie's steaming coffee mug while trying to figure out the best way to finesse regular visits from Meals on Wheels. A dose of nutrition would do more for him than a shelfful of medication.

Dougie's cleared a space on the side table and looks up expectantly as I deliver his coffee. "Here you go. Liquid tar, just the way you like it."

"Nothing finer," he says, after sipping the scalding brew.

"So, how's everything else with you?"

He knows what I mean. Evie has been dead for five months. The neighbors have stopped delivering casseroles. I've told him I'd help with any clearing out whenever he's ready, but my offer's been met with silence and a vacant look. Her clothing has hung in their closet for forty-eight years and there isn't a lot of motivation to change things. He hugs his coffee mug in both hands and looks into the middle distance as though giving my question a considered response.

"Good. Okay. You know, miss her." His voice is thin.

I sip my tea, backing off, letting the silence do its healing. A minute or two later, he reaches down and scratches Ridley's ruff, then runs his hand along the dog's silky, titian coat. "We've got each other here. Can't ask for more." He rocks back and turns his rheumy gaze on me. "What about you? I hear you got a new gig. Keeping it a secret?"

"Boy, you don't miss a thing!"

He nods toward the newspapers on the side table. "It's in the trades. Besides, I got a piece of the action, remember?"

"Of course! My God, what an idiot I am. You created *Holiday*! Sorry, Doug. I wasn't thinking." Then the obvious finally dawns on me. "Wait a minute. You knew the series was coming back and didn't tell me. Damn it, why not?"

"Couldn't. All under wraps. Besides, I'm no longer in the saddle. Not even on the ranch. I just did my deal and climbed into my rocker." The corners of his mouth settle into a clown's pout.

"Yeah, right. Poor, sad old you! C'mon Dougie, you're not out to pasture. If I know you, you're in the thick of it. Wait!" I bounce to my feet, sloshing tea on my Costco jeans. "You're the reason I'm coaching Chelsea Horne. You made that happen."

A lazy smile slides across Dougie's face. "Had to provide some sort of antidote to that up-his-ass acting coach she's got."

I shake my head, thoughts tumbling through my brain too fast to give them voice. I sit back down, realizing what a dimwit I've been. "Okay, so you didn't give me a heads-up. But then, it didn't occur to me to call you, either, when I got the coaching job. So we're even on that score. Still, I'm sorry. What was I thinking?"

"That I'm past it. A tired, old geezer best left on the back burner." There's an edge to his voice, a flicker of anger in his tired eyes. "Okay, so I'm not the newest, shiniest pot on the stove, but it was my damn stove! I'm not going to let 'em forget it!"

"I know how you feel." My voice is barely a whisper and I know there's a shameful tinge of grief lurking in its undercurrent. "I couldn't say this to anyone else, but—"

There's no need to finish the thought. Dougie nods. "Some young kid's gonna be wearing your top hat."

"Yeah." It's my turn to look into the middle distance. "She's good, though. She wants to make Jinx grittier, tougher. More real."

The snort I hear is enough to make me laugh. I turn to see Doug shaking his head. "Slick. Lots of cookie-cutter attitude. They all know the game, but you're right. She leaped off the screen in her camera test. No one else was even considered."

His words hang in the air between us, lingering just long enough to make me think a change of subject is in order. Then Dougie adds, "Almost as good as you, kid. You knocked my socks off when I saw your screen test for Jinx."

I swallow hard, keeping tears at bay. This conversation couldn't happen with anyone else. I know not a morsel of it will ever be repeated. "Thanks, Dougie. I appreciate that."

We both sit back, savoring our shared confidences, but the echo of our sincere, heartfelt sentiments sets off my irresistible need to throw a curve. "In fact, Doug, I'm so darn grateful for your kind words I'd consider it an honor to make you a gravy biscuit."

Dougie bursts into laughter so explosive that Ridley lifts his head for the first time since my arrival. "If that's all it takes! Bring it on."

"Okay, coming up. But first, tell me about the scripts. Do you have approval? Are you going to direct?"

"Consultant. Advisory only. Yeah, maybe I'll helm one toward the end of the season. We'll see. What do you think of the pilot script?"

"Honestly? It feels more like a procedural. I realize it's a weekly hour format, not like our ninety-minute specials. But given that, a lot of the rich, character stuff is lost to plot and pacing. The story goes into territory we couldn't have touched. This pilot about sex trafficking is gripping, torn-from-the-headlines stuff, which I know is what audiences expect now, but I miss the humor, the fun. What do you think?"

Dougie leans over and takes his time stroking Ridley. He cups the muzzle in weathered hands and looks into the dog's watery, brown eyes.

"It's a tale for our so-called post-ironic times. These are not whimsical days. The news blares terrible stories that scripted TV drama can't ignore. The horrors have to be dealt with, albeit in an entertaining manner, because that's what the medium demands. Is that post-ironic enough?"

Doug seems to be asking Ridley, so I don't bother commenting. Ridley, on the other hand, looks bored. He snuffles wearily, obviously having heard these observations from his master before. He makes a throaty sound that could be a dignified growl and lays his head back down on his paws.

"You see that? Ridley knows," Doug says, his voice soft. "The scripts we did back in our day, with that style of acting and directing, just wouldn't work now. The audience is three steps ahead and probably texting or paying online bills if they're even watching. It's a new day. Did I say post-moronic?" He tousles Ridley's ears and leaves the dog in peace.

We observe a moment or two of silent contemplation. While irony is my friend, and whimsy gets me through a day of hard-knocks reality, what would I do without Dougie in my life?

"Listen, there's a kid I'd like you to meet. Wants to be a director. Writes his own stuff. And he's got a thing for Ida Lupino and I think you knew her. Anyway, I just wrapped a little film he did, a backyard kind of production. You mind talking to him?"

"He's in film school?"

"Nope. Don't think he'll be able to afford it."

"Excellent. Send him around. I'll have that gravy biscuit now, if you don't mind."

I nod. "Coming up, sir."

I head for the kitchen, thinking that if the man wants a gravy biscuit, shouldn't he ask permission from his swollen, throbbing big toe? But if a gravy biscuit is worth more than the gouty pain it invites, then give the man his damn gravy biscuit!

With that, I yank open the fridge. Inside are two Samuel Adams pilsners, a wedge of ham in cling wrap, a puckered tomato, three stalks of something stringy and beige that could be the ghost of celery, and a plastic container with congealed white stuff, resembling gravy, that's devoid of any suspicious hairy green bits on top. I look at my watch and take a moment to consider before retracing my steps to the veranda.

"Dougie, you want a beer with the gravy biscuit? It's lunchtime."

"Sure." He glances at my shoulder bag hanging on the back of a chair. "Is that your phone making that racket?"

Indeed it is. Set to vibrate, my cellphone is burring noisily inside its leather pouch. I snatch it from my bag and catch the call before it goes to voicemail. "Hello? Hello?"

"Hey, hi. I've been trying to call you. Where've you been?"

It's Dirck. He's barely spoken and I'm already on the verge of rage. Do I really need to account for myself to a former husband? "What do you mean, where have I been? What do you want?"

"Hey, easy. I left a message. I thought you'd get back to me."

"Sorry, I've been with a friend. What's up?"

"Not sure. It's just that I was supposed to have a Skype session with Chelsea and I can't reach her. It's not like her, you know? Just wondered if you'd heard from her."

I'm struck by an odd sense of foreboding. In the time it takes me to realize I'm holding my breath, Dirck's voice, his real one that just sounds like a guy from Queens with a rasp, says, "Hey, Megsie, sorry, but I just wondered if she's been in touch with you."

"No. No, I haven't heard from her this morning. Sorry."

"That's okay. If you do, tell her to call me. I got a couple hours free if she wants to work."

"Sure. Will do. And, Dirck . . . you still there? If you hear anything, let me know."

"Yeah. Yeah, will do."

I look at Doug as I disconnect. His eyes are alert. "What's up?"

"Chelsea." I shrug. "Probably overslept. She was supposed to work with Dirck this morning but didn't call in."

"No harm there. She'd do well to lose his number." Doug's comment is offhand, but I sense he's picked up on my concern. "Anything you're not telling me?"

"Nope. That's it." I head back to the kitchen. "Gravy biscuit coming up."

There's no reason to go into the story about Chelsea stealing my hat, or that I have cuts and bruises because I fell into a hedge while chasing her. How do you explain that without sounding infantile—or post-moronic?

A voiding rush hour is a luxury only the unemployed can afford. The teeming sprawl is a world away from Donna's doorstep, choking every boulevard and side street leading to the traffic-clogged parking lots known as freeways. It happens to other people and is safely over by the time either Donna or I venture out.

Therefore, the chug of a diesel-powered engine laboring up the driveway and the squeal of thick tread on paving stones is a rare and terrible sound intruding on the customary morning quiet. I sit up in bed, listening to the metallic scrape of a roll-up door opening, followed by the sound of a hand truck rattling across cobblestones.

Still drowsy, my first awful thought is: *Donna's moving! The packers are here!*

I leap out of bed and stagger to the window. Indeed, a large truck is parked in the driveway, but the driver appears to be delivering, not picking up. The doorbell rings. I yawn. My bed is safe for another night.

I consider crawling back under the covers, but with sunlight streaming through the window, sleep loses its appeal. It hasn't been a good night, and for that I can blame Chelsea. I tossed and turned, playing out one scenario after another, complete with overwrought dialogue in which I chastised her for being irresponsible, ungrateful, disrespectful and duplicitous. Even as I spent sleepless hours churning out choice diatribe after choice diatribe, I realized I probably wouldn't deliver a single word of it.

Trumping all my scenarios is the one where Chelsea hands over the hat with a sly smile and no apology. "Oh, were you looking for this?"

When I finally did descend into sweet oblivion I was met with one of my strenuous Furniture Dreams, in which I leap from

end tables to chiffoniers and sofas while being chased by someone. But I was also searching for something lost—what? My hat?
Chelsea? Why would I lose sleep over a spoiled, arrogant little
thief? I'm not her babysitter. Besides, I'm on the production pay-
roll whether or not I give her the coaching she needs, and it's
money I sorely require.

But then, in the wee hours of the morning, when I awoke in
a panic, it struck me that what I might be striving to recover was
the lost role of Jinx. Admitting that to myself permitted me to
sleep dreamlessly until the arrival of the delivery truck.

I wash my face, skirting the red, puffy scratches on my cheek
and forehead. I'm hoping a dab of makeup will cover most of the
damage, but the deeper cut on my chin will take a couple of days
to heal. Dressed in blue jeans and a tee shirt, my feet stuffed into
well-worn Uggs, I pad into the kitchen to see what Donna's up to.
I stop in my tracks at the sight of the breakfast nook. I was expecting hot coffee and Donna's usual gourmet spread, but not
served this way: in an elaborate display of vintage crockery in a
mocked-up movie set. She is not a slapdash sort of person, but
this is way over-the-top even by her standards.

"You shouldn't have," I manage to say. "Just buttered toast
would be fine. Maybe cornflakes."

"It's my new venture!" Donna, decked out in a chef's toque,
traditional white jacket and black-checked pants, beams at me.
"What do you think?"

"Nice outfit. Have I stepped into *Moulin Rouge*?"

"Guess again. Sit, please."

She pulls out a chair. I sit and she snaps a napkin into my
lap. Above me, a crystal chandelier wobbles at a strange angle,
glittering brightly in the darkened alcove. Red velvet drapes cover
the mullioned windows. Red roses burst from a silver vase on a
sideboard that's overflowing with a sumptuous still-life of artfully
arranged delicacies. A crystal pitcher of orange juice nestles in an
ice-filled urn on a table laid with gold-rimmed china and fine cutlery. On a small scroll of parchment curled around a pair of or-
nate opera glasses, I see my name written in fancy script.

"Place cards for breakfast? Who else were you expecting?"

"For now, just you. But I want to get the atmosphere right
for guests. You know, set a theme."

I look at her in horror. "You're not opening a bed-and-
breakfast here!"

"No, but that's an idea. Actually I'm starting a catering business called . . . ta da! Hollywood on a Plate!" She spreads her arms wide and beams at me. "Get it? Meals based on old movies. Hollywood. On. A. Plate. I love to cook. I like keeping busy and I have all these vintage props. So I came up with the idea for Dine with the Stars! Hollywood on a Plate."

"Got it. And this is *Gaslight*?"

She shakes her head vehemently, almost toppling her chef's toque. She points a finger at an antique Venetian mask that I somehow overlooked, lying near a trio of jams and marmalade. "*Phantom of the Opera*!"

"Of course. But do you think *Phantom of the Opera* lends itself to breakfast?"

"Dinner, probably, but I wanted to try it out."

She hands me a shiny black business card emblazoned with silver lettering: *Dine with the Stars! Hollywood on a Plate.*

"My business cards and stationery were delivered with my new computer this morning, so I'm set to go. The plan is that you choose your menu based on a vintage movie. I figure it's a way I can put all this memorabilia to work for me." She waves her hand at the props on the table. "Ingrid Bergman's opera gloves. Fred Astaire's top hat."

"Great idea. But you better hope nobody tries to swipe your décor, thinking they're party favors. When are you starting up?"

"I'm already open for business. My first booking is lunch for my golf partners. We're doing *Shanghai Express* because everyone liked the idea of Chinese food, and I can show off my Anna May Wong kimono collection and Marlene Dietrich's lace fan."

Donna is almost breathless with excitement. I'm parched, longing for a plain cup of coffee in a mug no one famous ever used. I reach for the orange-juice pitcher, but Donna deftly beats me to it. "Please, allow me. Coffee?"

"Yes, please. Maybe we could have it in the kitchen?"

"Sure. Whatever you want." She looks disappointed, but leads the way to the bright, airy kitchen. "Are you in a hurry? I was going to do eggs Florentine."

"Maybe just an English muffin? I want to sit in on the table read at the studio this morning. With a bit of luck, Chelsea will show up."

"You still haven't heard from her?"

I shake my head. "She and your hat are apparently doing fine on their own."

"It's so disrespectful!" Donna splits an English muffin and slides the halves into the toaster oven. "I hope she hasn't wrecked the hat. It's irreplaceable. By the way, your face is better this morning, but it still looks like you tangled with an alley cat. Have you got some concealer?"

"That bad?" I gingerly touch my chin, feeling the sore ridge of the cut. "I'll put more makeup on it."

"Careful, don't let it get infected. Are you in for dinner tonight?"

"What's the theme?"

"Nothing special, but I want to try a recipe for pot roast in Guinness."

"Sounds good. Count me in." I devour my muffin and head upstairs to shower. On my way, I pass Donna dismantling her *Phantom of the Opera* set. "Would you mind if I bring a friend home for dinner?"

"Not at all. Who?"

"A guy who could use a good home-cooked meal. And he's Irish."

Bounding up the stairs, I somehow know I've made Donna's day. She loves company, especially someone new who will appreciate her collection of old Hollywood memorabilia. And Dougie Halliburton could use some tender care and attention, if not pot roast soused in Guinness.

On my way out the door, Donna hands me a stack of flyers advertising Hollywood on a Plate. "Pass these out at the studio, would you? I'd love to cater some movie star supper parties. Maybe even a premiere," she says, without a hint of modesty.

"Sure thing. There's always the chance I'll bump into Steven Spielberg." I tuck the flyers under my arm. "See you tonight."

Most people in Los Angeles have nothing to do with the movie business, but Hollywood leaves its mark everywhere and always attracts an audience. I swing my Volvo around a slow-moving van filled with tourists gawking at what was once the site of a Sunset Boulevard mansion known as the Pink Palace. It was the home of 1950s bombshell Jayne Mansfield, mother of actress Mariska Hargitay, and boasted a pink heart-shaped swimming pool. Built by 1920s crooner Rudy Vallée, the house was also home to Beatle Ringo Starr, and singers Engelbert Humperdinck and Cass Elliot. The house was demolished in 2002, but apparently the location is still worth ogling on the tour of celebrity homes.

I have my own Hollywood map of places that no longer exist: eateries, boutiques and even film studios that were once special places to me. I still find it hard to think of MGM, where I filmed the original *Holiday* series, as Sony Studios. The new *Jinx* is to be filmed in the heart of Hollywood in a studio where Mary Pickford made her first film. Small, with only twelve working soundstages, the studio is dwarfed by giant Paramount across the street. I pull off Melrose Avenue and turn into the Bronson Avenue gate, wondering if the production assistant in charge of such things has left me a drive-on pass.

No, the PA has not arranged for me to park inside the studio gates. I'm obliged to make an awkward three-point turn to pull out of the entrance and look for street parking. Fifteen precious minutes later, I squeeze into a spot, technically legal, with only a few inches of my fender protruding on the red-painted curb. I chance it, stuffing enough quarters in the meter to give me two hours, and sprint up the street.

Unfortunately the PA hasn't arranged for a walk-on pass, either. The guard, eyeing me frostily, calls the production office. No one answers, of course. Everyone is probably at the table read, which I am missing. Fuming, but unwilling to give up, I call Dirck on his cellphone, which he's probably turned off for the duration of the table read.

Surprise. He answers immediately. "Meg? Where are you? Everyone's expecting you."

"Oh, please, don't tell me they're waiting for me. I can't bear it." My cheeks grow hot with mortification. "I'm here at the gate. There's no pass for me and the guard won't let me in."

"What? Hey, stay where you are. I'll be right there to take care of it."

Swell. Former husband to the rescue. *He* probably got a drive-on pass. Lovely. But then my rational self asks, why would they wait for me? My presence isn't critical. I've only been invited to the reading as a courtesy. I shift from one foot to the other, misery seeping into every fiber of my body.

The Actor's Waking Nightmare attacks: I'm late because (a) nobody told me I had the job; (b) nobody sent a script; (c) nobody gave me a call time; (d) my alarm clock didn't go off; (e) "I died.

Didn't my agent tell you?" I would happily die rather than be late. By the time I see Dirck sprinting down the hallway toward me, I have lost feeling in my legs.

"Did you tell them why I'm late?" I yelp. "There was no drive-on pass!"

"Hey, easy. It's okay." Dirck grips my shoulders. "You all right? What happened to your face?"

"I walked into some tree branches. Nothing to worry about. God, how I hate being late!" Then I see the panic in Dirck's eyes and calm down. "What? Tell me, please, what's going on?"

"Chelsea's late. She's not here. Looks like she's a no-show." Dirck reiterates, as though I may not have gotten it, "She's. Not. Here."

"Where is she?"

"Wish I knew."

"But it's a table read."

I have now stated the obvious. No actor would miss a table read. Dirck knows this. I know this. Chelsea must be dead. We take a moment to let this sink in before Dirck eases his grip on my shoulders.

"I'm taking a lotta heat in there, Megs." He shakes his head and I hear the voice of a little boy owning up. "I sort've gave the impression Chelsea and I were really tight, you know? Like she doesn't make a move without me? Truth is, she's one very secretive chick. How the hell am I supposed to know what's going on with her? But everyone's looking to me for answers. I'm supposed to know where she is, why she isn't at the table, you know?"

"It's okay. I understand. Take it easy." Even as it registers how quickly we've fallen back into our former marital roles, I forge on, taking over. "Did you bring me a pass? Let's get in there and find out what's going on, okay?"

"Yeah, yeah. Here." He hands the guard a pass, then turns his troubled eyes back to me. "This could wreck me, you know. I shouldn't have shot my mouth off."

Dirck leads the way. With so much riding on Chelsea, my hunch is that Dirck's become a convenient scapegoat, paying the price for having overplayed his role as the guy holding the strings in her career. Chelsea's agents and manager must despise him!

We enter the space set aside for the table read, a corner of a soundstage with bare lights illuminating a long folding table and a dozen or more chairs. People mill around, voices low, no one looking happy. It feels as cozy as a KGB interrogation center. A short man sporting a shiny baldpate, encircled with a fringe of steel-wool hair, glares at Dirck. "So? You found Chelsea yet?"

Showman that he is, Dirck flings a hand in my direction. "Not yet, ladies and gentlemen, but I've brought you Meg Barnes, the original Jinx!"

Faces light up and there's a smatter of applause. I bow my head, smile and eat it up. "All in a day's work!" I respond, enjoying the hearty comments.

"So glad you made it!"

"Hoping you'd come!"

"Wow! You look great, Miss Barnes!"

"Thanks! Thank you so much for inviting me today. It's a privilege to be here and I wish you all the best with the new series."

More squeals of "My God! I loved you! I grew up with you!" I even hear someone say, "Miss Barnes, you haven't changed a bit!"

The balding man claps his hand on my shoulder. "Hey, I'm Ed Ackerman. We wouldn't be here without you, Meg. You created the iconic Jinx, after all. Glad to have you aboard teaching Chelsea the hat stuff." He turns and calls into the darkness, "Billy? Come on over. I want you to meet Meg."

Emerging from the shadows is a slim, lanky young man in blue jeans and a bomber jacket, who gives me a tentative smile before taking my hand. "Hi. Billy Gibbons. Nice to meet you."

"He's our director," Ed tells me. "I gave him all your DVDs to watch. You know, to get the tone, the flavor. Of course we're going our own route. Believe me, no same-old, same-old, you know?"

"Yes, of course. I understand, Ed." *Well, so much for my iconic contribution.* "It's nice to meet you both. Thanks for bringing Jinx back. I'm grateful to be here."

"Well, lemme just say," Ed says, glancing at Billy, "we'd be grateful if you could solve our real-life mystery. Where the hell's Chelsea? She's forty minutes late. No one's seen her since—when?"

I shrug. "I haven't heard from her." Out of the corner of my eye, I see Dirck slinking into the shadows. "I'm sure she'll turn up."

"Yeah, well, her agents are onto it. We even sent a car to her house to check. Anyway, we gotta get this show on the road. Everyone else is here. How about you reading her part until she shows up? That okay with you, Billy?"

"Yeah, cool. Sure." Billy nods, looking uncertain.

"Me? I couldn't, really."

"Why not? It would be an honor." Ed grabs my elbow. "You've read the script, right?"

"Of course, love it. It's great, but ... "

But what? Ed is already leading me to the table and I'm not dragging my feet. The actors, coffee containers in hand, take their seats. Ed steers me toward a tall, pale man with flaxen hair and a hawklike nose, who peers at me in round-eyed wonder.

"Meg, this Cedric Mickelthwaite, who plays the Magician. Cedric, meet Meg."

My first thought is that there is something to be said for made-up names. The second: *Omigod,* he's *taking over for Winston Sykes?*

Winnie, who has since grown portly, was matinee-idol handsome, with a raffish air that perfectly suited a debonair sleuth. Cedric Mickelthwaite looks like an addled egret anxious to take flight. He stares at me for a moment and says, "You were so marvelous as Hattie."

"Hattie? You saw me play Hattie? How amazing!" It's my favorite role, one written for me in a play I hoped would make it to Broadway. Instead it died a grim death after a brief run, mired in backers' woes and litigation. "You must be from Chicago."

"I am. My parents took me to see you. My dad loved you as Jinx."

"Of course, of course. He must be thrilled you're playing the Magician."

"And Cedric is a real magician!" Ed says, jumping in. "Does all his own stuff. Wait until you see!"

Cedric gives me a crooked smile. "I took it up as a kid because of *Holiday.* I can't believe I'm going to read with you."

"Well, let's see how it goes, Cedric."

I take a deep breath and sit. Only a moment before, I wasn't nervous. Now I am. I open the script the PA has placed on the table in front of me and turn to the first page.

Ed settles back in a director's chair, with an assortment of writers and staff members seated behind him. Billy perches on a stool. The script woman, stopwatch in hand, sits in a chair next to him. "Ready, everyone? Let's begin act one, scene one. We fade in on Jinx backstage."

I settle in quickly and find Cedric to be a deft sparring partner for Jinx. His timing is sublime. He infuses the role with a sly, elegant wit, a light comedic touch that doesn't undermine those moments when he has to be tough and serious. His eccentric appearance works for him. He's mesmerizing as the Magician. I imagine him with Chelsea, her deep-throated voice and cocky manner playing to his suave man-about-town, and realize why they were cast opposite each other.

Chelsea, you fool! Don't blow this! If only I could reach her, shake some sense into her. As much as I loved playing Hattie Osborne in a turn-of-the-century stage drama, I know that Jinx Fogarty is the role I'll always be remembered for and the one that made so much else possible. It could be Chelsea's ticket, too.

Approximately fifty-two minutes later, Cedric and I stand and give each other a hug. It's over, and I am both relieved and elated. It was fun. Cedric stretches his arms out, still looking like a bird about to take flight, but his pale face is glowing. He's grinning. I'm sure he's imagining the phone call home to his father.

I look around the room, listening to the buzz of voices. Ed is huddled with Billy and a cluster of people I'm sure include the writers and key crew members. The actors have broken into small groups hovering near a craft services table laden with snacks.

Where's Dirck? I realize he's the one I've been looking around for, but he seems to have disappeared. Then my eyes fall on him, half-hidden in shadow, leaning against a wall near the soundstage entrance. His arms are folded tight against his chest, his head tilted to the side, and he's looking directly at me. Our eyes lock for a moment and I realize that he's not going to come over to me. I sling my bag over my shoulder and go to him.

"So?"

"So? Nothing like the limelight, eh? You jumped right in." His lips curl in what tries for a smile, but his voice is cold.

"Hey, wait a minute! I didn't ask to read Chelsea's part. Ed asked me to sit in."

"But it felt good, didn't it? You liked letting 'em know you still have the chops. That's okay, but I wouldn't try to show the kid up anymore. You make yourself look bad. It's a little embarrassing, you know?"

"Dammit! That wasn't my intention and you know it!"

"Yeah? Okay. And just for the record, you held your own. Not bad. You still do that thing with your mouth, though. That nervous thing. You should work on it."

"Oh, really? Thanks for the critique. On the house, I hope, but feel free to send a bill." I smile, just to show there are no hard feelings, and brush past him. "Good seeing you, Dirck. As always."

The heavy soundstage door isn't conducive to slamming, but the loud click of the lock has a satisfying sound of finality. Jaws clenched, I march down the cement walkway toward the studio entrance. All I need is a parking ticket to make my day truly dismal.

I pick up speed and almost knock over the young redheaded PA barreling full steam around a corner. We bump into each other and I instinctively grasp her upper arms to steady her. "You okay?"

"Sorry, wasn't looking." She takes a deep breath. "I'm Eden, Mr. Ackerman's assistant. Please forgive me for not leaving a pass for you. But it's been such a day, you wouldn't believe!"

"I know. Any word from Chelsea?" I venture.

"Not yet." Eden groans and shows me her clipboard full of messages. "I've called and called. Even sent a car to her house to check if something happened up there. Her agent is beside himself. I don't know what we're going to do."

"It's not good," I mutter while my eyes scan the clipboard for Chelsea's address. "She's up in Laurel Canyon somewhere?"

"Yeah, a rented house off Wonderland Avenue. Sorry, I'm not supposed to give out the address." She hugs the clipboard to her chest, which is fine since I've already memorized the street number. "You were just great in there. It must've been fun for you to play Jinx again."

"Thanks! I hope it was okay for me to do that. After all, it's Chelsea's role now. I don't want to butt in."

"Oh, you didn't! I sat in on all the casting, so it's fascinating to see what each actress brings to the role. You're funny and lighthearted. Great timing. Chelsea's really strong, tough, but she's got this vulnerable side."

"I know. And her voice. Great voice." We smile at each other. I'm aware that Eden is jiggling her clipboard against her chest, anxious to move on. "Well, you've got to get back, so I'll let you go. Nice to meet you, Eden."

"And you! Sorry, got to run." She takes off at a gallop, then turns back. "And, hey! You were really great! So funny!"

"Thanks! See you around." It's a terrible thing to acknowledge, but I really needed to hear those reassuring words. The fact that a young personal assistant, a neophyte in the business, who essentially works as a gofer for the producer, thinks I was "great" and "funny" carries more weight than I care to admit. Why do I let Dirck get to me?

I race to my car, grateful to see that there's no ticket stuck under the windshield wiper. I open the windows to let in cool air, fasten my seat belt and head for Laurel Canyon Boulevard. The winding, congested thoroughfare snakes up a hilly route from West Hollywood to the crest on Mulholland Drive, then down to the San Fernando Valley on the other side.

Along the way, my eyes travel up to the hodgepodge of bungalows clinging to the canyon walls, surprised to recall how many of these houses I've visited over the years. Laurel Canyon, long known as a counter-culture haven, has always attracted its share of actors and celebrities, beginning with cowboy star Tom Mix, up through musician Frank Zappa and his family. I even lived for a few months in a small rental on Lookout Mountain.

I swing off the boulevard and head up Wonderland Drive, the streets becoming narrower and more winding. Eventually I find the house Chelsea has rented, an almost shack-like structure painted pale blue with white trim. A brick walkway twists uncertainly up a grassy rise, skirting around a giant sycamore shadowing the house, and ending at a set of cracked cement steps. The windows are shuttered. There's no car parked in the sagging carport.

I continue on up the street, turn around and park about twenty yards north of Chelsea's bungalow, my wheels turned tight to the curb. I'm in no hurry. I wait, occasionally checking my cellphone for messages. Few cars drive by. No one appears on the street or leaves any of the houses.

Slowly I get out of my car, an old envelope from my glove compartment in hand. If anyone is watching me, I want an excuse for opening her mailbox. I find a handful of circulars and an envelope inside, perhaps two days' worth of junk mail and a telephone bill. I slide my envelope, an untraceable advertisement, inside the box. There are no newspapers yellowing on the doorstep, but then Chelsea is young. If she reads a daily paper, she probably does so online. I glance around, then head up the twisting walkway to her front door.

I give the buzzer a poke, wait a moment, then knock, almost jumping when I hear the sound of a telephone ringing inside. It rings five times, then stops. I wait another minute or so, trying to peek into the narrow cracks of the shuttered windows. The phone begins to ring again. I turn around and walk toward my car.

Just as I reach the trunk of the sycamore, a green sedan pulls up to the curb and stops. A woman peers through the windshield, first at me, then at the house. The car reverses a few feet, then pulls into the driveway. It's not Chelsea at the wheel, but something about the woman's jawline and the set of her shoulders looks familiar. I hitch my bag further up on my shoulder and grip the strap with both hands, feeling wary and not sure why.

The woman is tall with broad shoulders and sandy-blond hair pulled into a loose knot at her neck. Without even seeing her face as she eases out of the car, I realize who she is. She turns around, her movements quick and decisive as she takes me in. She's recognized me, too, and glares.

I smile warmly, which is sure to get her goat. Elaine Farris was a ferocious, hard-drinking, tough-talking broad back in the days when we worked together, and it appears she's lost none of her edge. I stand a little taller, sizing her up as she stares me down, her glower intensifying.

Her long legs are clad in jeans tucked into boots, and she's wearing a chamois jacket over a ribbed blue sweater, an outfit I swear I remember from twenty-odd years ago. She strides toward me, Amazonian in stature.

Growing up on a farm in Nebraska, I was a tomboy. I climbed trees, built forts out of cabbage crates, drove my dad's Allis-Chalmers tractor, and was even capable of plowing furrows as deep and straight as his. But I could never match Elaine in sheer muscle strength, skill and daring. That's why she was my stunt double on *Holiday* and, for my money, one of the best in the business. She also has great legs, long and beautifully shaped. If her body is mistaken for mine in action sequences, I'm not about to set the record straight.

As she approaches, I see a soft belly bulging beneath her jacket, a sign she may still be chugging down a beer too many. Her eyelids are heavy and her jowls sag where once her skin was taut. She has a weathered look, attesting to too much sun and hard living. I may have aged better in the close-up department, but I'd still welcome her standing in for me in the long shots.

She stops, looks me up and down, and shifts her weight before speaking.

"Barnes. What the hell you doing here?"

"Hi, Elaine. I just dropped by to see if Chelsea Horne was in. Don't tell me you've been called in to coach her, too? It's like old-home week all of a sudden." I know I'm talking too much, but I can't seem to break Elaine's impenetrable stare. "Like the whole gang's back."

"The gang?" She looks at me as though I've lost my marbles. "What the hell you talking about? I've been called in to work with her? Like a stunt double? I'm her mother!"

6

It's my turn to look at Elaine in disbelief. "Chelsea's mother? Horne?"

"Yeah, there was a Horne along the way. I'm Elaine Farris Horne. I kept my husband's name. I guess you couldn't ever be bothered to use the name Heyward?"

"No. No, kept my own name. A good thing, since we got divorced."

"Yes, of course. It's not the only thing we don't have in common." Her smoky-gray wolf's eyes, with their steely glint, stare at me, inscrutable as always.

"So, you live around here? I haven't seen you in years."

"That's not a bad thing, as far as I'm concerned. No need to get chummy now. I'm not in town for long."

"You just arrived?"

"What's it to you if I did?" She eyes me more closely. "You walk into a wall or something?"

"My face?" I cup my chin in my hand. "No, just some branches, that's all. Anyway, Chelsea's a terrific girl. Lots of talent."

"Yeah, she's my daughter. I know. She doesn't need you moving in on her, okay? This is her gig. She's not walking in your shadow."

Heat rises in my throat, constricting my voice. "Look, I was hired to coach her. I didn't ask for the job. I only worked with her once, okay?"

"Good. That's enough. Back off." She tosses the words over her shoulder as she strides up to the front door. "No need to hang around here."

"She's not home."

Elaine turns around, her eyes flashing angrily. "So leave already."

"Do you know where she is?" Despite Elaine's fury, I hold my ground. "I mean it. Do you know where she is? Nobody's seen her and we're concerned." As though punctuating my words, the phone rings inside the house. "That's probably the studio. She didn't show up for the table read this morning."

Elaine's mouth falls open as she absorbs the significance of what I've said. "She missed . . . a table read?"

I nod. "Do you know where she is?"

Elaine wavers for an instant, uncertainty clouding her face. A moment later, she springs into action. With a single sweep of her eyes, she determines the most expedient entry point to break into her daughter's house. Watching her hoist her trim body up to a windowsill, lift a sash, push aside shutters and sling a leg inside the room, it's clear to me the woman has lost none of her muscle tone.

In one easy motion, she dips her head and slides her body through the open window—then vanishes. I hover below the window frame, impatiently calling out, "Hey, Elaine, everything okay in there? Could you open the front door, please?"

In response, Elaine slams the window down and closes the shutters. Why has this woman never liked me? But I'm not one to let a little animosity stand in my way. I walk up the steps and press my ear against the front door.

I can hear Elaine moving around, her boots pounding across hardwood floors, followed by sounds of doors opening, the scrape of a sliding panel, the snap of a latch and then the click and whir of an answering machine. The words aren't distinct, but I recognize the voices of Dirck, Elaine, Ed Ackerman and his secretary, Eden. Several unfamiliar voices, some sounding urgent, even harsh, could be those of her agent and manager, but I'm not able to comprehend anything in the rise and fall of faint garbled speech.

I'm so intent on listening at the door that I barely register scuffling footsteps on the walkway until I jump at a sudden loud *skrawking* sound. Whipping around, I see two police officers walking toward me, one of them adjusting a noisy radio device attached to his belt. The tall, dark-haired officer stops under the sycamore and speaks into a mouthpiece. The other officer, squat with a barrel chest, adjusts his belt and advances to the bottom of the steps.

"Miss, you mind coming down here, please?"

"No, not at all." I walk down three steps and face the husky officer, looking directly into his cold, pale eyes. "Hi, I'm Meg Barnes. I'm just here checking on a friend."

"Could I see some identification, please?"

"Sure, right here in my wallet." I slide my shoulder bag onto the crook of my arm, slowly unzip it and spread the opening wide so he can see the contents. I pull out the wallet, flip it open and show my driver's license. I replace my bright smile with a look of concern. "We haven't heard from her. I last saw her night before last."

"Could you take your ID out of the plastic, please?"

"Of course. We didn't report her missing because we just weren't sure what was happening." I take my driver's license out of my wallet and hand it to him. "She's an actress and didn't show up for a read-through this morning. Have you heard of a show called *Holiday*?"

Without looking at my license, he passes it to the other officer. "We're here because we had a complaint that someone's breaking in. You happen to know who lives here?"

"Chelsea Horne." I look toward the street. A squad car is parked several houses down from my Volvo. Directly across from Chelsea's house, an elderly woman, arms tucked close to her chest, stands on her doorstep watching. "I just came by to check up on her. We didn't have a key, so—"

"Who's we?"

"Her mother. She's inside."

"And she had no key? How did she get in?"

"The window." I indicate the bedroom window, now closed and shuttered. "But it's her mother. From out of town, I think. She just got here."

"Maybe there's a reason she had no key. You want to step aside, please?"

"Sure. Absolutely. There's no need for me to even be here, so maybe I'll—"

"Just stand over there, please. Do not leave." The good-looking dark-haired officer moves up next to me, still holding my license.

Husky Cop mounts the steps and presses the buzzer while at the same time calling out, "Open up. Police."

Frankly, I'd like to see Elaine get arrested—as long as I'm not charged as her accomplice. If we were hauled in and booked, it could make an interesting story: Jinx and Her Stunt Double Charged with Breaking and Entering New *Jinx* Star's Home. The story would probably gain even greater traction as Young Star Disappears on Eve of Filming, a headline I'm sure Ed Ackerman doesn't want to see. These thoughts zip through my brain as we wait for Elaine to unlock the door and open it.

When she does, I'm not prepared for the look of horror on her face when she sees a cop standing on the doorstep. "My God, is it my daughter? Is she okay?"

"Ma'am, we have no knowledge of your daughter. We're here because of a report that someone was breaking and entering. You know anything about that?"

Elaine shifts gears, planting a boot on the threshold, and seems to fill up the doorframe. Even her voice is commanding. "My daughter lives here. I just arrived from Indiana and misplaced my keys. I've found them now." She raises her hand and jingles a ring of keys. "Case solved."

"Your daughter's not at home?"

"She's working."

"Wait a minute, Elaine." I can see where this is going and I'm not about to let her get away with it. "Chelsea wasn't at work. That's why I came by."

"Now, look!" With lightning in her eyes, Elaine points a finger at me, thundering, "You're nothing but an opportunist! Get out of here and leave my daughter alone!" She glares at the police officer on her doorstep and says, "Sorry, but I don't want this woman harassing my daughter. And I don't have time for this!"

"Ma'am, please step out of the house."

Elaine shakes her head, sighs, but complies. The husky officer enters the house, leaving the other officer standing on the steps between us.

Taking a different tack, Elaine says confidingly, "I'm sorry, Officer. I didn't mean to be disrespectful, but this woman has no business being here."

I suck in a breath, struggling to remain calm. "In fact, Officer, I've been hired to work with her daughter as a coach, but she's disappeared. I'm not at all harassing the girl. I just came to see if she was home."

The officer looks from me to Elaine and asks, "Has a missing persons report been filed?"

"Of course not," Elaine says. "I just arrived. We've only got *her* word that my daughter is even missing."

"Maybe we need to check with her employer? Did they send you here to look for her?" he asks me.

"No. I came on my own, but it's not necessary to check with them."

It occurs to me to stop talking. I could be digging myself into a hole. Not only Ed Ackerman, but also the studio and the network would be unhappy to have the police involved. "She hasn't really been missing long. Probably with a boyfriend, you know? I'll head back to the studio. She's probably turned up by now."

"Good idea," Elaine says. "Why don't you do that. Thank you, Officer. I'll just go back inside."

"Just wait where you are, please. Both of you."

The husky officer returns from his inspection and the two confer on the sidewalk, leaving Elaine and me cooling our heels in the hot sun. The dark-haired officer turns to me, then looks back at my license. "Meg Barnes? You live at this address?"

"Um, no, not exactly. I moved out a while back. Meant to change the address, of course. I'm actually staying with a friend."

"So this isn't your address? Where are you currently living?"

I reach into my shoulder bag and grab a handful of Donna's flyers. "Here, this is where I currently live. I'm also in the catering business. There's the telephone number and address. Keep it. If you know anyone that needs a party catered, call. Anyway, I need to get back to work."

Elaine doesn't even ask, just snatches a flyer from my hand.

"That your car over there?" Husky Cop nods toward my Volvo.

My chest feels tight, probably gearing up for a heart attack, which would at least provide distraction. "Sure, take a look. Everything's in good order," I say, wondering if indeed everything's in good order. The officer and I walk down the gentle slope to my Volvo, which at least no longer looks like I live in it.

"You've got some nasty scratches on your face. Mind telling me how you got them?"

"No big deal. I slipped, fell into some bushes." He nods but says nothing. "It was dark and I was running. You know, wet grass."

I promise myself not to say another word. Still waiting to have the heart attack, or maybe just a garden-variety panic attack,

I imagine myself being cuffed and hauled off under suspicion of being a stalker. The dark-haired cop gives me a long look, then hands me my driver's license.

"Thank you, Miss Barnes. It might be best for you to be on your way. I wouldn't hang around here."

"No, of course not. Thanks so much."

Under his watchful eyes, I climb into my car, fasten my seat belt and drive off with a wave of my fingertips. I exhale, letting the news sink in that Chelsea is Elaine's daughter. Perhaps that's why Chelsea looked familiar to me, not so much facially, but the long-limbed body and easy carriage. She doesn't have Elaine's smoky-gray eyes, but the haughtiness is certainly an inherited trait. However, Chelsea's demeanor, which could be off-putting if it weren't accompanied by a sardonic sense of humor, is an improvement on her mother's sourness.

Elaine was always tough sledding; frosty, with a chip on her shoulder. I avoided her as much as possible, but I also knew she made me look good in the action sequences. More than once, I stood off camera watching in awe as she leaped from one tall building to another or escaped from a burning car just before it exploded. Despite my praise and early attempts at camaraderie, Elaine treated me with disdain. Her attitude rankled, and over time, I loathed being around her. It appears the antipathy between us hasn't diminished in the twenty years since we last saw each other.

Checking my rearview mirror as I head down the hill, I see Elaine enter the house accompanied by both officers. Fifteen minutes later, I reach the bottom of the long, winding canyon road and pull up at a stoplight, uncertain which way to turn. I'm about to call Dougie to invite him for dinner at Donna's when my cellphone rings. Bluetooth kicks in and I answer.

"Meg, hi. It's Eden. Could you hold for Mr. Ackerman?"

But Ed Ackerman is already on the line. "Meg, what's this I hear about you and Elaine Farris having a run-in with the cops? She just called me. What were you doing over there?"

"Sorry, Ed. I just stopped by to see if Chelsea was home. I'm concerned about her."

"Yeah, we all are, but why'd you pick a fight with her mother, for chrissake? She said the police showed up."

"Elaine broke into the house. It had nothing to do with me. I just told her nobody had heard from Chelsea—"

"Yeah, right. So now her mother wants to file a missing persons report. That's all we need. Any way to stop her?"

"Elaine?"

"She's screaming at me, like I had something to do with this. I told her last time anyone saw her daughter, she was working with you. So what's up? Chelsea's got a boyfriend or something? This better not turn into some Lindsey Lohan stunt."

"You know, Ed, I only worked with her a couple of hours. We didn't get into any personal stuff. I only know that she was supposed to work with Dirck Heyward the next morning."

"Dead end. He says she didn't call."

"Then maybe filing a missing persons report is the way to go."

"Hell, no! The press will pick it up. They'll turn it into a carnival. This can't get out. Not until we get everything together on our end, understand?"

"Wait, you're not thinking of replacing her already?"

"Can't say." There's a long enough silence to make me think I've lost the connection in the canyon. Then, as though talking to himself, Ed mumbles, "Hate to do it, you know? She's the best, but . . . "

"I'm sure she'll turn up with a good excuse. Let's hope so."

"Yeah, for everyone's sake." His voice grows harsh. "Maybe she got cold feet, or ran off with a guy. Who knows? But she can be replaced. We're looking over camera tests, figuring out what to do. But nothing about this gets out, understand?"

"Okay. I understand. I'll let you know if I hear anything."

"Thanks. And stay away from the mother, okay? She's bonkers."

Before I have a chance to agree with him, he's hung up. Staying away from Elaine suits me fine. I regret letting her grab a flyer and hope she doesn't get in touch. What can I tell her, anyway? Aside from my assumption that Chelsea spoke to Dirck shortly after my session with her, I have no idea what the girl's movements might have been.

I head down La Brea Boulevard and pull into Pink's for one of their celebrated hot dogs. The line is long, but I don't care. I've nothing pressing to do but think things through. I punch in Dougie's number and let it ring until voicemail picks up. I leave a message about dinner at Donna's and ask him to let me know if he can make it. I'd half-expected him to be at the reading this morning, but clearly he's keeping his distance from the production—or wasn't invited to attend.

I take a seat at the end of a crowded picnic table behind the food stand and settle in with my chilidog. I'm about to sink my teeth into my favorite way to consume a gazillion sloppy calories when my cellphone rings. I glance at the ID before answering, relieved to see it's Jack calling.

"Hey, there! Nice surprise. My God, I miss you! Are you still in Seattle?"

"Actually, I'm in Minneapolis, but I'll be back in LA soon. Can't wait to see you, darling. I'll catch a flight as soon as I finish up with HSI out here."

"I appreciate you keeping our homeland secure, thank you very much. Why are you in Minneapolis? Aren't you still investigating the death of the Ukrainian girl in Seattle?"

I can picture Jack raising an eyebrow, wondering how I figured out which case he's on. "Yes," he says wryly, "there's a connection I'm following up on."

"Do you know yet what happened to her?"

"We've picked up some leads, but it's the tip of an iceberg. Nothing I can go into now. Anyway, I'm back in the office writing up a report. I've been thinking about you and had to call."

His voice is warm and intimate, making me smile. I picture him at a desk, wearing a crisp white shirt, tie loose at the collar, and brushing his hand across his short-cropped hair.

"What's happening with you? Weren't you going to start coaching the new Jinx?"

"Chelsea? Oh, very top-secret stuff I can't go into now," I tease. "She stole my hat, but that's just the tip of my iceberg. Now she's disappeared and I'm looking for her and my hat. What's the world coming to?"

"I ask myself that every day. Besides missing you. I'm really sorry we didn't get out to Two Bunch Palms."

"Hey, no apology necessary. It's your job. But I miss you, too, Jack." Not that anyone in the vicinity is listening, but I turn my knees away from the table and cup my hand around the phone. "If you were here, I'd invite you over to Donna's house for pot roast in Guinness tonight."

"Sounds delicious. Save a plate of leftovers in case I make it back tomorrow."

"Really? Great! Want me to pick you up at the airport?"

"Thanks, but I'll have to go directly to a debriefing. How would you feel about dinner at Chez Jay, if I can break away?"

"I'd love it. Whatever works for you, just give me a ring."

"Take care, Meg. See you soon."

"Bye. See you." I can't make myself press End Call. I wait until the screen goes dark, then tuck my cellphone back in my pocket.

My chilidog is cold, but I don't care. Thoughts of Jack race through my mind, lifting me out of the morass left by my encounter with Elaine and the police. I have a job, change in my pocket, a roof over my head and a full belly. That's far more than I had a year ago and enough to put me back in a good frame of mind. If only Chelsea would turn up, life would be close to perfect.

One irritant, of course, remains. Of all the acting coaches in the world, why would Chelsea end up with Dirck? I can imagine their sessions together, with him urging her to make Jinx grittier, more real than I played her. But one of the reasons the original *Holiday* series was such a success is that Winston and I found that sweet balance between humorous jousting and the serious aspects of the crimes we solved.

Take the Fourth of July episode. Jinx played a tough undercover role in a story about a terrorist cell, with a final chase sequence in the Statue of Liberty that paid homage to Alfred Hitchcock's *Saboteur*, one of Dougie's favorite films. Perhaps Dirck has forgotten how much research I did to prepare for episodes dealing with gun smuggling, identity theft and child abduction. For a plot that hinged on domestic violence, I arranged to live in a women's shelter for several days.

What kind of preparation did Chelsea do, other than learning some hat tricks from me? Even as the question crosses my mind, it jolts me into sitting up straighter. Could Chelsea have run into trouble delving too deeply into research for her character?

I push the basket with the remains of my chilidog aside and pull up Dirck's number on my cellphone. He answers instantly.

"Hey, you heard from Chelsea?"

"No, sorry. But that's what I was calling about."

"I hope you're not still sore I said anything about the read-through. You know me, I don't hold back."

"No, no, it's not about that." I decide not to distract him with the news about Elaine's arrival. "I was just wondering if you could tell me a little about how you and Chelsea worked on the role. This pilot episode involves Jinx infiltrating a high-end escort service. A woman's been killed, someone the Magician knew, so Jinx has to go undercover."

"Right. Sure thing. Like I tell all my students, you want to get your imagination in play, but first you have to spend time learning about the real-life people portrayed, delve into their world—" Dirck's voice has gone into professorial mode; time to cut him off.

"Right. In this case, it's the world of high-class prostitutes. Did you encourage her to do that?"

"Yeah, you know, you gotta dig deep, go all the way. The attitude, motivation, the actual experience of hooking up with a john, that's all part of it."

"Do you think she actually set herself up as a call girl? Did she give any indication she'd checked out an escort service?"

"All I know is that there was an actor who dropped out of my class in New York that she kept in touch with. Apparently he had some connection to an escort service and she followed up on it."

"You know his name?"

"Yeah, Jerry Schlitz. He goes by Jeremy Sloan. A few bit parts, works as a bartender."

"You know where?"

"No, the guy left owing me money for class. I don't expect to hear from him again."

"Okay, thanks. If I hear anything, I'll let you know. Bye."

"Hey, wait—" I press End Call and jot the name Jeremy Sloan on a napkin. Could the guy in the red convertible be the bartender and sometime-actor? If so, the fact that he allegedly skipped out on paying Dirck for his acting classes but can afford to drive a pricey convertible, leased or owned, is intriguing. It's not a secret that most bartenders earn more than most actors, but this guy—if it's Jeremy Sloan—has managed to strike it rich.

I settle back to explore the apps on my fancy smartphone, a castoff from Donna when she upgraded. It's a godsend, and one I can afford on her family plan. In the browser search bar, I slowly tap out *Jeremy*, which becomes *heavy* for no good reason. I am well aware that my atavistic fingertips manage to clumsily misspell everything, and autocorrect only corrects that which needs no correcting. It's my supposition that the next generation of newborns will come equipped with small knobs on their thumbs that relate to the size of miniature keyboards. Lucky them.

I finally manage to enter his full name. What pops up on my screen are many Jeremy Sloans, but only one of the candidates is depicted in what looks like an actor's eight-by-ten glossy: a dark-haired, handsome babe-magnet with a brooding expression.

"Well, aren't you cute," I murmur as his other headshots appear on the screen. "Where do we find you, Mr. Sloan?"

It turns out Jeremy wants to be found. Even without requesting to become his Facebook friend, I discover he bartends at Gilligan's Bar and Grill. I also check IMDb and discover he recently costarred in episodes of two TV series and has a role in a horror film that's in post-production.

I look up Gilligan's, located in Westwood Village, and see that they have happy hour beginning at four o'clock. The location and timing suit me fine. It seems almost too easy. I check my watch and head back to my car.

Parking in Westwood Village requires cunning and native knowledge. With the UCLA campus and hospital on one flank, Wilshire Boulevard on another, and museums, theaters, shops and dense housing packed in the middle, unmetered parking is virtually nonexistent. But I find a spot two blocks from Gilligan's at five minutes to happy hour. With a bit of luck I'll find the place not yet jammed and Jeremy Sloan already on duty behind the bar. At happy hour prices, I can probably even afford a glass of wine to aid in digesting my chilidog.

Gilligan's, occupying a pie-shaped corner on the southeast reaches of the commercial area, is in a quaint, low-slung hacienda-style structure of the sort that once defined Westwood Village. But while the building is old, the bar and grill is relatively new to the neighborhood and looks far more upscale than the pizza joint previously located there. Bushes planted in large earthenware pots form a hedge lining the sidewalk, partially concealing a flagstone patio with heat lamps, oversized upholstered ottomans and two-seater couches.

I pause on the corner to check messages on my cellphone, but also to peer surreptitiously through the curtain of greenery to get the lay of the land. Even at this hour, the bar is more crowded than I hoped it would be, but there's an empty stool available and a dark-haired bartender that could be Jeremy Sloan.

The interior is cool, bathed in bleached sunlight filtering through a domed skylight. A giant urn filled with eucalyptus and yellow day lilies perfumes the air. I perch on one of the stools at the curve of the bar near the entrance to get a good view of the room as well as the two bartenders on duty. I look at the menu teepee on the bar to check the happy hour prices, waiting to catch the eye of the lanky young man I'm pretty certain is Jeremy.

He nods and makes his way toward me, moving in a leisurely amble that doesn't cost his long legs too many strides. He gives me a welcoming smile and tosses his head back as though that would keep his hair from flopping becomingly across his forehead. Haircuts like his don't come cheap.

"Hey, how you doing?" he says, wiping his hands on a bar towel.

"Good, thanks. I'll have a glass of your happy hour pinot grigio."

"Make it two," says a deep-throated, all-too-familiar female voice. I know without a sideward glance that Elaine has joined me at the bar. My stomach takes a quick elevator ride, but I manage to cover my shock.

"Coming right up, ladies," he says, sliding a napkin in front of each of us before going off to get our wine.

"This where you do your drinking these days?" Elaine asks.

"Thought I'd give it a try. What a surprise. Are you meeting someone?"

"Who would I meet?"

"Whoever you want." The stool next to mine is occupied, but Elaine manages to wedge herself close to the bar, her face inches from mine.

"Guess I'll just keep you company. You mind?"

"Why would I?" I smile, wondering how long she was watching me before announcing herself.

Elaine smiles, too. "You might have some business here, something you wanted to do without me hanging on your shoulder. You going to be here long?"

"I don't know. Happy hour is over at seven. Are you waiting for my seat?"

"Nope. I'm good standing."

I could probably keep this up as long as Elaine can, but having a few minutes alone with Jeremy doesn't look like it's going to happen. Out of the corner of my eye, I see him ambling back toward us with two damp-looking glasses of white wine. He sets each down on a napkin. "There you go."

"Great. Thanks." Elaine picks up her glass, peeling the napkin from the bottom where condensation has soaked into it. "Cheers," she says before taking a sip.

"Cheers yourself, Elaine."

I catch the quick look the bartender gives Elaine when I mention her name. "You ladies want any bar snacks?" He slides the teepee in front of us. "Calamari. Lobster sliders. Tuna rolls. Lotsa good stuff here."

"Thanks. Maybe later," Elaine says. "Did I catch your name?"

"Me? Hey, I'm Jeremy. Welcome to Gilligan's. You gals been in here before?"

"First time," Elaine says. "Why? Do I look familiar to you?"

"Yeah, yeah," he says. "I was gonna say you remind me of someone."

"I wonder who that might be." She looks directly at Jeremy, and I can tell she's going for the zinger. "Maybe you know my daughter, Chelsea Horne? People say we look alike."

His face tells me he knew this was coming. He raps his knuckles on the bar and says, "Yeah, I know Chelsea. You two could be sisters." He gives her a winning smile. "I bet you hear that all the time."

"Not often enough." She leans in, her hands tight hammers on the bar. "You look like a good kid, Jeremy. I've got a hunch you know where my girl might be. You want to spill it?"

"I wish I knew." He looks down the bar, takes a breath. "Look, could you just hang on a minute? I'll be right back."

"Jeremy, wait. You're not going off to call Chelsea, are you?" My voice is soft, but I see a look of alarm on his face.

"Now? No. I texted her again before my shift started. She hasn't gotten back to me." He looks at Elaine. "I mean, I don't know what's going on with her. Sorry, but I gotta close out a check. I'll be back."

We both watch Jeremy head to a computer screen at the end of the bar. "So how did you find him here?" I ask.

"He left messages for her on the answering machine. No number, but he mentioned Gilligan's. You?"

"Just heard they knew each other, so I Googled him. Nothing's a secret anymore."

"Except where she is. That's what I came here to find out." Elaine takes a long swallow of wine and sets her glass down. "I don't know what you have in mind, but she's my daughter. If this jerk knows where she is, I'll get it out of him. Not you. This is between my kid and me, got it?"

"Got it. I'll just finish my wine."

Maybe that's all she needed to hear from me. The tension ebbs from Elaine's face, her fist relaxes on the bar. "Sure, take your time. Drink up."

We both watch Jeremy deliver the check to the customer, take a credit card, then return to the register. He gives us a quick glance before dropping the leather folder back in front of his customer. The bar is filling up, the noise level increasing as people crowd around us. Jeremy pours beer, makes two margaritas and delivers a plate of calamari.

Minutes pass, my tension rising. Elaine finishes her wine and signals Jeremy for another. He looks at me and I shake my head.

"Going easy on the booze, Meg? Probably a good thing. This could take a while."

Jeremy hurries toward us, setting a glass of wine down in front of Elaine. He picks up the empty glass, his head swiveling between us. "You know, the place is jumping this time of the evening. I'm not going to have a chance to talk. Besides, I really don't know where Chelsea is. I've been trying to reach her."

"I know. I heard your messages," Elaine says, clamping her hand on his arm. "You knew who I was, right?"

"Sort of. I mean, she mentioned you once or twice. I saw a picture of you at her house, that's all." He turns to me, smiling. "And Chelsea was thrilled she'd be working with you, Miss Barnes."

"Really? If that's the case, Chelsea's an even better actress than I thought."

"Oh, yeah, couldn't get over it."

Elaine looks at him in disgust, releases his arm and grabs her wine glass. Seeing her reaction, I can't resist goading her.

"I love coaching Chelsea. We had a great time together. I heard you've got a movie coming out soon—a horror flick, right? Congratulations."

"Enough with the sucking up, you two!" Elaine slams down her glass, sloshing wine. "Where's my daughter?"

"I really don't know." He wipes up Elaine's spilled wine with a bar cloth. "I just wish she'd get in touch."

"But everything was good between you two?" I ask.

"Yeah, great. I just figured she was immersed in preparing for the filming. You know how it is. Look, it's really busy here. I'll try to get back over later, okay?"

"And bring me another glass of wine," Elaine calls out as Jeremy hurries off. "That framed picture of me is on her bedside table. I guess they know each other pretty well."

"Are you surprised?"

"Can't say I am. She knows how to pick a stud, I'll give her that. But he looks like a dope to me."

I glance down the bar. Jeremy is far enough away that he couldn't have heard Elaine's comment above the din. I'm not sure she would care if he had.

I flinch at the tug on my hipbone, then realize my cellphone is vibrating in my pocket. I pull it out, see *Donna Bendix* on the ID and turn to Elaine. "Sorry, I'm going outside so I can hear this call. Please, take my seat." I rush for the door as Elaine slides onto my stool.

"Donna? Hang on. It's noisy in here." I step outside and hover near one of the giant flowerpots. "Can you hear me?"

"Where are you? Sounds like a party."

"No, just happened to bump into Elaine, my stunt double on *Holiday*. We're having a drink. I'll tell you about it later. Anything you want me to pick up on the way back?"

"No, I was just hoping you could give me a hand with something before dinner."

"Fine. See you soon."

There's no point in hanging around for a quiet word with Jeremy. With Elaine in earshot, I'm not about to ask him if he set Chelsea up to meet with a call girl for research.

Before going back inside Gilligan's, I reach into my shoulder bag for a ballpoint and quickly write my phone number and *Please call me!* on a scrap of paper. I fold the note inside my in-case-of-emergency twenty-dollar bill and head back inside. Without looking at Elaine, I push through the milling crowd to the far end of the bar, where Jeremy is standing at the computer monitor.

"Hey, Jeremy, I gotta run." He looks up and I reach across the bar to press the money into his hand. "Here, this should cover my drink." Impulsively, I hand him one of Donna's flyers from my handbag. "I'm also in the catering business."

"Thanks. It was great meeting you."

"You, too." I nod toward the twenty. "Please, call me."

Before he can respond, I turn away and speed-walk toward Elaine, who's been watching me. "Hey, sorry, but gotta run. I'm meeting someone. I paid Jeremy, so you're on your own. Enjoy!"

"Wait, what were you saying to him?"

"Nothing. Just paid. Bye!"

I hurry out of Gilligan's and almost run down the street toward my car, eager to put distance between Elaine and me. My hope is that Jeremy won't divulge my note to her. Besides, I doubt guys like to mention it when a woman presses a phone number into their hands.

I only hope he calls—and that I haven't squandered my precious twenty dollars.

As I head up the street to Donna's front gate, a late-model Ford sedan pulls out of her driveway. I hope it's a client booking Donna to cater a party. I have to admit, she's come up with a good idea, as long as she doesn't get carried away with the design elements involved. Hauling food around is one thing, but constructing elaborate theme meals with vintage props and furniture is quite another.

Knowing I'll somehow figure into her plans as sous chef or serving wench, possibly both, makes me uneasy, but I owe it to her to do whatever she asks. However, I will draw the line at doing impersonations or serving food while wearing sarongs, kimonos or French maid's outfits—and I have a feeling such an occasion will present itself.

The kitchen is fragrant with the musky, rich smell of simmering pot roast. Brussels sprouts, washed and trimmed, are on the counter in a colander next to a mound of peeled carrots. I'm beginning to regret chowing down on a chilidog. I hear Donna humming and find her standing on a ladder in the spacious pantry, taking inventory of her china cabinets. She's wrapped in a long bib apron and wearing white gloves.

"Hey, good timing!" she says, handing me a clipboard. "I need to get to these upper shelves."

"Let me do the counting."

"Don't worry. I can reach." There's an edge to her voice, her natural response to any implication that she might be short. She is short, but not giving in to it, which means I have to watch her tottering on her tiptoes at the top of the stepladder.

"Did you get another booking? I saw a car in the driveway."

"No such luck. It was a detective following up on the theft. He just left."

"Wait, what theft? Is that why you called me? Were you robbed?"

Donna peers down at me with a look of exasperation. "Yes, remember? The detective said he was following up on Chelsea. Apparently you gave the police a flyer and said you lived here. I assume you're the one who reported the hat missing, right?"

I shake my head, feeling my hair tighten on my skull. "Donna, I did not report that your hat was stolen. And it's not the sort of thing they send a detective out to investigate."

"Then why did he come by? He mentioned Chelsea Horne and asked about your connection to her, so I told him. I said she took the hat when she left and it was the last I saw of her." Her voice squeaking with indignation, Donna plants her white-gloved hands on her hips. An image of Minnie Mouse comes to mind.

"And me? What did you say about me?" I ask.

"I told him the truth, that you were teaching her hat tricks and then she took off with it. I said you ran after her, but she got away."

"Donna, could you come down here? We need to talk."

I'm sure it's my tone of voice, but Donna hesitates only a moment before climbing down from the ladder. She gives me a worried look. "What is it? What happened?"

"The detective wasn't here because of a missing hat. It's Chelsea who's missing. She didn't show up at the studio today. I went to her house looking for her and ran into her mother, who turns out to be Elaine Farris, my stunt double on *Holiday*."

"You're kidding. Chelsea's her daughter?"

"I know, small world and all that. Anyway, to make a long story short, the police showed up." I lean against the wall for support. "I just don't need to get mixed up with police. Not ever again."

"I don't get it. What did you do to her mother?"

"Nothing! The police were called because she didn't have keys and broke into Chelsea's house. It's nothing to do with me. But now she's filing a missing persons report, which is probably a good idea. But everyone is going to figure out that apparently I'm the last one to have seen Chelsea. You didn't happen to mention anything about me getting hurt falling down, did you?"

"Sort of." A flicker in Donna's eyes tells me she's beginning to get it. "I said you were scratched pretty badly, you know, falling down in the garden. I mean, they couldn't possibly think—what?"

I shrug. "I don't know what anybody's thinking, but Elaine is a loose cannon. She could be saying anything."

"But it's only a hat."

"Not anymore." I shake off the bad vibes and look at the clipboard. "Anyway, let's finish up here. Dougie Halliburton may come for dinner tonight, but I don't think we need to break out the Limoges."

Donna brightens. "I thought the Fiesta plates, something casual." I hold my breath as she climbs back up to the top step and rises to her tiptoes. "Ready? We'll do the Wedgewood next." She claps her hands together and the image of Minnie Mouse springs afresh.

With time out to braise Brussels sprouts, add carrots to the pot simmering on the stove and set the dining room table, we manage to count every last cup, soup bowl and piece of cutlery. One three-drawer canteen of silverware alone contains 124 pieces, including an assortment of soup, dessert, tea, coffee, mustard, salt and egg spoons. I'm ready for a break. I check messages and see that Doug has confirmed for dinner.

I take a quick shower and change into pants and a light jersey top before joining Donna in the kitchen for a cup of tea. Looking over her eight pages of inventory, Donna decides high-end catering for dinner parties of up to twelve people would make the most sense.

"There will be breakage," I warn.

"I know, but I like seeing these things used, not just stored in a dark pantry. Maybe I could do dinner parties in my dining room. What do you think?"

"I think you'd need valet parking and a liquor license, but what do I know? Why don't you just do rentals until you get the hang of things?"

The intercom for the front gate buzzes, sparing further discussion of a truly terrible idea. "That'll be Dougie. I'll let him in." I press the button on an antiquated panel in the hallway and go to the door to meet him.

The night is surprisingly cool, the rain a novelty for July. A faint mist hangs in the air, shimmering around the fairy lights in the trees. Headlights sweep around the curve of the driveway, shining on the slick, wet panes of the orchid pavilion. I hug myself in the chill, imagining the look on Dougie's face when he sees the contents of Donna's living room. But anticipation fades when a dark green sedan pulls up at the side of the portico. It's Elaine, and there's no smile on her face.

She climbs out of her car, slams the door and stomps up the steps, each footfall like a clap of thunder. She's still wearing jeans, boots and a chamois jacket, but her hair is loose under a black cowboy hat, which means she's made a pit stop at Chelsea's house before coming here. If she were wearing six-shooters strapped to her waist, she couldn't look more menacing.

"Hi, Elaine. I wasn't expecting you." In fact, I have half a mind to go back inside and shut the door in her face. "What's up?"

"My daughter's missing and now you're accusing her of theft? What's with you?" She's standing directly in front of me, but her voice is loud enough to be heard in Holmby Park.

"Take it easy. I made no such accusation."

"Someone did. I just spoke to the police again."

"That was me," Donna says, standing at the open door. "I'm sorry your daughter is missing, but she took my hat. It was right here on the hall table and she walked off with it."

Elaine glares down at Donna, her mouth trembling. "I don't believe this. Do you have any idea what I'm going through? You're worried about your hat when I can't find my daughter? Is this a joke?"

"I'm sorry. I didn't mean it like that. Excuse me, that's the front gate," Donna says, turning to go back inside. "I have to open it."

"I'm sorry, too, Elaine. We're all concerned about Chelsea."

She looks at me, her eyes brimming. "Are you? Well, you have no idea how frightening this is for me. If you had children, maybe you'd understand. My daughter has disappeared. I have no idea where she is!"

"Jeremy wasn't helpful?"

"Are you kidding me? Once you left, he barely said two words to me. Then I go back to Chelsea's place and get a call from this detective asking me about a hat!"

I stare at her dumbly before it registers that she's actually crying. Vulnerability is not a trait I've ever associated with Elaine.

"Elaine, I'm sorry. We'll find her." I move toward her, my hand reaching to touch her arm, but she turns away, wiping her face with the sleeve of her jacket.

"Just leave me alone! I don't know why I bothered coming up here."

Headlights fan across the portico as Doug's Jeep wheels around the fountain and pulls up next to the green sedan. "Elaine, it's Dougie Halliburton, remember? I invited him for dinner."

"Omigod, he's still alive?"

"Yes, very much so. I think he had a lot to do with casting Chelsea."

I'm walking down the steps to greet Doug, who's slowly climbing out of his car, when a light-blue compact squeals across the wet pavement and whips around the fountain to park next to Elaine's sedan. I squint into the headlights before they're doused and let out a small groan. It's Dirck. I turn to glare at Donna, who stands holding the front door open.

Seeing my reaction, she shrugs and gives me a helpless look. "Sorry! He buzzed the intercom and said you were expecting him."

The light mist turns to drizzle, but summer rain isn't the biggest surprise of the evening. I only hope Donna has enough pot roast to feed the multitudes. I steer Dougie under the portico and up the steps as Dirck bounds toward us.

"Hey, what luck! I was hoping I'd see you, Doug. I thought you'd be at the table read this morning."

"Hiya, Dirck. I figured I'd sit that one out. How're you doing?"

"Great! Couldn't be better. You know, Chelsea Horne is in my acting class. Great talent. I discovered her."

"Really? You discovered her?" Elaine steps out of the shadow of the portico, her eyes still glistening with a wash of tears. "Good for you, Dirck. But I gave birth to her. What do you think of that?"

The sight of Dirck's jaw going slack is deeply satisfying.

Dougie shakes with laughter. "You been trumped, pal."

Dirck, pale in the cool light of the portico, lets out a low whistle. "Can't top that one." He shakes his head and looks Elaine up and down with a rueful smile. "Yeah, yeah, I can see it now. There's definitely a resemblance. Hey, you know, I got a daughter, too." He whips his wallet from a back pocket and flips it open. "Priscilla. Ten months old and already walking. She's gonna be a star someday."

"Well, that's great, Dirck," Elaine says. "I'm sure you'll make a terrific father."

"Hey, it's cold outside." Donna holds the door wide and beckons everyone inside. "How about some cheese and wine?"

"Why not? The gang's all here." I put my arm around Doug and squeeze his ribs. "I could go for a drink. How about you, Elaine?"

"A drink? Okay, looks like we have something in common," she says, giving me a look that for once doesn't seem unfriendly.

"And I'm hungry," Doug says. "There was some mention of dinner."

"Coming up," Donna says. "Enough for everyone. Elaine, please join us. Dirck, you're welcome, too."

Very cozy. Too cozy, I think, as I bring up the rear and close the door. But the gang's all here and if it eases some tension, what's wrong with that?

If nothing else, the sight of Donna's living room is an ice-breaker. I stand back, watching Doug, Elaine and Dirck get an eyeful of the vintage treasures. Donna, in her element, takes everyone on her special tour, even unlocking the credenza in the library to show off vintage film scripts and handwritten notes from the likes of Cecil B. DeMille, Charlie Chaplin and Mary Pickford.

I hang back, listening to them pepper Donna with questions, but mostly observing with amusement the subtle body language and choreography of three people who can't stand each other trying to be sociable. The trio manages to maintain physical distance, avoid eye contact and dodge any direct communication. None of this is apparent to Donna, who relishes their rapt attention. Dinner should be interesting. I excuse myself to get cheese and wine.

I uncork a bottle of pinot noir, pour myself a glass, and then open the Sauvignon Blanc that Donna has been chilling. I place an assortment of cheeses, including Brie, Roquefort and an aged Gouda, on a board with olives and crackers, hoping my arrangement passes muster with Donna. I carefully lift the lid from the Dutch oven, breathe in the singular aroma of melts-off-the-bone pot roast, and take another sip of wine. With a green salad and a crusty loaf of bread, there's more than enough food for everyone. Certainly it will be a feast for this motley crew that would otherwise have made do with diner food or leftovers in the fridge. The downside is that they will have to eat their dinner in each other's company and possibly be forced to exchange a word or two at the table.

I would guess none of them have seen each other since *Holiday* went off the air, and never desired to. Dirck, who considers himself an authority on almost everything, dropped by the studio daily, hung out in my trailer and had free access to our "closed" set. He became a thorn in everyone's side, including mine, but in the interest of marital harmony, I put up with his near-constant presence and noisome intrusions. Others were less accommodating.

Elaine loathed Dirck, who never took the hint that she didn't appreciate having him on the sidelines offering helpful little tips on how she could better "double" me. During one arduous day filming stunt scenes on location, Dirck confided, "I told Elaine she should watch her posture in that fight scene and she took offense. But good posture is the one thing you have going for you, Meg."

It would not have occurred to Dirck that both Elaine and I would bristle at that comment. His suggestion to Elaine one afternoon that she "might want to suck in her belly" marked the last day Dirck was allowed on the *Holiday* set. She complained to Doug, who was only too happy to have a reason to ban him from hanging around.

"Man, is she touchy!" Dirck said, back in my trailer. "Look, baby, if her gut hangs out, people will think it's yours!"

I looked at him aghast. "You didn't say that to Elaine, did you?"

"Well, yeah. If she's a pro, she needs to hear the truth."

"Dirck! No woman wants to hear she has a gut!"

"I'm only thinking about you, baby. Don't forget, she's hired to make you look good. Remember that. Her gut is *your* gut."

I was pretty sure that particular comment went a long way toward explaining why Elaine despised me. Little wonder she looked for ways to retaliate. Even I was amused the time I came across her giving a hilarious impression of us in bed. "Not bad, Meg," she mimicked in Dirck's sonorous voice, "but roll over and try again. We're going to keep at it until you get it right." As funny as it was, her mimicry stung, especially when I saw how appreciative her audience was. I smiled, told her she must have been eavesdropping at our bedroom door—earning nervous laughter from everyone—and slid into a makeup chair.

In not-so-public ways, Elaine, who also served as a stunt coordinator, had other means of showing her disdain for me. She'd find a way to end a stunt sequence with her face in the mud or her body wrenched in some grotesque, painful pose—and I would then have to step in and assume the position for my close-up. I once had to stand waist-deep in an icy river, without the benefit of Elaine's wetsuit gear, waiting to emerge and play a scene following a fight sequence. Chilled to the bone, with my teeth chattering so badly I could barely speak, I prayed we'd wrap the scene in a single take.

Doug had his own issues with Elaine. While he appreciated her skill, he wasn't much enamored of her habit of second-guessing him. She, like Dirck, always came up with a better way of doing things.

"Never met a more contrary woman," he'd say through gritted teeth.

He offered to replace her before the next season, but I turned him down—I knew there was no one better to take her place. But I also didn't want her to think she'd gotten the better of me, that I couldn't handle whatever she dished out.

The last time I saw Elaine was at the final wrap party when *Holiday* went off the air. She was hoisting a beer, hanging with the stuntmen and doing a good job of ignoring me. She vanished after that, presumably to Indiana in the company of someone named Horne, and gave birth to Chelsea. Dirck and I stuck it out for several more years, largely because I got enough long periods of location work to give us some distance from each other.

"Hey, are you hitting the bottle on your own in there?"

My head snaps around. Dirck is walking down the hall toward the kitchen, followed by Donna. I set the pinot noir back on the counter, uncomfortably aware he's seen me topping up my glass.

"Don't worry. Left some for you. Did you enjoy the grand tour?"

"You bet I did. You landed in some swell digs, kid." He's doing his best Bogart imitation, and it's clear he's out to impress Donna.

"You're really good!" she says, looking up at him with bright-eyed admiration. To me, she says, "You should hear him do Clark Gable and Spencer Tracy. Brilliant!"

I nod. "No one better."

Elaine and Doug join us in the kitchen, both of them tight-lipped and somber. I suspect Dirck has entertained everyone with samplings of his movie star impressions.

"Let's stay in the kitchen," Donna says. "It's so much cozier."

I hand out glasses as everyone groups around the butcher-block table where I've set out the cheese. "Red or white wine? We have both."

"Red for me," Elaine says. "Thank you."

"I'll try the red," Doug says.

"Me, too," Dirck says. "Salud! To old times and good friends. Or is it the other way around?"

"Works both ways," Donna pipes up, adding a log of hard salami to the board.

The rest of us sip our wine quietly, not bothering to respond to Dirck's toast. Donna, on the other hand, raises her glass of white wine and says, "To *Holiday*! It's so nice to have you all here. I was a great fan of the show."

"Thank you," Doug says. "It's good to finally meet you. Meg told me how kind you've been to her."

I see Dirck's ears prick up. There's too much I would prefer he not know about my life in the last year or so. I move swiftly to divert him. "Tell me, Dirck, how long have you been working with Chelsea?"

"Yes, how long?" Elaine echoes. It hits me that I haven't chosen the best diversion.

"A good two years," Dirck says, turning to Elaine. "She probably told you I gave her free classes until she got her first acting gig."

"No, she never said a word about it. And you never heard her mention my name?"

"Not once. I had no idea you were her mother. But I set her up with an agent. Did she mention that?"

"No," Elaine says, her voice icy. "Not once. She never mentioned you at all."

"You're kidding! She wouldn't be out here without me."

"Maybe she wouldn't be missing without you, either. Did you think of that?"

"Wait a minute! I was in New York when she vanished. She was supposed to call in for a Skype session and didn't. Is that my fault? First I knew she was missing is when I called Meg. Right, Meg? You said you hadn't heard from her."

Thanks to Dirck, I'm back in the hot seat. Elaine turns her gaze on me and I take my time sipping wine. Do we need to get into this now?

"Cheese, anyone?" Donna holds up a cracker slathered with Brie. "There's some nice salami here."

With Elaine's eyes still boring into me, I look at Dirck and shrug. "I was visiting Doug when you called. I had no reason to think she was missing, because there was no reason for her to be in touch with me unless she needed some help with the hat."

"*My* hat," Donna says, under her breath. She hands the cracker to Doug, who slaps a slice of salami on top and eats it.

"Is this the hat my daughter is supposed to have taken?"

"She did take it," Donna says firmly. "She walked out the door with it."

"My daughter is not a thief!"

"Maybe she just borrowed it," I say, hoping to placate her. "The hat she was using didn't amount to much. Flimsy, hard to control." I flick my wrist as though to demonstrate, but my hand knocks Donna's empty wine glass off the counter. Elaine, in a move so swift I barely register it, catches the glass before it hits the floor and sets it back on the counter near the kitchen sink.

"Nice one," Dirck says. "Good catch."

"Thanks, Elaine," I murmur. "That was quick." But my eyes are on the business card she's spotted on the counter.

"Detective John Muldauer?" Elaine picks up the card, reads the name and looks at me. "He's the one who called me."

"That's mine," Donna says, reaching for the card. "I'm the one he came to see."

Elaine glares down at Donna, holding the card too high for her to grab. "So that's when you told him my daughter stole your frigging hat?"

"Actually, I think he was inquiring about me, trying to confirm that I lived here, but Donna thought he was here about the hat," I say, also reaching for the card.

Elaine swings back to me, holding the card an arm's length away. "So you were here, too?"

"No," Donna answers for me. "I was alone. Detective Muldauer said he'd call back to speak with Meg."

"He did?" I look at Donna, unable to check my surprise.

"Didn't I tell you?" Donna and I lock eyes. "I guess he meant tomorrow."

"It sounds like you two need to work out your stories," Elaine crows. "I'm beginning to wonder what else you two know and aren't saying."

"I'm wondering that myself," Dirck says, pouring himself more wine. "Let's get this straight. Where did you actually last see Chelsea?" I'm not mistaken that Dirck's voice has taken on the unctuous sound of Columbo about to entrap the guilty party.

Dougie picks up on it, too. "C'mon, Dirck. Let's not get too carried away, here. There's no reason to think anyone's hiding anything."

The scorn in Doug's voice does not deter Dirck, who has assumed the mantle of Lieutenant Columbo in all but the shabby raincoat. "Sure, sure. I get what you're saying, Doug, but let's hear it from the ladies. When did you last see Chelsea?"

"I invited her for dinner," Donna says, "then went back to the kitchen."

"I said goodbye after our session. Then I saw that the hat was gone from the front table."

"That's it?" Dirck says, disbelief oozing sweetly. "End of story? You didn't give chase?"

"Of course I did!" Immediately realizing my mistake, I backtrack. "I mean, I saw the hat was not where I'd left it, so I asked Donna if she'd seen it."

Dirck, his "aha" moment at hand, quietly says, "I thought Donna was in the kitchen."

"I was," Donna says, "but then I came out to see if Chelsea was going to stay for dinner. But she had already left."

"And then?" Dirck says, shifting focus back to me.

"I went out to look for her," I dutifully respond, "but she was gone. That's when I slipped and fell into some bushes. That's it."

"Wait, that's when you got the scratches? I thought you said you walked into some branches," Elaine says, zeroing in. "Maybe you caught up with her . . . "

"Bushes, branches and a lot of wet grass, okay? I tripped and took a bad fall, that's all. I did not harm Chelsea."

"I can attest to that," Donna says, hurriedly supplying an alibi for me. "I came to the doorstep just after she fell. She was all alone."

"In any case, Chelsea was gone," I say with finality, trying to keep the exasperation out of my voice.

"And so was my hat," Donna mutters. "Look, dinner is ready. I'm just going to toss the salad together and then we can eat. If you want to wash up, now's the time."

"Thanks," Elaine says, "but, if you don't mind, maybe Meg could show us where she was working with Chelsea."

"I was going to suggest that," Dirck says, his "aha" moment still waiting in the wings.

Doug rolls his eyes. "I'd rather watch a salad being put together." He makes a show of looking at his watch. "Donna, how long would that take?"

She looks at Doug appreciatively. "Let's say ten minutes until everything is on the table."

"Nine minutes," Doug says. "We assemble in the dining room, hands washed in nine minutes. Meg, clock's ticking."

8

I fortify myself with a topped-up glass of pinot noir, pour another glass for Elaine, and lead my party of two down the hall to the den. "Off we go, this way, please."

"How did you and Donna meet?" Dirck asks, sidling up next to me.

"A charity group. We just hit it off." There's no need to mention that we met while distributing Meals on Wheels to the housebound elderly. Donna's motivation was entirely altruistic. I did it to get a free meal.

"Lucky you, kid. I know you fell on some hard times for a while, but this more than makes up for it."

"Don't get any wrong ideas. I was looking to downsize." As much as I'd like to know how much Dirck has delved into my past legal and bankruptcy problems, I don't want to give him an opening for more probing. "This is temporary until I find something of my own."

"I don't know why you'd ever leave," Elaine says, looking around the book-lined den with its quaint mullioned windows.

"Funny, that's just what Chelsea said to me."

"Really? So she got the grand tour, too?"

I shake my head. "Donna offered, but I don't think she was that interested. Some people see this as nothing more than clutter."

"Junk, I know. First thing I'd do is clear it all out. But I wouldn't mind having the closet space, you know?"

Elaine's dismissive tone does not mask her envy, nor does the appraising look in Dirck's eyes fool me. "Pru would give her eyeteeth to live in a place like this," he says quietly. "A backyard would be nice for the kid."

I unlock the French doors and give them a shove. The moisture has caused the wood to swell. "Watch out, the grass is slippery. That's how I fell."

It's also cold and drizzling. I hurry across the lawn to the pool house, Dirck and Elaine on my heels. The lock sticks, but I manage to push the door open. "Sorry, it's chilly in here, but we'll just be a minute."

I flick a switch on the wall that turns on every light in the room and illuminates the outdoor pool. Elaine and Dirck stop on the threshold to look in awe at the wall of French doors that open on to the pool, tennis court and rolling, landscaped lawns. The Olympic-sized pool, lit underwater, glows a jewel-like turquoise, its surface ruffled with gently falling rain. Inside, shabby-chic sofas and chairs clad in chintz are grouped in front of a fieldstone fireplace. Snug in an alcove is a fully equipped kitchen with such charming 1940s touches as a vintage stove and fridge and a soda fountain ringed with shiny stools. A jukebox stands in the corner next to an old-fashioned pinball machine.

I hear a sharp intake of breath and turn to see Elaine gazing at the lunch counter with its soda siphons and malted-milk machine. "Did Chelsea talk much about home?" Her voice is soft. I almost miss hearing the question.

"Home? No, not at all, Elaine. To tell you the truth, we had very little time and a lot of work to do. We shoved aside the Ping-Pong table so we could work with the hat." I flip my hand around as though tossing a hat in the air and catching it on my head. "You remember?"

"How could I forget your precious hat?" Her tone is cold and dismissive again, but I understand. I insisted on doing all of the hat tricks myself, even in the action sequences. It was a matter of pride with me and irritated the hell out of Elaine.

"So, that's it. Chelsea and I worked for a couple of hours. That's all. Ready to go? I know we're all hungry."

"Wait a minute," Dirck says. He stands at the base of a spiral staircase, looking up into darkness. "What's up there?"

"Nothing. Storage. Nobody goes up there." I clap my hands together and head for the door. "Okay, ready to go?" But Elaine is looking out on the pool and Dirck can't seem to pull himself away from the spiral staircase. "Really, nothing more to see here, Dirck. The route we took out here is the same one Chelsea and I took."

"You mind if I look up there?" He's already climbing the stairs.

"There's no light. It's storage." I'm firm, but it has no effect on Dirck. "Would you please come back down? We did not go up there." For a moment, all I see are Dirck's pants legs from the knees down, then he slowly makes his way back down the stairs.

"You never know," he says.

"I think dinner's on the table. Let's go." I stand in the drizzle, holding the door open until both Elaine and Dirck are outside. While they hurry back across the lawn to the den, I turn out the lights and lock the door. By the time I return to the kitchen, Elaine is pouring herself the last of the pinot noir.

Donna has managed with lightning speed to give the dining room a pub-like atmosphere. The long oval table is set with tin chargers under colorful Fiestaware plates on a blue-checked cloth. The lights are low and candles in ye olde English pewter candlesticks are lit. On a chilly, rainy night, what could be more welcoming than pot roast and good conversation with old comrades? Actually, one out of three is welcome. The pot roast is delicious but, for the most part, the old comrades eat in silence until Dirck clears his throat and turns to me.

"You know, I've been meaning to ask if they ever caught that fugitive husband of yours, the one that robbed you blind?" His voice is casual, but the question lands on the table with a thud.

"Excuse me?" Elaine's cutlery clatters onto her plate. "What's this? Nobody told me about a fugitive here. You were married to a criminal? You, Miss Perfect?"

"Dirck, please." I sit back and take a deep breath. "This isn't something I want to go into. Not now."

"Hey, sorry I brought up a touchy subject."

"Well, I'd like to know! I mean, what'd my daughter walk into here?" Elaine asks, her words slurring. "This guy's still on the loose?"

"No. It's over, okay? Let's not get too dramatic here, Elaine." In his stern, quiet voice, the one that brought instant silence to a set, Doug says, "We have moved on."

"Not so fast," Elaine counters. "How do we know Chelsea ever left here? Think about it—no one saw her leave." She reaches for the Cabernet and drains the last of the bottle into her glass. Swirling the wine, she looks at each of us. "Meg didn't see her go out the door. Donna didn't see her leave. Who knows if my daughter even left here? And if Meg, who was the last to see Chelsea, is harboring this fugitive—"

"I'm not!" I gape at Elaine as she polishes off her wine. "That's crazy!"

"Is it?" Dirck intones with doomsday portent. "I wonder."

"I was thinking a search warrant," Elaine says. "Getting the authorities up here to investigate just what's going on."

"Enough!" Doug thunders. "Let's not spoil this lovely dinner. There is no fugitive lurking here, never was. Nor is Chelsea hidden here. Who would benefit from that?" He puts a leathery hand on the table, stands and picks up his glass. "I would like to propose a toast to Donna. This is the best meal I've had in years."

"Hear, hear!" Dirck says. "To Donna!"

I lift my glass. "To Donna, thank you!"

"Yes, to Donna," Elaine says, raising her empty glass and looking almost contrite, but definitely tanked. "Look, I barged in here uninvited, so it was nice of you to ask me to stay for dinner. I also gotta thank you for making a big, stinking deal of the hat, because the truth is the police will investigate breaking and entering or some lousy theft, but they don't give a hot damn about a missing person, you know? According to them, because my daughter's not a child and doesn't have a mental disorder, she has every right to disappear if she wants to. So, here's to you and a nosy neighbor and some cops who wanted to check out Meg's address." Elaine puts her glass down and buries her face in her hands. "I'm sorry. I just don't know where to turn."

"I'm sorry, too, Elaine. I know this is hard." I take a breath, then quietly add, "Especially when she knew you were coming today."

Elaine shakes her head. "No, she didn't know. It was supposed to be a surprise. I just don't understand what could've happened to her. Not showing up for work? It's not like her. That scares me."

"Actually, the police have a point," Doug says. "She may not be missing at all. Sometimes kids do dumb things. I'm a father, so I know."

"Maybe she'll just turn up," Dirck says. "It hasn't been that long since Meg saw her the other night."

"Why would she take off now?" Elaine demands. "Why? Her car is gone, but then I assume she took it with her. Where would she go?"

"She didn't drive her car here," I say. "Someone dropped her off."

"That means someone was going to pick her up," Elaine says. "Who?"

"I don't know. She said she had to meet someone, but she didn't say who it was."

"Damn it, you've got to know more than you're letting on! I just wish to hell she hadn't got mixed up with any of you in the first place. I told her not to take this job. I knew it would be a disaster for her. It was for me."

"Man, I'm glad she didn't listen to you," Dirck says. "*Jinx* is her big break. I told her it would launch her film career if she played her cards right."

"Like you know everything. Why the hell she had to study with you—"

"Whoa, there. Let's rewind a bit," Doug says. "You wanted her to turn down the role, but she took it anyway, right?" He rests his elbows on the table and leans toward Elaine, his gaze shifting into a middle distance that seems to fall somewhere to the side of her left ear. Elaine, too, must recall that when Doug gave notes on set, he never looked directly at you. He spoke in a kind of deathless whisper that was mesmerizing. "You must have had a pretty good reason. And she knew how angry it made you. A kid somehow always senses a surprise visit coming. And there's always a reason the visit is a surprise. Why not let her know you were coming out?"

I hold my breath for the answer to a question I was dying to ask. Out of the corner of my eye, I watch Elaine bite her lip before answering.

"We hit a rough patch a couple years ago. Normal, I suppose. We were close, maybe too close. She needed to break away. We had a falling out, didn't speak for a while, but things seemed to be getting back on track until she told me she was coming out here for this role. I blew up, said things I shouldn't have said. I could've told her I was coming out, but—"

Doug lets the pause linger, then says softly, "There's always the chance—"

Elaine shakes her head slowly. "If she'd said don't come out to visit, it would've killed me. I couldn't take the chance."

Doug nods. "I know. I'd sooner die than hear that from my kid."

"Worse, maybe she somehow did know I was coming—"

Speaking in a low voice so as not to break the spell Doug has cast, I ask, "Elaine, why are you concerned she might have known you were coming out here?"

"What an asinine question!" Elaine snaps irritably. "I don't want to think my kid disappeared just because she didn't want to see me. I wanted to surprise her, that's all."

"Sorry, I didn't mean to upset you."

"Forget it. I'm just glad I got a chance to talk to the cops today. At least they've listed her as a missing person, so if she's taken to a hospital or something and the police are called, they'll know—" Elaine shakes her head, her eyes welling. "Sorry, I can't bear to think about it."

"You shouldn't, Elaine. After all, there's no sign anything bad happened. Her house was in good order?" I ask. "No indication of anything out of the ordinary?"

"That's what the cops asked. I told them everything was fine, as far as I could see. You know, dishes in the sink. Bed unmade. Clothes on the floor, but that's not unexpected. I cleaned it up. As usual."

Got it. I now know Elaine's visit was a surprise and, according to her, there were no signs of, as the police would say, foul play. I also have some insight into at least one aspect of their mother/daughter relationship, which sounds pretty normal. Kids are messy. Mothers clean up. But the tension between them runs deeper than just sloppy housekeeping and Elaine's interference in her daughter's career. I'm about to ask why she was so against Chelsea taking on the role of Jinx when Donna stands up and clinks a spoon against her glass.

"Well, I'm glad you're here tonight, Elaine, and I'm looking forward to having Chelsea at my table, too. I'm glad all of you are here. This is a very impromptu meal, so all I have for dessert tonight is ice cream and cookies."

"Needless to say, the ice cream and cookies are homemade." I raise my glass to Donna. "Thanks for everything."

"Stay where you are, everyone," Dirck says, picking up his plate. "I'm going to help the little lady with the clearing up."

"That's John Wayne! You walk and talk just like him." Donna beams at Dirck. "You're hired, pardner."

The two of them, ferrying plates and cutlery to the kitchen, push in and out of the swinging door, Dirck carrying on with his

John Wayne impression. He may be the most irritating man on earth, but I did a picture with John Wayne and I could swear the Duke has returned from the dead to clear the table. Doug, who once directed Wayne in a cowboy flick, drums his fingers on the table, possibly having similar thoughts to mine.

Elaine checks her cellphone, a worried look in her eyes. "You know, maybe I should get back to Chelsea's place. She could be there and just not picking up the phone. I keep texting her, but—" She lays the phone on the table, face up, staring at it.

"If you want to go now, I'll follow you," Doug says, his voice tender. "I'd like to make sure you get back safely. We don't have to stay for ice cream."

"Thanks, Doug. That's really kind of you, but I'll be fine." She picks up her phone and pushes away from the table. "I'm just going to say goodbye to Donna and be on my way."

"Of course, but I'm still going to see you home."

"Hold your hats, folks!" The dining room door swings open and Dirck walks in carrying bowls on a tray, followed by Donna holding a platter of cookies. "We've got homemade cinnamon ice cream and snickerdoodles!" He sets the tray down on the table and looks at Elaine, who stands up. "You're leaving?"

"I'm afraid so. Thanks, Donna. This was really nice of you to do."

"You're welcome. But why don't you just stay for some ice cream?" Donna offers her a bowl, but Elaine shakes her head. "I'll pack up some cookies for you. It won't take a minute."

"Well, thanks to Donna," Dirck says, "it turns out I'm not leaving here. Not anytime soon, anyway."

"What? Why not?" I glance at Donna, who frowns and looks away.

"Meg, you didn't tell me that pool house has a guest room above the spiral stairs. It's the whole top floor! Just needs new light bulbs and the space heater turned on to clear the damp, right, Donna?"

"Well, I guess so. Nobody's stayed there in years."

"But if it's okay with you, I'd really appreciate it. The hotel I was staying in is too expensive and the studio's not paying for it. I had to check out this afternoon. My luggage is in the trunk of my car. Would you believe it?"

Yes, I would believe it. I stare at Dirck, feeling numb. He had this all figured out. That's why he showed up uninvited.

"Well, good for you, Dirck. You sure know how to work it."
Elaine puts on her cowboy hat and reaches unsteadily for her bag.
"Anyway, I better be going." She walks out of the dining room
without looking back.

As the front door closes behind Elaine, Doug turns to Donna.
"I'll be off, too. I want to make sure she gets home safely. Thanks
again. Dinner's on me next time."

"Hey, I'll walk you out, Doug," Dirck says, heading for the
door. "I have to get my stuff from the car."

Doug hangs back and wraps an arm around my shoulders,
whispering in my ear, "I'll round up a posse and run him out of
town, sugar. Hang in there."

I nod. "If only you could," I whisper back.

The door closes behind Doug and Dirck. Donna and I remain in the dining room, silence hanging heavy. "I'm really sorry,"
she says. "He caught me off guard."

"Not your fault. He's good at that. C'mon, I'll help you clean
up. We can have our ice cream in the kitchen." How can I blame
Donna? I snookered her into taking me in as a houseguest, too.

I pick up the tray of ice cream bowls and push through the
swinging doors, my mind turning to Dougie. Thanks to him, I
know Elaine's arrival was meant as a surprise, one that Chelsea
may not have appreciated. If he's able to follow Elaine home and
walk her to her front door, perhaps he'll find out even more about
the falling out between mother and daughter. Is Elaine the reason
behind Chelsea's disappearance?

I set the tray next to the sink and begin cleaning up. But just
as I'm about to close the dishwasher, I hear a sharp sound, rapidly
followed by another that sounds like gunfire.

"Meg? Is that fireworks or—?"

I turn to Donna, who looks at me inquiringly, then we both
race for the front door.

I run down the slippery steps, past the portico, Donna at my
heels. The rain has stopped, but a foggy mist shrouds the grounds
below the orchid pavilion. The trunk of Dirck's car is open, but I
catch the dim outline of his body running down the driveway toward the open gate. Fear clutches my throat, hoping nothing's
happened to Dougie.

My cellphone erupts with a noisy buzz, vibrating in my hand.
I glance down, see Doug's name. Donna hurries past me as I
pause on the walkway to answer the call.

"Dougie? My God, what's happened?"

"Down the street. It's Elaine. I already called nine-one-one."

I hear the distant sound of a horn blaring, then the scream of sirens approaching from Fire Station 71, located only blocks away on the corner of Sunset Boulevard. "I'm coming!"

I sprint down the driveway, passing Donna, my sandals squishing in the muddy puddles. I almost trip on the embedded metal bar as I run past the gates, then slow up when I turn onto the street. I hear sirens, but can barely make out the fire engine on the other side of a cascade of water shooting into the air. The plume, a silver streak spouting skyward some thirty feet, almost obscures Elaine's green sedan tipped up against a fire hydrant.

Fearing the worst for Elaine, I raise my cellphone and record a sweeping video, catching glimpses of her car in the pulsing waves of water. I arc the camera up to catch the cascade against the black velvet sky, then dip and pan back across the street. Shooting video at a time like this may seem callous, but some instinct tells me these first moments may be important.

I zoom in, picking up Dirck waving to me. He calls out and I lower my phone, trying to catch his words. I can't hear him above the noise of shrieking sirens and gushing water. I cross the street to avoid the blowing spray and dash along the sidewalk to a stand of trees. A handful of neighbors have come out, some with umbrellas, to stand under the sheltering branches of a native oak tree. An SUV skids around the wall of water, gains traction, then comes to a stop on the far side of the hydrant, blocked by the fire truck and two squad cars.

I spot Doug standing partly concealed behind a pickup parked across the street from Elaine's car. He's soaked to the skin, hanging on to the rim of the truck bed for support. I crouch down and run to join him, sprinting through water lashing the pavement. I shield my eyes from the thick spray, trying to get a closer look at the car.

"Can you see her? Did she get out?" I shout.

Doug shakes his head, his eyes on the car. His arm encircles my shoulders, the sodden sleeve of his safari jacket clinging to my soaked jersey.

"Drunk. She was drunk," I mutter, staring at the sedan shuddering under the pounding water pressure. "We shouldn't have let her drive!" I cover my eyes with my hands, the image of Elaine's tear-stained face haunting me. I picture her reaching unsteadily for her handbag, then heading for the front door. "Why didn't we stop her?"

Doug's hand squeezes my arm, kneading the flesh below my shoulder. I know he must be thinking the same thing. *We shouldn't have let her drive.*

For long minutes, we watch firefighters in helmets and heavy black gear and paramedics in yellow vinyl coveralls and boots struggle to wrest the car off the curb. Once the hydrant is shut down, the cascade of water quickly diminishes. Through the throng of emergency workers, I catch glimpses of Elaine slumped over the wheel.

Donna and Dirck move in next to us. "Not looking good," Dirck says, shaking his head slowly.

"She shouldn't have been driving," Donna whispers, tears welling. "It's my fault. I shouldn't have let her leave in that condition."

"We're all to blame," I say, mentally counting the glasses of wine she drank, beginning with happy hour at Gilligan's. But then the loud cracking sounds we heard reverberate in my mind. "Maybe she struck something and had a flat tire. You know, lost control. What'd you see, Doug?"

"Just the sedan plowing into the fire hydrant, then all hell broke loose with the water. Could've been a flat tire, I guess. When I turned onto the street, all I saw was the sedan swerving, then sort of cruising up the street." He looks down at the ground as though trying to recall something else. "It had to be an accident. A terrible accident."

"I heard some loud backfire sounds," Dirck says. "Maybe something was wrong with the car."

"I've got to find out how she is," Donna says, breaking away from us. She dashes across the street toward paramedics wheeling an empty stretcher to the sedan.

I follow. Before Donna gets within ten feet of the car, a young, ruddy-faced police officer blocks her. "Whoa, there, ma'am."

"She was my dinner guest," Donna protests. "I want to know how she is."

"Elaine was a friend of ours, Officer," I say, stepping up. "We just spent the evening together. Is she going to be all right?"

"Could you move over there, please," he says brusquely.

Dirck and Doug join us as we're all herded to the side of the fire truck. Two other vehicles pull up, both with emergency lights flashing. A short, stocky African-American woman climbs out of the first car and stands for a moment, surveying the activity around the sedan. A tall, wiry man, cameras slung around his neck, jumps out of the second unmarked car, leaving its lights flashing, and joins her. The two exchange a few words before he starts taking pictures of Elaine, still slumped over the wheel. I follow his movements as he photographs her being removed from the car and lifted onto the stretcher. Her face and chest are bloody, her chamois jacket streaming dark red in the headlights of a squad car.

I turn back to the officer. "Please, we're friends. We know her. If those are detectives over there, could you ask if we could speak to them? We want to know if she's alive."

He looks around, then nods. "Wait here, please. Don't move. We'll likely want information from you."

The officer moves a few steps away to speak to the detectives, an older man with a thick chest and steel-gray crew cut who is conferring with the female detective. The male detective listens to the officer, looks over at us and nods, then turns back to watch as EMTs load Elaine's stretcher into the paramedics' van. The doors close and the red van speeds off, sirens blaring, in the direction of Sunset Boulevard.

"She's alive," Dirck says. "If they're taking her to the hospital, she's alive."

"You're right. She's alive," the older man says, approaching. "I'm Detective McCauley, West Los Angeles Police Department. You know the driver of this vehicle?"

"Yes," I volunteer. "Elaine Farris Horne. She lives in Indiana and just arrived in town today. She was here to visit her daughter."

He looks around. "Her daughter is here?"

"No, unfortunately she's missing. We've been trying to locate her."

"Did any of you witness what happened?"

"I saw her car hit the fire hydrant," Doug says. "It could've been a flat tire that sent the car swerving. The road was slick, too. It just seemed to happen in slow motion."

"How far away were you?"

"I'd just pulled out of that driveway down there"—he turns to indicate the open gates to Donna's place—"and saw her car veer to the right. That's my car parked at the curb."

"You didn't see anyone else in the vicinity? No other cars? People on foot?"

Doug shakes his head. "No. Nothing. There was some light up ahead, but it was hard to see in the mist. Where did they take her? UCLA?"

"Yes. Did you notice anything else?"

"We heard some loud sounds. Could've been backfire," Dirck says.

"We could hear it up at the house," Donna says. "Like fireworks or gunfire."

"Yes, two loud shots," I say. "It sounded like gunfire."

He nods to the younger officer. "Officer Ragon is going to take down your names and contact information. You'll all be available in case we need to talk to you?"

"Wait, why? What's going on?" Dirck asks. "I'm going to be around, but why do you need to talk to us?"

"Maybe we shouldn't have let her drive," Donna interrupts, her voice rising. "I mean, she seemed fine, but—"

"Donna, let's leave it at that, okay?" I turn to the officer. "Elaine was upset about her daughter. She was probably fatigued from traveling, but there was no reason to think she'd have an accident like this."

"Nothing happened? A few drinks too many? An argument, maybe?"

"What? No! It was a nice dinner," Donna says. "Why would you think that?"

"This wasn't an accident." He looks at each of us in turn. "Your friend was shot."

9

I wake up to a world that got a whole lot more complicated overnight. Listening to the early morning chorus of chirping birds, I feel no thrill at the start of a new day. My eyes are gritty from lack of sleep, but I'm wide-awake. I sigh and roll onto my back, a heavy weight settling on my chest as I recall the events of last night.

In the stunned silence that followed the news that Elaine had been shot, Detective McCauley departed. While we provided Officer Ragon with our contact information, Detective McCauley walked swiftly toward a newly arrived black van from which a middle-aged woman, heavyset, with cropped gray hair, had emerged.

As Officer Ragon led us back behind a police barrier, I glanced over my shoulder to see curious onlookers gathered in small groups behind a yellow-taped perimeter. I snapped pictures with my cellphone, then took video of Detective McCauley conferring with the middle-aged woman, who appeared to be taking charge. She glanced our way, her eyes on me. I put down my cellphone. She turned back to Detective McCauley and shook her head slowly. A sick feeling settled in my stomach.

Turning to Doug, I whispered, "I don't think Elaine made it."

"That's what I'm guessing," Doug said. "Seems like we've got homicide investigators arriving. This is a crime scene," he mumbled. "Looks awfully damn familiar, and we're smack in the middle of it."

I knew what he meant. The surrounding scene had the look of a night shoot, the sort where the makeup call is in the late afternoon but filming doesn't begin until after sundown. Holmby Park was the perfect base camp for a production crew shooting in one of the surrounding mansions: It was easy to envision the arc-lit alien encampment of honey wagons that housed dressing rooms parked curbside, their generators churning lustily, next to a string of prop, wardrobe and camera trucks.

How many such scenes, with squad cars, fire trucks and hundreds of extras, had the two of us shot together over the years? Normally Doug would be at the center of the action, calling the shots, not stranded uselessly "smack in the middle of it." Therein lay a huge difference. This setup was unscripted and he had no control of the action.

Again I had an eerie feeling about what had taken place, that the circumstances behind the shooting were still unfolding. I turned slowly, taking a sweeping panoramic video of the moonlit park and the street where Elaine's sedan sat crumpled on the pavement. Still recording, I zoomed in on Elaine's cowboy hat mired in a muddy puddle below the door of the sedan. For once, she wasn't the stunt double, but the star of the show, and she wasn't even on set. Alive or not, she was in a hospital three miles west, while the drama was playing out here. Had she known, she would not have been pleased.

It was my turn to give Officer Ragon my name and address. "You can just ditto the address you have for Donna," I said, and gave him my cellphone number. "We should probably go to the hospital now, okay?"

"Hang on, breaking news," Dirck said, staring at his own cellphone. He looked up and pointed to a news van, its antenna visible on the other side of one of the fire trucks. "They're saying an unidentified woman was shot and killed in a drive-by on South Beverly Glen—that's gotta be Elaine." He turned to the officer. "They're saying dead on arrival at UCLA emergency, is that right?"

"I have no confirmation on that," Officer Ragon said, flipping his notebook closed.

"Yeah? Then I guess I'll check it out with the people who have inside dope."

Doug rolled his eyes as Dirck stalked off toward the news van. "You can bet he'll be on a live news feed doing interviews in no time."

"Should we go to the hospital?" Donna asked fretfully.

"Not much point if the newswire got it right," Doug said. "She'll be in the care of the medical examiner."

"Poor Chelsea. It's her mother!" Tears sprang to my eyes as it sank in. "I hope she's okay, wherever she is. If only we knew how to find her."

"I know," Doug said, "I've been thinking that, too." He turned to Officer Ragon. "We'll be up at the house if you need us. There's no reason to stay here."

"Thank you, sir. Appreciate it," he said. "Sorry for your loss."

We headed back to Donna's house, passing Dirck's car in the driveway, its trunk still wide open.

"We better take his things inside," Donna said, peering at the luggage.

"I'm not his damn bellhop," Doug said, slamming the lid down on the trunk. "He can drag his own stuff in."

Elaine's death was confirmed on a late-night news bulletin during a stand-up interview with Dirck, his collar up, shoulders hunched, seemingly bearing up under the terrible weight of "the loss of a good friend." He was positioned with his back to the sedan as a tow truck hoisted it up. His voice husky, he said, "Elaine Farris was one of the industry's great stunt gals, no one finer. She's going to be deeply missed by all who knew and loved her."

Doug, watching the interview on the flat screen in Donna's den, cracked his knuckles, mumbled an expletive and said he ought to be going home.

Donna and I went to bed, neither of us feeling up to waiting for Dirck to arrive back once the news vans shut down for the night. Donna set a plate of cookies on the kitchen table with light bulbs, a set of towels and some brief instructions for the guest quarters in the pool house.

"I gave him a key and the code to the gate. You think he'll be okay? This seems sort of inhospitable," Donna said.

"Don't worry. Dirck has a way of figuring things out."

Alone in my room, I sent a text to Jack. I ached to call him, but he was in Minneapolis, where it was three o'clock in the morning. *Call me whenever you can*, I tapped out. The news was too big, too complicated for my tired fingers to type.

This morning, awake only hours after I drifted into fitful sleep, I feel no urgency to get up. I pick up my cellphone and look at the video I shot of the pulsing geyser of water shooting up from the fire hydrant spraying Elaine's car. The headlights of a car I hadn't noticed last night shine across the darkened north side of the park. A bicyclist cuts across the road as a squad car, lights flashing, approaches the boulevard. The video is choppy, occasionally blurred, but grows sharp as I focus on the female detective looking into camera, nodding and looking back to Detective McCauley.

I reach for the remote to turn on the small flat-screen mounted on the wall. I'm in time to catch the top-of-the-hour local morning news, not surprised to see that the death of Elaine Farris heads the broadcast. The adage "if it bleeds, it leads" is entirely appropriate for a story that crackles with such hashtag piquancy as *Hollywood, murder* and *stunt girl.* The fact that the incident occurred in one of the toniest neighborhoods in Los Angeles only adds to the allure.

A sweeping early-morning shot of the crime scene shows a substantial length of the boulevard cordoned off. The reporter, toothy, busty and blond, indicates that where Elaine's sedan mounted the curb, there's now only the toppled fire hydrant and an array of candles and bouquets forming a small shrine. *Who would leave flowers for Elaine?* The moment that cynical thought crosses my mind, I try to scrub it away, but I still can't help but wonder—*Who? Why?*—unless it's simply a gesture of humanity for someone inexplicably and tragically killed.

In a cutaway to Dirck, looking fetchingly haggard, filmed sometime during the night, he's identified as "a family friend and the acting coach for young Chelsea Horne, the missing daughter of veteran stuntwoman Elaine Farris, killed in a drive-by shooting." A news conference is scheduled for later this morning. I wonder if Dirck will be on deck as a "family" spokesperson?

Thank God Dougie notified Ed Ackerman last night, because the producer's phone must be ringing off the hook by now. Sadly, and ironically, Elaine's death also means Chelsea's disappearance will become a top police priority. If there's a connection between her disappearance and her mother's murder, is there the grim possibility that Chelsea's body will now be found? I can't bear to think about it. Feeling sick with dread, I turn the television off and toss the remote to the foot of the bed.

Sun streams through the open windows like a slap in the face. The birds are finally chirped-out, but I hear splashing in the pool. I clamber out of bed to take a look, but realize almost immediately that it's probably Dirck swimming vigorous laps.

I push my arms through the sleeves of a robe and crouch next to the window, shading my eyes from the glare of sun glancing off the pool. The lawns glisten with the last of yesterday's rain, wisps of steam rising where the warm sun bakes the grass dry. The air smells sweet, perfumed with jasmine and fragrant English roses.

The only sight marring the idyllic scene is Dirck flipping around at the far end of the pool for another lap.

I watch him slither through the water, back and forth, lap after lap, almost forgetting he used to be my husband. I manage to take an abstract view of a lean, powerful swimmer, with arms stretching out in long, clean strokes. The water churns in his wake, sparking in sunlit crystals that seem to burst and fizz in the bright sunlight. My eyes follow the figure gliding through the water until he emerges from the pool, dripping onto the flagstones and shaking himself like a wet dog.

Every inch of that body is familiar to me. It's held up well since I last saw it in as natural a state as this. The shoulders are broad, the waist narrow and the legs strong and finely shaped. If I did not know this package housed Dirck—God help me!— there's a chance I might've been interested in getting to know it better.

He picks up a towel from a lawn chair, uses it to ruffle his thick, curly hair dry, then tosses it around his shoulders like a loose cape. Hands on hips, he surveys the tennis court, the rolling lawns and the orchid pavilion, then turns to gaze at the entrance to the den. I know what he's thinking: *Breakfast.*

Then, in a swift move that catches me off guard, he glances up at my bedroom window. I shift sideways, wondering if he's caught my movement or if he can even see me through the glare of sun. His head swivels as he takes in the entire house, then turns to look back at the pool house. I watch him pad across the flagstones to the French doors and vanish into the shadowy interior of his new guest quarters.

I admit it's churlish of me to begrudge Dirck free use of Donna's unoccupied guest room. After all, she took me in, too, providing me with safe haven when I had no shelter other than my car. But I resent the intrusion. He should not be here. The last thing I want is to bump into him in the kitchen, where I'm sure Donna is whipping up a sumptuous breakfast. I'm so unhappy about this turn of events that I consider going back to bed to brood. If my cellphone hadn't rung its merry tune, I probably would have done just that.

Instead, I snatch up the phone, instinctively knowing it's Jack calling.

"Hey, sunshine, you texted at three in the morning. I hope I didn't wake you up."

"No, I'm so glad you called. Have you seen the news reports about Elaine Farris, the woman who was shot last night near Sunset Boulevard?"

"I was just watching a news bulletin now. Did you know her?"

"She was my stunt double years ago. She was here for dinner last night with Dougie Halliburton and Dirck Heyward. We all worked together on *Holiday*. Someone killed her just after she left here to go home. It was awful! Elaine also happens to be the mother of the young actress I was coaching for the role of Jinx."

"The one who took your hat. Is she still missing?"

"I'm afraid so. It's been three days now. The worst of it is, she and her mother were estranged. Elaine came out here to patch things up and then this happens. It's anyone's guess if there's a connection between the murder and Chelsea's disappearance."

"The report I heard indicated it was a random drive-by shooting."

"But according to Dougie, who was on the scene, there was no one driving by—I mean, no one anywhere on the street when it happened. I can't figure it out."

"The police will, Meg. Just tell them what you know and leave it to them. Have they interviewed you yet?"

"We talked to a detective last night. He called Donna after we got home and said he'd be coming by today. The only one who really saw anything was Doug. When are you getting back?"

"I wish I could get on a flight right now, but maybe we'll wrap this up before tomorrow. Sorry, but there's not much I can do about it."

I hear his sigh and follow with one of my own. "I understand. I just miss you."

"Me, too. I wish I could be there for you. Keep me posted on this. I'll try to find out what I can, but please keep me informed, okay?" There's a hesitant sound in Jack's voice, and before I can respond, he adds, "There's no way to know what's at the bottom of this. Just watch yourself, Meg. A breaking story like this brings out the—"

"No, I know. Don't worry. Donna and I will look out for ourselves, and besides—" I stop on the verge of telling Jack that we'll be safe because my former husband has moved into the guest house—definitely TMI. There is no way this information is beneficial. I laugh to ease the tension and shake off a terrible mental image of Jack encountering Dirck lolling at Donna's pool.

"What? Besides what?"

"Nothing. I was going to say that I haven't seen Elaine in years and barely know Chelsea. There's nothing to connect me to them, so don't worry." I laugh again. "Hey, I miss you! Get your buns back here as soon as possible."

Jack laughs, too. "Working on it. But stay in touch, okay?"

The doorbell rings. "I promise." I walk to the window with the phone to my ear and peer down at the driveway. "There's a Chevrolet Caprice parked out front. I have a feeling the police are here to interview us."

"Then I'll let you go. Call me when you can."

"Bye, darling. I'll stay in touch." I hold the phone to my cheek a moment, feeling its warmth, not wanting to be the one to push End Call.

Then, figuring Donna will be happily plying Detective McCauley with flapjacks and applewood-smoked bacon, I take my time showering. Something tells me I've got a long day ahead.

10

Donna has staged no elaborate mise-en-scène in the dining room this morning. There are no props or fancy china on display, just Dirck sitting at the kitchen table, working his way through a plate of eggs over easy, bacon and whole-wheat toast, his favorite breakfast. He's wearing a flannel shirt, sleeves rolled to the elbow, jeans and boots, his essential manly-man outfit.

Donna sits with a cup of coffee, elbows on the table, apparently captivated by Dirck shoveling food into his mouth. She looks up as I enter, rapture glittering in her eyes.

"Good morning. I just made fresh coffee for Dirck. Want some breakfast?"

"Best I've ever had," Dirck says, tapping a napkin to his lips. "The applewood-smoked bacon is great!"

"Thanks. I'll just have coffee. I thought the police were here."

"They are," Donna says. "I was about to come up and get you. They already talked with Dirck. I didn't have much to tell them. They're out front now, looking around, but they'll be back. They want to talk with you, of course."

"Don't worry," Dirck says. "I pretty much filled them in, gave 'em all the background."

"That's helpful," I murmur, wondering what in the world he's managed to dredge up. I sip my coffee and size up the situation. Given that Dirck has a wife and kid back in New York, he can't stay here that long, but he's looking awfully comfortable. With luck, he'll spare us a burp of satisfaction. "You slept okay?"

"Got in a couple of hours, all I need. Man, I must've done five, six stand-ups out there last night. Exhausting. I shoulda got paid for those interviews, but it's the least I could do for poor Elaine." He leans back in his chair, gazing at Donna, his voice honeyed. "I can't tell you what a pleasure it is to wake up here. And the pool's even heated."

"You're more than welcome," Donna coos, pouring more coffee.

"Did the police have any news about Chelsea this morning?"

"I asked. Nothing new," Dirck says, looking up at me. "I wonder if she's heard about her mother."

"Who can say? I just hope she's alive and well, wherever she is." I pull a chair up to the table. "You know, I've been thinking about what you said yesterday, that Chelsea was really into researching her role. You don't think she'd sign on with an escort service and actually hook up with some guy, do you?"

"Hey, c'mon, I didn't suggest she do that," Dirck chuckles, "but you never know. Chelsea's pretty gung ho. I had another gal in class, who got herself arrested for shoplifting. The judge wouldn't buy her story that it was just research for a role. But at least she's got that experience under her belt, and a little community service, to boot."

"Nice. A criminal record always looks impressive on an actor's resume."

"You always got to put me down, don't you?" Dirck scowls. "I didn't tell her to shoplift!"

"Okay, okay, the girl was a little too gung ho. But what about Chelsea?"

"Chelsea's got great instincts. This call girl, whoever she is, must have given her some good background dope, because it really comes through. I saw honesty and real depth to her work. I like to think I had a hand in getting her to that place, you know? It's what I live for."

"That's swell of you, Dirck. What have you got on for today?"

"I'm hanging loose. I've got a couple of Skype sessions scheduled later with some actors in New York." He looks out the window at the pool glimmering in the sun. "Thought I might catch a few rays until then."

"Be my guest," Donna beams. "Let me know when you'd like some lunch."

"Thanks, Donna. Let's go a little light, if it's okay with you. Maybe some salad and a slice or two of cold pot roast?" He stands and stretches. "How about you, Meg? Joining me at the pool?"

"No, I think I'll stay dry until I've talked to the cops. See you later."

"Sure thing. Thanks again, Donna." Dirck ambles out of the kitchen, taking an apple from a bowl on the counter as he goes.

"Wow," Donna breathes. "He has some appetite."

"Especially when it's on the house." Then, realizing I've done my own share of mooching on her hospitality, I add, "It's very good of you to put him up. Any idea how long he's staying?"

"He didn't say, but he did offer to help me move some furniture around later this week." She lowers her voice and gives me a teasing look. "You two really don't get along, do you?"

"It shows?"

She laughs. "I'm hiding the sharp cutlery for the duration. Look, I can see he gets under your skin, but he's really kind of a nice guy."

Alarm bells ring. Dirck's charm offense is working. I smile. "You're absolutely right, Donna. Nice guy."

"And he sure loves to eat! Are you hungry?"

"No, thank you. I'll finish my coffee and go outside to make friends with the police."

The thought of Dirck on the premises through the week is enough to rob me of my appetite, but it occurs to me that Donna's look of rapturous adoration has as much to do with having a man around the house paying attention to her as it does with his appreciation of her cooking.

This thought is confirmed when Donna says, "Okay, see you later. I'm off to the market to pick up some fish. Dirck said he liked the idea of a nice bouillabaisse for dinner, and then we're going to watch a movie together. He's knows as much about film as Robert Osborne!"

"Sounds like fun, but I'll probably miss out on it. I'm hoping to see Jack tonight if he gets back to town. I'll call and let you know."

"Please do. You could always invite Jack to dinner here," she says with a sly smile, "but something tells me that's not in the cards."

"I can't imagine anything worse. Dirck would have a field day and I'd be mortified."

Donna laughs. "Don't worry, I won't even mention Jack's name to him."

"Much appreciated. By the way, I'm dropping by to see Doug later. Any leftovers you want me to bring him?"

"You bet!" she says, glowing with the anticipation of feeding yet one more human being.

I swish my coffee cup with a spray of water and leave it to dry in the dish drainer. Fortified with a strong shot of caffeine, I step out the front door. I know Jack probably won't be back until tomorrow, but if a little white lie to Donna saves me another dinner in Dirck's company, it's worth it.

Detective McCauley isn't hard to spot crouching in the grass at the bottom of the driveway, nor is the squat woman with cropped hair that I saw with him last night. She appears to be inspecting the intercom pad to the side of the front gates, but glances up when she sees me amble down the walkway. Looking composed in an ill-matched navy jacket and black pants, she watches me approach.

When I'm within greeting distance, I call out, "Good morning. I'm Meg Barnes."

"Good morning. Detective Christine Yarrow, West Los Angeles Homicide Division. I understand you live here?" She hands me her card.

"Yes. Donna probably told you I've been staying here for a while until I find my own place."

"She mentioned that. And, of course, I'm familiar with you from *Holiday*. I used to watch the show growing up." I detect a hint of a smile and suspect she's probably a fan, which is always helpful. "I understand that last night was sort of a reunion for all of you."

"It was. Of course, we hadn't seen each other in a good number of years. It was great to get together again, all very serendipitous." For some reason I'm speaking in an inappropriate party voice. I switch gears, reminding myself that the evening ended with Elaine's death. "It's tragic what happened, a complete shock. We'd said goodbye just minutes before."

"That's what I hear." She looks at me intently, her manner unhurried. *What is she thinking?* My cheeks burn. If only that noncommittal look was just her way of concealing her excitement at meeting Jinx in person—*that* I could handle.

The silence between us lingers and I begin to feel uneasy. Perhaps she's taking her time assessing just how guilty I might be—*of what?* My caffeinated heart pumps rapidly, wondering just how well acquainted she is with my recent history. Thanks to the Internet, my life is an open book, with several lengthy court documents and news articles about my conman husband that anyone can access. She must be aware that I was implicated in Paul's business fraud.

"Maybe we could find a place to talk out of the hot sun," she says finally. "Detective McCauley will join us." She motions to McCauley.

"G'morning," he says, lumbering over, wiping his hands on a large plaid handkerchief. He's wearing a black nylon jacket with khakis and looks uncomfortably warm. "How're you doing?"

"Okay, all things considered." I wave my hand toward the wrought-iron garden furniture arranged on a patio that's shaded by the orchid pavilion. "How about over there?"

I start up the walkway, the two detectives on my heels, and try to shake off free-floating anxiety. *I have nothing to hide!* But then, I remind myself, I've done nothing but hide for more than a year. It's become habit forming.

"My goodness, it's warm this morning," I say, reverting to my gay party voice. I sit in one of the garden chairs across from Detective Yarrow and turn to Detective McCauley, who settles into a chair next to me. "And awfully humid after all that rain last night."

He nods. "Unusual for this time of year."

"Very," I say. In the lingering silence, I tap Detective Yarrow's card on my knee, glancing at the lettering. "Homicide Division. Hard to believe, you know? Do you have any idea how it happened? Or who could've done this?"

"That's what we're working on," she says. "Maybe you could tell us about the last time you saw Elaine *before* your dinner here."

"Before? You mean at Chelsea's house?" The prickling on my scalp tightens. I'd invested my anxiety in what happened to me a year ago, forgetting entirely about my run-in with the police just yesterday afternoon. "Of course. I dropped by the house just as Elaine arrived. She didn't have keys, so she climbed through a window and then a neighbor saw her breaking in and called the police." I smile at Detective Yarrow. "Looking back, it was sort of funny, like the old days when she was my stunt double, you know?"

Detective Yarrow makes a note, then looks up, her face registering puzzlement. "So it was all good-natured? She wasn't upset to find you there? According to a police report—"

"I see what you mean. Well, she was surprised to see me, of course, but then I told her that I'd been hired to coach Chelsea. You know she's playing Jinx in the new series, right?"

"Did you know Chelsea was her daughter?"

"That was a surprise. But then Elaine got very upset, understandably, when I told her Chelsea hadn't shown up for an important table read. That's the reason I went to the house looking for her in the first place."

"I understand you were the last to see her?"

"Seems like it. We'd been working together. I was teaching her hat tricks."

"You're talking about the famous hat that went missing? Apparently she took it and you were trying to get it back from her?"

Donna drives her Mercedes out of the garage and waves to us before heading down to the gates. I wave back. "I'm sure Donna told you—"

"We'd like to hear about it from you. Apparently you were injured chasing her? Can you tell us about that?"

"I wasn't really chasing her. She was already gone. I happened to trip and fall into some bushes. Just a few scratches, that's all." I try to swallow, but my mouth is dry. "Look, I don't think any of this has to do with Elaine getting shot, but why don't I just tell you what I know. She certainly wasn't killed because of a missing hat!"

"Go ahead, tell us," Detective Yarrow says, looking almost affable. "That's what we want to hear."

"Okay, you got it." I settle back, trying to work up some saliva. The last thing I want to suggest is going into the house for water, where we'll likely run into Dirck. Beginning with our work session in the pool house and Chelsea's abrupt departure, I cover the same ground but in more detail. In going over my encounter with Elaine at the house, I stick to the bare facts. Aside from a natural reluctance to speak ill of the departed, I see no point in delving into our occasionally contentious working relationship. She was doing her job. I was doing mine. What can it matter now?

"And what about her husband, a Mr. Horne?"

"I have no idea who he is. I didn't know she'd married or had a child until I saw her yesterday afternoon. Have you reached him? He probably doesn't know his daughter is missing."

"We're on top of it," Detective McCauley says, standing up. "You know how to reach us. Get in touch if you think of anything else."

"Of course." I shake his hand. "I know you have to question the last people Elaine was with, but it's unnerving. It must be obvious that none of us were involved in what happened to her. It had to be something random. Maybe a carjack attempt."

"Anything's possible," he says.

"It's a real pleasure to meet you," Detective Yarrow says, smiling warmly now that the interrogation is over. "Who would ever think I'd be on this end of things with Jinx. I guess it's all in a day's work."

"Jinxed again!" I laugh and shake her hand. "It's nice to meet you, even under these circumstances."

I watch them go to their car, then head inside for a glass of water, relieved to have made it through the interview without getting arrested.

There's no sign of Dirck, but Donna has left a picnic hamper for me on the kitchen counter. I peek inside, finding sliced pot roast, a jar of horseradish mustard, green beans in vinaigrette, crusty bread and oatmeal cookies—a feast! I race upstairs to grab a jacket and my shoulder bag, hoping to be on my way before running into Dirck.

After taking care of a few errands, I pull in to Dougie's driveway. As usual, he's sitting on the front porch with Ridley at his feet.

"Hungry?" I ask on my way to the kitchen with the hamper. "It's just past noon."

"Bring it on," he says, clearing the rattan coffee table of newspapers.

I pull a couple of Samuel Adams pilsners from Doug's fridge, but otherwise Donna has included everything we might need: napkins, vintage 1940s red Melmac plates and miniature shakers of salt and pepper.

"You always get to eat like this?" Dougie says, a note of wonder in his voice.

"What can I say? She loves to cook. I love food. The trick is to keep exercising." I take a sip of pilsner and settle back in a roomy wicker chair. "So what's your take on what happened to Elaine?"

"I don't know. Some detective is coming by this afternoon. I can't think of anything to add to what I said last night."

"They came by Donna's this morning. I certainly wasn't able to shed any light on how Elaine was killed, but they wanted to know about my run-in with her at Chelsea's house."

"You know, until last night, I hadn't laid eyes on Elaine in two decades. I was thinking it's funny that she hadn't seemed to mellow over the years. I can see where Chelsea gets her edge." Doug strokes Ridley, ruffling the dog's ears. "But I also understood what Elaine was going through. You never want to leave issues unsettled with your wife or kids because you just never know what's around the bend. If she came out here to patch things up with her daughter and something bad happened to Chelsea before she could see her, she'd never forgive herself. But no one could have predicted this outcome."

"You didn't get to ask her what caused the falling out?"

He shakes his head. "She was already in her car when I got outside."

"If we knew what their blowup was about—"

"It was between them. Private." Doug sips his pilsner and sets the glass down with a thud. "In fact, I wonder what the kid would say if she knew her mother had forced her way into her house. After all, we're talking about an adult woman, a working actress living her own life. If there were real problems between them, I'm sure Chelsea didn't want her mother snooping into her life."

"But Chelsea's missing. It's odd that she'd disappear the night before her mother arrives. Whatever went on between them might be a clue to where Chelsea is—maybe even to what happened to Elaine. That's all I'm saying."

"I hear you and I know where this is going. You've got your Jinx hat on and you want to go poking around. I wouldn't advise it." Doug balls up his napkin and tosses it into the hamper. "Elaine is not anyone I would ever have wanted to hang out with, but she's dead under terrible circumstances. We were the last to see her and that's reason enough to stay clear of this. You don't know what you could stumble on, and it could be dangerous, hear me?"

"Maybe—"

"No 'maybe' about it. Stay out of it!"

Doug's response is more heated than I would have expected. I push my pilsner aside, unnerved by his vehemence. Why is he taking such a hard line? We sit quietly for a moment or two, letting things settle. I know I shouldn't pursue this, but I can't stop myself.

"Okay, but this isn't just about Elaine. You're a producer on the new series. Your lead actress doesn't show up for work. Aren't you concerned about finding her?"

"Of course, but that's a different matter. It's Ackerman's headache. He's the executive producer, a pay grade above me, and he's on top of it. They're looking at camera tests as we speak. I don't want to see Chelsea blow this, either, but my feeling is that she will turn up. Believe me, she better have a damn good reason for going AWOL, but I'm guessing it's a personal matter. I'm just telling you to keep your nose out of it. You hear me?"

"You're coming across loud and clear."

"Good, then get this. You could stir up things that maybe shouldn't be stirred up. So let things be."

"You're right. Not another word. How about if we take Ridley for a walk? I need to work off lunch."

"You're on, kid." Doug smiles, looking relieved.

But it's that very look of relief that makes me wonder why he's so adamant I stay out of it. Perhaps it's advice worth heeding. After talking with Dirck, I'd momentarily flashed on the notion of suggesting to the detectives that maybe Chelsea got in over her head researching escort services. I'm glad I dropped the idea. The consequences of raising that line of inquiry could have made matters worse for everyone involved, including Ed Ackerman—but most especially for Chelsea herself.

While I clean up, Doug attaches the lead to Ridley's collar. As we start walking down the winding street, he chuckles and says, "Knowing Ed Ackerman's ulcer is flaring up over this shouldn't give me so much satisfaction, but it does. And that's all I'm going to say."

I refrain from any further reference to Chelsea, but Doug's insistence that I not meddle has stimulated my curiosity. There is something he's not telling me, and I have no idea what it is. But then, I'm not telling him everything, either. I switch subjects before I'm tempted to reveal more.

"By the way, Donna wants you to know you have an open invitation to her table anytime you want to come. She's serious about that. Nothing gives her more pleasure than feeding people and entertaining guests. Unfortunately, if you come by this week, you'll be dining with Dirck."

"Then I'll take a rain check until you give me the all-clear that he's decamped. I can't take more than a small dose of the man. I don't know how you stuck it out with him as long as you did."

"I wanted to make it work." I shrug. "If his career had taken off instead of mine, it might have made a difference. Who knows?"

Doug doesn't respond.

We walk through the neighborhood until Ridley gets winded. We turn back and, as we're walking up Doug's driveway, my cellphone rings. Caller ID flashes *Jack Mitchell* and I quickly answer. "Hey, there! Are you on your way back?"

"I'm already here. I caught a red-eye and spent the morning in meetings. It looks like I can break away early, maybe around six thirty. You up for dinner at the beach?" By that, I know he means a walk along the Santa Monica Pier, followed by pepper steak at Chez Jay, a venerable old haunt on Ocean Avenue.

"Sounds good. Want me to meet you on the pier?"

"Why don't I swing by and pick you up at Donna's?"

"No need. It's out of your way." It could also mean an awkward introduction to Dirck, which I'm determined to avoid at all costs. "I'll pick you up for a change. How about six thirty, unless I hear from you in the meantime?"

"You're on. Everything okay with you?"

"Couldn't be better. We'll catch up later." Doug gives me a knock in the ribs. "And Dougie sends his greetings. We're out walking Ridley."

"Say hi to him, too. Can't wait to see you."

"Now there's a man worth his salt," Doug says as I pocket my cellphone. "Even when you thought he was giving you a hard time, I could tell he cared about you. Wish you'd hooked up with him in the first place."

"If only." In this case, "if only" means I could have avoided two ill-fated marriages, the first a disaster, the second a calamity.

Doug settles himself back in his chair on the porch, Ridley dropping into a fur puddle at his feet. "Try to hang on to this one, okay?" he says, his reference to Jack clear. "I don't want to worry about you anymore."

"Me?" I laugh, surprised by his comment. "C'mon, when did I ever give you reason to worry?"

"Always!" He gives me a tepid smile and shakes his head. "You're always getting yourself into some damn fix."

"That's what makes life worth living." I lean down and kiss him on the cheek. "See you soon."

I leave the last few slices of pot roast in his fridge, then stow the hamper in the back seat of my car. I wave to Doug and pull out of his driveway, wondering if he has any idea how much I worry about him living on his own and missing Edie. But he's right; if only I'd hooked up with Jack in the first place, life would be a lot sweeter.

It would also allow me to drive back to Donna's house without having to weigh the risks of running into Dirck, which I just don't feel up to doing. The irony that I've been forced to take refuge in my car once again is not lost on me. I feel a stab of irritation that Dirck has moved in, but it also serves as a reminder that I've practically become a squatter in Donna's house. However much she insists that she wants me to stay on, it's time I found a place of my own. The two of us will remain friends forever, but not roommates—and I would never want to be dropped as a dinner guest!

Thinking of dinner guests, I wish I'd somehow managed to ask Elaine why she was so opposed to having her daughter play Jinx. But as soon as my mind turns down that path, Doug's warning echoes in my ears: *It could be dangerous, hear me? You could stir up things that maybe shouldn't be stirred up. So let things be.*

11

Instead of returning to Donna's house, I pull into a shady space up the street from Holmby Park. In my present frugal circumstances, I can't afford to aimlessly drive around using up precious gas I'll need for the trip to the beach and back with Jack this evening. I'm reminded of my salad days as a young actress in New York, choosing to walk rather than squander a subway token. I'm again counting my nickels and praying a good-paying job will come along so I can afford a roof over my head.

The reboot of *Holiday* could provide a regular paycheck if I snag a recurring role in the series. I hope that filling in for Chelsea at the table read inspires Ed Ackerman to think of me as more than her coach and hat wrangler. As it is, my present gig could end if Chelsea doesn't return soon, an added incentive to track her down.

I sling my bag onto my shoulder, lock up and amble over to Holmby Park. On my way, I pass the spot where I saw Chelsea wriggling her bottom while talking to the guy in the red convertible. It occurs to me that during the interview with the detectives I somehow neglected to mention either Chelsea's bartender boyfriend or my happy hour encounter with Elaine at Gilligan's. I'm curious to know if Jeremy got in touch with the police after hearing about Elaine's death. If he did, Detective Yarrow will probably wonder why I didn't bring up my visit to Gilligan's. Oddly enough, it simply didn't come to mind.

I sit on one of the shaded benches just past the putting green and punch up the number for Gilligan's on my cellphone. After several rings, someone answers and I ask for Jeremy. I'm told he'll be in later.

I look across to the far side of the park where large red cones strung with yellow tape surround the broken fire hydrant, the bright colors giving an air of festivity to the grim scene of Elaine's murder. Cello-wrapped bouquets of flowers, balloons and candles in tall jars rest against the curb. Traffic slows as one car after another passes slowly by, invariably with someone leaning out a window to aim a cellphone camera at the makeshift shrine.

I watch for a few minutes, then walk across the park to take a closer look at the offerings. Are these tributes from friends, fans or just kind strangers saddened by a shocking act of violence? I flash on the unlikely possibility that whoever killed her might've left a brazen, perhaps even remorseful note that could provide a clue. I sprint across the street, dodging a slow-moving car full of looky-loos.

Stooping down to read the messages, some hastily scrawled on the backs of envelopes and tucked under candles, I make a show of rearranging bouquets for the benefit of anyone observing me as they drive by.

As it turns out, someone does recognize me and calls my name. I turn around and see Corky Shaw, camera in hand, hanging out the window of a car driven by his mother, Julia. "Hey, it's me! We'll pull over."

As Julia maneuvers the Honda to the curb, I walk over. "Hey, buddy, how's it going?"

"Good, really good." He nods vigorously, then, remembering, says, "Hey, sorry about your friend. She was Chelsea Horne's mother, right?"

"Yes, she was."

"Poor Chelsea. How's she doing?"

"As well as can be expected." I see no reason to reveal that Chelsea has disappeared. I reach through the window to shake hands with his mother. "Hi, Julia. I see he's got you driving the camera truck again."

"I should join the Teamsters," she says, rolling her lively brown eyes. "My condolences. So sad. Do the police have any idea who did it?"

"No, not according to the detectives I talked to this morning."

"Wow," Corky says, his eyes alight. "What's that like? I mean, are you a suspect and everything?"

"Corky!" Julia knocks his elbow with her plump arm. "Mind your manners!" She looks at me and shakes her head, her dark brown curls framing a face that closely resembles her son's. "You live around here, don't you?"

"I told you already, Ma!" Corky says loudly. "You don't listen. She lives behind that gate down the street." He turns back to me. "Did you see it happen?"

Mother and son look at me expectantly, their curiosity palpable. "No, I was still up at the house. By the way, Corky, you were filming the other day when Chelsea was here in the park. Did you save whatever you recorded?"

"Oh, yeah. You want to see it? I could also show you the trailer. I just finished it."

"It looks great," Julia says. "Come on over to the house anytime."

"Thanks, how about today?" I check my watch and see that I'll have plenty of time to go back to Donna's to change clothes before meeting Jack later. "Maybe in a couple hours? Want me to call first?"

"No, just come on over," Julia says.

"See you later," Corky says as the car pulls away from the curb.

I glance back at the scene around the fire hydrant as a middle-aged woman climbs out of a red compact carrying a spray of gladiolas. She steps up onto the curb and turns to face a man sitting behind the wheel of the car and focusing his cellphone on her.

"Take it vertical, too," she calls out, "so you can see the house up there in the back."

I look up the hill above the hedge lining the high wrought-iron fencing, aware for the first time that, from this angle, the mansard roof of Donna's house is visible. I can also make out a sliver of the portico, front door and my upstairs window through the trees. From my perspective inside the house, I feel completely hidden from view even though I can see the street. How strange that it hadn't occurred to me that if I could see people in Holmby Park, someone could see me as well.

I look back at the middle-aged woman climbing into the passenger seat of the red compact, the gladiolas still in her arms. Chances are their next stop is the house nearby on Carolwood Drive where Michael Jackson died, still a ghoulish must-see on the celebrity-homes route.

I retrace my steps, then stop at the oak tree to look back at the scene from my viewpoint last night. As I do so, I see the gates to Donna's house swing open and watch Dirck drive out, turning toward Sunset Boulevard. He drives slowly past the shrine to Elaine and doesn't see me standing in the park.

All clear. I walk back to my car, assured that I won't bump into Dirck. Donna's Mercedes isn't parked in the garage, either. I set the hamper down in the pantry and pass through the kitchen, somewhat regretting that I'll miss out on bouillabaisse. But in Dirck's absence I have the pool to myself to swim a few laps and lie in the sun before showering and changing for tonight.

It's been way too long since Jack and I had some time together. Even though we'll be walking on the beach and having dinner in a ramshackle dive, I want to look my best. From my limited wardrobe, I manage to produce a pair of cropped pants and a flattering boat-necked jersey that I wear with sandals and a lightweight jacket. My less-is-more living arrangement has its advantages: fewer decisions and less bother. I look just fine without having tried on an assortment of outfits. By the time I head out to the Shaw home two hours later, neither Dirck nor Donna has returned.

The flip side of Donna's multimillion-dollar estate is the Shaw residence, a gray stucco tract house south of the airport, built at a time when much of Los Angeles was still orange groves and bean fields. The trim two-bedroom houses with single-car garages and small backyards catered to the post-war flood of GIs settling in Southern California, looking for sunshine and security. Nearly seventy years later, the once identical bungalows have taken on some individual character, but the neighborhoods, squeezed between freeways and giant box stores, look run-down, some with junk-strewn front yards.

On an otherwise unremarkable street of houses with peeling paint and broken sidewalks, the Shaw home is an exception. The lawn is green and freshly mowed. A neat canvas awning shades the picture window, the white trim looks freshly painted, and a basket of petunias hangs on a hook next to the front door. I park directly in front of the house as Julia opens the screen door and waves.

"Good timing!" she says as I head up a walkway lined with more petunias. "Howard just got home, and Joe's here, too. We're all in the backyard."

I follow Julia through the small living room and adjacent dining room, both choked with large pieces of good quality furniture better suited to a more spacious home. The kitchen is a '40s relic with original tile, a Hotpoint fridge and matching white enamel range. A window over the sink looks out on the backyard, where Corky's father and Uncle Joe are seated in metal lawn chairs, both men smoking cigars.

Julia picks up a pitcher of lemonade and a plate of homemade sugar cookies from the counter. For a moment I'm transported back to my own mother's old-fashioned kitchen in rural Nebraska.

"Come on out and say hi before looking at the trailer. Corky's in his room still making some changes to it."

"I can't wait to see what he's come up with. I'm sure you're both happy to have the garage back."

"For the time being," Julia laughs. "He'll be back in there next week doing some more reshoots."

The moment I emerge from the kitchen, Joe and Howard both rise, holding their cigars behind their backs.

"Please don't mind me," I say with a big smile as I walk across a small patch of lawn to a cement patio. "I love the smell of cigars." The fact is, I do like the pungent aroma of a good cigar, but both men look at me suspiciously. "Really, I mean it."

"Normally women can't abide the smell," Howard says, with a glance toward Julia. Neither man extends a hand for me to shake. As jovial and open as Julia is, her husband and brother-in-law seem more reserved, perhaps a shared family characteristic. But since I've met each of them just once before, perhaps they're only guarded around relative newcomers.

"Outside is fine," Julia says, standing at a picnic table, pouring lemonade into tall plastic glasses. "Smoking cigars inside is a no-no."

"I'm sorry to hear about your colleague," Howard says abruptly. "It's been on the news, of course. One has to be so careful on the streets at night."

"Indeed, such a terrible thing to happen," Joe says. He's the taller of the two, and a few years younger than his brother, but still has the unhealthy pallor that I'd assumed was Corky's attempt at makeup the other day. "My condolences, Miss Barnes."

"Thank you. Actually, I hadn't seen Elaine in many years, but I'd been working with her daughter."

"Who was studying acting with your former husband," Julia says, handing me a glass of lemonade. "He gave Chelsea her start."

"How did you know that?"

"I heard him on the radio this morning. He was talking about all of you getting together for dinner last night."

I might've known Dirck couldn't resist trumpeting his insider status. I take a gulp of lemonade, wondering what else he might have said.

"It's a complete tragedy and they have no idea who killed her mother or why. Meg was interviewed by detectives this morning."

"Really? They don't suspect you, do they?" Joe asks.

"Of course not," Julia answers for me, "but she was one of the last to see her."

"I'm so sorry. Being interviewed by the police can't be pleasant," Joe says.

"It's their job. Anything to help," I respond, trying to be non-committal. The police can't be too happy about Dirck's interview, either.

"It was probably a carjacking attempt," Howard says. "Completely random. We should all be very careful."

"Hey, Meg!" Corky bounds out of the kitchen, letting the screen door slam behind him. "It's done! Come and take a look at it." He grabs a handful of cookies and a glass of lemonade.

"Thanks, I will," I respond, grateful to avoid any further conversation about Elaine's death. "Nice to see you again," I say to the brothers before going back into the house with Corky.

It does not feel at all cool to follow a sixteen-year-old kid to his bedroom in his parents' house, especially a man/boy such as Corky, who exhibits at once both virile manhood and brash adolescence. I'm even less thrilled when I enter a cramped, cluttered room with the curtains drawn and see that there's no place to sit except on an unmade twin bed shoved against the wall. The space is crammed with action figures, posters, DVDs and bunched-up tube socks.

"My room," Corky says, spreading his arms wide and grinning. "Just push stuff aside and sit."

I leave the door open and decide to remain standing, keeping a respectable distance.

Corky plops down onto a swivel chair in front of a bank of computer equipment. "Uncle Joe works in a print shop and did these up for free," he says, handing me a color flyer from a stack on the floor.

The artwork for Corky's film, *Forsaken*, consists of a photoshopped image of my face tacked onto a seductively posed female body with breasts heaving out of a tight-fitting, shimmering red dress. The design is '40s lurid pulp, with an overlay of a spider's web and a knife-wielding figure seen in silhouette. "Nice," I say, "but this looks somehow familiar."

"Wow, good eye," he says, pulling up another image of a woman in a red satin dress, but with Ida Lupino's head, not mine. "Works, doesn't it? I found it on the Internet. You're so like her!"

"Thanks," I say, dubious about any resemblance at all between the 1940s film siren and me. "But can you do that? I mean, just use it?"

"It's a 'homage,'" he says, pronouncing the H. "Besides, I don't have much of a budget. If I pick up a distributor, that'll all change." He busily taps the keyboard, opening a file with the teaser he's been working on. "I've almost got the music right. I need to hear what you think."

What I hear is more "homage" ripped from the soundtrack of another old film, but it's evocative and suits the mood of *Forsaken*. What's enthralling is Corky's inventive use of backgrounds he's filmed around the city, including train tracks, old Hollywood bungalows and creepy industrial sites. Scenes that seemed so static when we shot in front of blue drapes hung in the Shaws' garage are transformed when set against the underpinnings of an old bridge with people moving around in the background.

Despite his bumptious childlike demeanor in person, Corky shows a surprising degree of sophistication in his composition and editing. The kid clearly has talent as a director, and the fact that he can write a good screenplay is a huge bonus.

"Well done, Corky! Nicely cut together."

"Would you mind doing some narration? It's the only thing missing."

"Sure. Why not?"

"I figured you'd be okay with it, so I'm all set up." He grins, handing me a sheet of paper he whips from the printer. He shuts the door and hands me a mic while I review the text. We do several takes, alternating phrases and changing the tone, until Corky is satisfied.

"Now, let me see what you shot the other day."

I kneel in front of the computer to get a better view of Corky's scenes recorded around Holmby Park, including a shot of Uncle Joe seated on a bench, wearing his fedora. There are also shots zooming in on Donna's house and the old Spelling mansion. Finally I see the segments with Chelsea arriving in the red convertible. I smile at her gyrations, but also try to focus on the man behind the wheel, who I'd assumed was Jeremy. Having now met Chelsea's boyfriend, I have my doubts that he was the driver.

I have Corky run the piece three times, enlarging images as much as possible. I jot down the license number, but can't get a good fix on the man behind the wheel, whose face is shadowed by sun-dappled leaves.

The video follows Chelsea sauntering toward us, then abruptly cuts to her close-up, looking directly into camera. "That's when she told me to stop filming," Corky says, blushing. "Said it was pervy."

"I remember. But then you drove by later when we were going up to Donna's house. Could I see that?"

"Actually, I kind of sneaked some more filming before getting into the car."

He plays another clip, this one a sequence, shot at some distance, of Chelsea and me, completely unaware we're being photographed. We look chummy, gesturing animatedly while walking toward a picnic table. We're about the same height and coloring, both of us in jeans and tee shirts. Chelsea is thinner and a little taller, but our age difference is not as apparent in the long shot. I can't help but wonder how much of me Doug saw in Chelsea when he and Ed Ackerman cast her as Jinx.

The video ends abruptly, just after I pop my top hat open and set it on the picnic table. "That was when Uncle Joe told me to stop filming and get in the car," Corky says. "Man, if only I had my own wheels! I really wanted to film the two of you working together."

"I'm glad you got this much. What about the next bit?"

"It's just you," Corky says. "Chelsea had already left."

The strip is brief, catching me at Donna's gate as I turn to see Corky filming from the blue Honda. I flip the top hat onto my head, pose, then laugh as he strains to film me from the accelerating car.

But then I hear the distant sound of a man's voice say, " . . . disrespectful! No good can come of it." Corky abruptly freezes the film on me waving to him.

I look at Corky's flustered face and ask, "What was that? It sounded like Uncle Joe."

"Sorry, it was. I accidentally flicked the sound on when I was shooting." He grips his knees with the palms of his hands, his pale face growing pink. "Sorry you heard that. It's not you, really, it's, um . . . they don't think I should be doing what I'm doing."

"You mean they want you to do something more respectable than making movies, right?" I take his hands in mine, looking him in the eye. "You've been at this since you were a kid. I thought your parents were behind you, especially your mother. She seems very supportive."

"She is, they are . . . but it's just that—"

"Wait a minute. Is it me? I hope your folks aren't upset that I'm encouraging you."

There's a swift rap on the door that coincides with it opening wide. The timing could not be worse.

"Oh, dear," Julia says, wearing a look of surprise as she sees me on my knees holding her son's hands. Uncle Joe is behind her, his face a mask of revulsion.

"Ma, don't just barge in!" Corky bellows.

"Hey, hey, it's okay, Corky. That's enough rehearsal. We got it." I smile as I slowly rise to my feet, the thought occurring to me, perhaps for the first time, that Julia and I are around the same age. Still smiling, I turn to her and say, "The nice thing about working with your son is that he's so open to rewriting and reshooting if I don't like something. We were just going over a scene that wasn't working."

"Oh, of course," she says, glancing at the grinning image of me in a top hat on the computer screen. She looks uncertainly from me to Corky and back again. "I just wanted to say that I'm dropping Joe off at the bus stop. Be back soon."

"I'm leaving, too." I reach for the door knob. "I'm off to meet a friend for dinner. You want me to drop you off, Joe? Or I could take you wherever it is you need to go."

Instead of answering, Joe turns on his heel and walks down the hallway. Julia watches him leave, then turns to me. "Don't mind Joe. He and Howard had a bit of a squabble, as usual. They seldom see eye to eye on anything."

"I'm really sorry. I hope it's not because I've intruded here."

She gives Corky a quick look, then says, "Of course not. And I hope no one's given you that impression. We're just so grateful you've taken Corky under your wing. It means a lot to have someone like you go out of their way for a kid just starting out."

"I'm learning a lot from him, too. Wait, I'll walk out with you." I turn back to Corky. "Good work, pardner. As soon as you have a rough cut together, I want to see it."

"Oh, yeah. Hey, thanks!" He rocks from one foot to the other with an expression teetering between blissed out and mortified.

"So you have nice plans for tonight?" Julia asks as we walk to the door, where Joe is waiting.

"Yes, actually, a date with a man I've been seeing for a while."

"Good for you! Sounds like it might be serious. Is he in show business, too?"

"No, actually a completely different world from mine. We're going out to dinner at a place near the beach." For Joe's benefit, I add, "You know, Corky really does have a bright future. I'm just paying forward the encouragement people gave me at his age."

"Thank you so much for saying that!" She throws her arms around me, squeezing hard. "It means everything." I hug her back, my eyes on Joe, who stares at me coldly. Obviously nothing I've said has swayed him.

"You ready?" he asks. "I'm going to miss my bus." He stalks down the driveway toward the Honda.

"Sure thing, Joe. Coming." She gives my ribs another squeeze. "Don't take any of that to heart. Sometimes he and Howard get into it, but he loves Corky like a son. He just wants the best for him. Maybe he's a little too protective sometimes."

"I understand. See you soon!" I hurry off down the walkway to my car. By the time I've buckled my seat belt, Julia has pulled out of the driveway. She waves as she passes me, but Joe stares straight ahead.

Imagining the pressure Corky is under, I think back to my own youth. At age eighteen, I was so determined to be an actress that I catapulted from my small hometown to New York. Nothing could hold me back, and I had my parents' blessing. What must it be like to be in Corky's shoes, with his father and uncle hoping he'll outgrow his obsession with moviemaking? When it comes to family strife, it's not my place to get involved. After today, I'll steer clear of visiting the Shaw home.

I drive to the corner, turn right and park, leaving my Bluetooth active to call Gilligan's. The hostess answers and puts me through to Jeremy, who finally picks up on the seventh ring. I hear happy hour in full cry in the background.

"Jeremy? Meg Barnes here. You were going to call me."

"Sorry, listen, this isn't a good time."

"I know, but just two questions, okay? I'm sure you heard Chelsea's mother was killed last night, right?"

"Some friends came in to tell me. Man, I can't believe this! And I still haven't heard from Chelsea."

"Have the police been in touch?"

"No, why would they? I'd just met her mother, like, hours before. Do they know who did it?"

"No, not yet. Did you talk with Elaine much after I left?"

"Not really." He lowers his voice and I sense he's cupped his hand over the phone. "Sorry to say this when she's dead, but she was something else, you know? A steamroller, like Chelsea said. But now I'm getting really worried about where she is. And I can't reach this girl I put Chelsea in touch with, the one who was filling her in on stuff for the role."

"That's who I wanted to ask you about. She's a call girl, right? How do you happen to know her, if you don't mind my asking?"

"She's more of a party girl, like with an escort service. And I don't actually know her that well. I mean, not like that. I got this gig bartending at some private parties. Pay's good. That's how I met her and we got to talking."

"Was Chelsea still meeting with her?"

"That's the thing. Chelsea said they were planning to get together again after she worked with you. That's the last I heard from her."

"Do you know where they were meeting? Or when?"

"She called me at work right after you guys finished. She said she was waiting to be picked up. I figured it was the girl and they'd go off and gab somewhere and then she'd drop Chelsea off at home. That was the last I heard."

"What's the girl's name?"

Jeremy sighs. "Sorry, I only know her as Lisa. She never gave me her last name and I didn't ask for it."

"Do you know where she lives? Anything?"

"These gals tell you only what they want to and that's it.

"Do you have her phone number?"

"Not on me. Look, I gotta go, okay?"

"Wait, you drive a red convertible, right?"

"Yeah, in my dreams. I'm driving my brother's old Mustang. Why?"

"Just wondered. Can you get back to me later with the girl's number? Or send a text?"

"Will do. And if you hear from Chelsea—"

"I'll let you know. Bye."

I punch End Call, wondering how I can go about checking the license number of the red convertible.

12

Jack. Just the thought that I'll see him soon makes my heart race. With ten minutes to spare before picking him up, I park on a side street in Westwood near the Federal Building. I flip down the sun visor and, before dabbing on lip-gloss, take a moment to size up what I see in the vanity mirror. Thanks to my afternoon swim and walk in the park, my skin has a healthy glow. My hair, bobbed in a chin-length version of the style I wore playing Jinx, catches the copper glints of the lowering sun. The fact that I've held up this well under the less than ideal living conditions I've endured in the last year is a miracle. Affording decent moisturizer was the least of my problems.

Then, without warning, dark thoughts I'd hoped were buried rise to the surface. I stare into the mirror, trying to find the happy face I saw moments ago. Will I ever come to terms with that terrible period of time? Even now, snapshots flash through my brain in a dizzying loop. The anxiety of nights spent in my car, parked at the curb, trying to sleep under a spread of newspapers. Dealing with the heartbreak of strangers moving into my home and old friends shunning me. Bills. Bankruptcy.

Stop! This won't do! I can't meet Jack while in the throes of a post-traumatic flashback.

I breathe, first in short, shallow breaths, then longer, deeper ones as my head clears. My mantra, the silent one I recite when black thoughts overtake me, forms on my lips: *There, there, all is well.* Those are the words my father spoke when I was a child, quiet and soothing, that comforted whether my feelings were hurt or I'd skinned a knee. Jinx had such a mantra, too, a catchphrase that I took as my own. In response to Winston's heartfelt, "Awfully good of you, my dear," I'd say, "All in a day's work"—words that, to me, meant the task is done, let's move on. All is forgiven.

I put my car in gear and pull back into traffic. I weave from one lane to another, zip through a light that is technically amber, and spot Jack standing next to a column outside the Federal Building, his eyes on his cellphone. I glide up to the curb and flash my lights, catching a brief sign of irritation as he looks up. I lower the passenger window and lean across the seat. "Sorry it took me so long. Traffic."

He nods and pockets his cellphone. "I figured as much. You okay?"

"I'm fine. Hop in."

Instead he walks around the front of the Volvo, his dark suit jacket flapping open. My heart thumps an extra beat seeing him in the headlights, looking trim, with his white shirt open at the neck, his blue tie loosened. I roll down the window and look up at him, his caramel-brown eyes taking me in.

"Why don't I drive? You mind?"

"Not at all." The trusty pheromones kick in. I'm already pushing the door open and standing, ready to give him a kiss. "You've had a long day," I murmur, my face nuzzling his neck. "Tired?"

"Not anymore. I've been looking forward to this." We kiss again and he says softly, "More of this later. C'mon, get in."

I hurry around to the passenger side and climb in, pulling the seat belt across me in one quick movement. Jack slides the seat back, adjusts the mirrors and takes a moment to look at me as he fastens his seat belt.

"How're you doing? You look great."

"Thanks! What about you? How was Minneapolis?"

"Muggy. Mosquitoes the size of B-2s—and just as stealthy. Otherwise it's a great place. I may be going back there."

"Soon? Not for long, though, right?"

Jack hears the note of apprehension in my voice. He gives me a quick, reassuring smile. "No, probably not. But Homeland Security tipped us to something we're following up on."

"Anything you can talk about? Terrorist cell? Bomb smuggling? Something else to give me nightmares?"

"No, nothing like that, but it's a dirty business. I've been in briefings most of the day. We're coordinating with HSI and local law enforcement."

"Sounds like I might see some headlines in the papers soon?"

"If it means we've put an end to sex trafficking, I'd like nothing better. But it's too widespread. Too difficult to effectively prosecute." He lays his hand on mine, giving it a light squeeze. "Anyway, I'm happy to be back." With that, he's signaled an end to any further talk about his work.

"I'm glad to see you again. Stick around a while. No mosquitoes and the weather's fine."

Jack laughs. "When is it not? Look at that sky."

In exuberant response, a burst of coppery light streaks along the railings spanning the overpass on Wilshire Boulevard, fanning the clear blue horizon with a molten glow.

Jack edges into the right lane, merging with the trail of cars entering the on-ramp to the 405 freeway. I settle back, the terrible anxiety I felt only a half hour ago barely a memory. I'm with Jack, the only person I care to be with, and all is well.

"How did it go with the detective this morning? Anything new since we talked?"

"They didn't give anything away, of course. I'm sure they're thinking it's a random drive-by shooting. I watched them scour the grounds, examine the gates and keypad. I can't imagine anyone was lying in wait for Elaine. Practically no one knew she was in town. I mean, she only arrived here yesterday. Less than twelve hours later, she was killed."

"What were you able to tell them?"

"Well, now that I think of it, I probably spent more time with her than anyone else. I was already at Chelsea's house when Elaine arrived, and then we ended up having dinner together at Donna's. I also bumped into her in the late afternoon, which I forgot to mention to the police, and all of it was unplanned."

"So no one could've known her schedule or where she would be going?"

"Well, not me or anyone else at the dinner last night. I'm sure we're off the list of suspects. At least I hope so. Besides, she arrived from Indiana without telling Chelsea, so her trip would've been a complete surprise. Actually, I told Detective Yarrow that our get-together was serendipitous, which certainly wasn't how it turned out."

"Did she fly or drive from Indiana?"

"I assumed she flew and rented a car, but I can't say for sure."

"And Chelsea's father?"

"They asked me, but I know nothing about him. I don't even know if they're still married. Or if he's even alive. But Chelsea's still missing and that's really troubling."

"Boyfriend?"

"Yes, a bartender. I managed to track him down, but he has no idea where she is, either. That's something else I need to mention to Detective Yarrow."

"You spoke to the boyfriend? How did you manage that?"

"He used to be in Dirck Heyward's acting class, which is how he knew Chelsea, so I just looked the guy up, found out where he worked—"

Jack glances at me, his grip on the steering wheel tightening. "Wait, you just decided to check him out on your own? And you also went to Chelsea's house looking for her? What else?"

"C'mon, it's what anyone would do. This was way before anything happened to Elaine. In fact, she was checking out the boyfriend, too. That's how I ran into her again. The only concern now is that the guy I saw Chelsea with before she disappeared turns out not to be her boyfriend."

"And you know this because—?"

"I just called and asked him. Boyfriend doesn't own a red convertible."

"I'm not liking the sound of this."

"Nor am I. I'd like to find out who the guy was that—"

"No, I mean, it makes me uncomfortable that you're looking into matters that should be handled by the police. You're better off telling the detective these things, not trying to investigate on your own. You can't withhold information they need."

His speech is conversational, but I recognize the shift in tone. Reasoned and cool, it's the voice of a professional trained in law enforcement. It's the voice I heard when we first met and Jack was grilling me about Paul's disappearance, his tone implying that I knew more than I was revealing. That voice, detached and impersonal, held no regard for me, only for the information I might supply.

As Jack deftly changes lanes, I choose my words carefully, resolving to be truthful without denying myself the ability to act on my own instincts. If it means keeping certain things to myself, it's with the knowledge that he does the same.

"I know what you're saying. Dougie accused me of doing the Jinx thing, too. On the other hand, it's just my intuition. Nothing

more. I wouldn't want to go pointing a finger that will cause someone a lot of hassle with the police for no reason."

"I'm sure the detectives will check out the boyfriend on their
own. It would be their first consideration, but you should still in-
form them of what you know."

"Again, it's just intuition, but the reason I wanted to talk to
the bartender is that he introduced her to a call girl with some
escort service. He thought she could give Chelsea insight for her
role in the pilot. I only hope she didn't take things too far and actually hook up with some guy. Sounds crazy, but you never know,
and it's not something I would want to tell the police."

Jack clears his throat, making a noise that sounds like exasperation. When he speaks, his tone is even more measured.
"You're right, you never know. So you might want to pass this
along to the detective anyway. Your instincts are good, but the
police should take it from here, okay?"

"Okay, good advice. As soon as I get home, I'll look for Detective Yarrow's number and give her a call." I look out the side window, grappling for a change of topic to lighten the mood. "By the
way, I don't think I mentioned that Donna's started a new venture, a catering service. I think she's already got her first client."

"Good for her! Tell me about it." I sense he, too, wants to
shift the conversation. Jack turns onto the less congested west-
bound Santa Monica Freeway. By the time we've parked on Ocean
Avenue a few minutes later, I've filled him in on Hollywood on a
Plate and recapped my *Phantom of the Opera* breakfast, produc-
ing more than a few appreciative chuckles.

We climb out of the car, breathing in the heady tang of sun-
warmed sand and sea. Jack rolls his tie and stashes it in his jacket
pocket before we head toward the walking path along the beach.
The air is still warm, but there's a cool breeze sweeping off the
ocean. We fall into step, strolling leisurely, as cyclists whiz past us
on the parallel bike path.

I reach into my shoulder bag for one of Donna's brochures
with the banner *Dine with the Stars!* above photos of some of her
treasures. "It's a great idea, but I don't think she fully realizes how
much work is involved. I have a feeling I'm going to be pressed into
service. Here, keep it in case you know someone who wants to dine
off Clark Gable's dinner service."

"You never know." Jack takes the brochure and tucks it into
his pocket. I laugh and reach for his hand. He pulls me close, kiss-

ing me lightly on the lips, then embraces me in a lingering kiss I'd like to have go on forever. Hand in hand, we continue our walk as a ball of red sun slowly dips to the ocean and long shadows drift across the footpath.

I lean into Jack, mentioning there's a free jazz concert coming up at the Los Angeles County Museum that we might want to attend. "Sounds great," he says, wrapping his arm around my shoulders, warming me against the evening chill. A sense of well-being washes over me and I realize how wonderful it is to be making plans with someone again.

"Hungry?" he asks, stopping on the footpath. "I booked a table at Chez Jay for eight o'clock."

"Starving!" With my arm wrapped around his waist, we turn back, quickening our strides as darkness falls. Ahead, the Santa Monica Pier gleams with colored lights from the amusement rides. The Ferris wheel makes its slow revolution, reminding me of the starlit night when Jack and I took a ride, necking like two teenagers. I'm about to suggest we ride the Ferris wheel again after dinner, when I see him checking his cellphone.

"Sorry, Meg, I have to take this." He turns away to speak.

I walk ahead, giving him privacy. Minutes pass and I realize his call must be important to take so long. I look up at the sky, star-filled now, and stroll off the path. The sand is cold, tickling my toes until I reach the damp, hard-packed beach. It's dark and quiet, except for a gentle lapping of waves along the shore and distant sounds from the pier.

I look over my shoulder and see Jack, his head down, back turned, still talking on his cellphone. This does not bode well for our dinner reservation at Chez Jay. I look at my own cellphone and see that it's well past eight o'clock. I call the restaurant. Mike Anderson, the owner, answers.

"Hey, Mike! It's Meg. Sorry, but Jack's detained and we're going to be late."

"That's okay. How long are you going to be?"

"I'm not sure." I turn to see Jack approaching, his face solemn. "Just a moment—"

"Sorry about dinner," Jack says, "but I have to get to the airport."

"That's okay. I'll take you there." I turn back to my cellphone. "Sorry, it won't be tonight. Something's come up and Jack has to catch a flight."

"That's okay. Anytime. There's always a table here for you guys."

"Thanks, Mike." I end the call, my eyes on Jack as we walk quickly back toward the footpath. "What's up?"

"Actually I don't have to catch a flight, but I need to get to LAX as soon as possible. Sorry about this."

"No need to apologize. I'm happy with a rain check."

"I'll make it up to you, promise." Jack grabs my hand and we hurry down the street. "I'll drive, if you don't mind," he says, pulling my car keys from his pocket.

Jack drives swiftly, taking a zigzag route that doesn't rely on GPS. As we near the airport, he says, "Thanks for understanding. This alert came up sooner than expected."

"I don't mind at all. At least we had some time together. Can you tell me what it's about?"

"We may have gotten a break. Immigration tagged a couple of arrivals we want to check out. I'm not sure how long they can be detained."

"So you have to get there fast. Does this involve the case with the Ukrainian student?"

Jack nods. "Very likely. Two young Latvian women arrived on a flight from Finland. One of them misplaced her papers. By the time she found them, an agent had done some checking. They were students entering on the visa waiver program, supposedly to work as au pairs, but their tickets were paid for by a party we've been investigating."

"So what happens now?" I ask, surprised that Jack is willing to divulge so much.

"They'll be sent back."

"How disappointing for them."

"It might be for the best if they were duped into thinking they'd be working as au pairs. Meanwhile, we've got a chance to find out more about the individual who got them over here. If it's not too late, I'll give you a call when I finish up."

"You don't want me to wait?"

"No, this will take a while. Someone will drop me back at the Bureau so I can pick up my car. Can you grab something to eat on your own?"

"Of course. Don't worry about me." I flash on the bouillabaisse I know Donna is preparing and can almost taste it. Then I picture myself sitting at the dining table with Dirck. *How hungry am I?* "Please call, though. I want to hear how this turns out."

"Don't worry, I will."

Dodging cars and hotel transport vans, Jack pulls into the curb some fifteen feet from the entrance to the massive Tom Bradley International Terminal. Unbuckling his seat belt, he leans over to give me a quick kiss. "We'll talk later." Before I can respond, he's out of the car, trotting toward the entrance.

I watch him darting around people pushing overloaded trolleys on the sidewalk, bucking the flow of newly arrived passengers leaving the terminal. I get out of the car and by the time I reach the driver's side, Jack has already vanished inside the building.

I sit behind the wheel for a moment, trying to decide what I should do. A traffic cop raps on my window, waving me on. I nod, put the car in gear and pull out, still unsure about heading back to Donna's. As I'm driving down Century Boulevard, approaching the on-ramp to the San Diego Freeway, my cellphone pings, alerting me to a text message. I pull to the curb and see that Jeremy has sent me a phone number with the message: *Lisa don't know her last name.*

I stare at the message a moment. Jack would want me to pass the information straight to Detective Yarrow. I deliberate another moment or two, pretty certain a girl working for an escort service wouldn't appreciate having her number passed to a homicide detective for no good reason. It couldn't hurt to check her out first, I decide, pressing my finger firmly on the number.

By the third ring, my mouth dry as flannel, I hear a click. I almost jump when Bluetooth broadcasts a soft voice purring, "Hi, there, Lisa here. I know you want me, so leave your name and number."

I hold my breath until the tone beeps, torn as to whether I should leave a message. Just as I'm about to end the call, I impulsively say, "Hi, you don't know me, but I'm a friend of Chelsea's. Please call me," and leave my number. My fingers are icy with nerves as I hit End Call.

I pull back into traffic and drive toward the freeway ramp. Even if Jack wouldn't approve, what harm have I done? If she calls, she calls. I only want to ask her when she last saw Chelsea, or spoke with her. Detective Yarrow will be pleased to have the information. But my thumping heart also tells me I'm exhilarated to be on to something no one else has so far considered. Chelsea had no idea her mother was arriving, so what connection is there between her disappearance and Elaine's murder? Perhaps none.

I take the Wilshire exit and cruise down the boulevard through Westwood. By now, Dirck and Donna have finished dinner and will be watching a movie in the den. I can grab something to eat in the kitchen, say a quick hello to them and go to my room. With a bit of luck, Jack will still call tonight.

With those thoughts in mind, I turn off Wilshire, several streets from Donna's house. But as I'm making the turn, I hear a crunching slap and feel a sting on my forehead. Glass shatters in my lap and I swerve abruptly, my foot hitting the accelerator as I realize I've been hit—someone is shooting at me!

I fight to regain control of the careening Volvo, but the wheels lock. The car skitters off the road up an embankment in what feels like sickening slow motion, then flips over. The last thing I remember is a sense of being airborne and then a teeth-jarring impact that sounds like a sonic boom.

13

After drifting through an eerie sort of twilight, I wake up to the sight of both Jack and Dirck gazing down at me. One looks concerned, the other merely curious.

"You've met." I state the obvious, then close my eyes again. This could be a bad dream. God willing, it is.

"Wow, off again. You see that? Like she's in a coma."

My eyes fly open. "I was sleeping, Dirck. I'm not in a coma!" *Wait, was I?* "What day is this?"

"You're going to be fine, Meg." I look up into Jack's warm brown eyes and see the shadow of worry. "You'll be sore for a few days, but at least nothing worse happened."

"Wait, I was shot! Wasn't I?" I raise my hand to my forehead and feel a thick bandage. "Somebody shot at me?"

"Do you remember what happened?" he asks quietly. "Did you see anyone?"

I flash on the shattering glass, then the blur of trees as I spun out of control. "I only remember turning the corner and swerving. It took a moment to realize there were gunshots. I'm not sure I really heard them."

"There were shots fired and you were hit. But you're going to be fine."

"Am I? Seriously, I want the straight dope. Do I look like a train wreck?"

"Car wreck," Dirck corrects. "You're lucky to be alive."

"It's nothing serious," Jack says evenly. "Nothing broken. How are you feeling?"

"Okay. Glad you're with me," I whisper to Jack. "I hate to even ask this, but how's my car?"

"Totaled, I'm afraid," Dirck says. "Donna has the receipt for the towing operation."

"That's right. I remember now. I talked to the police before I was put in the ambulance. Are you sure my car can't be repaired?"

Jack shakes his head. "But don't worry about that now. We can deal with it later."

"Too bad. I'll miss her. We went through a lot together."

"That car probably saved your life. Dirck's right about one thing. You're damn lucky. What else do you remember?"

"A free fall. Just hanging on. I must have been unconscious for a moment, but I remember being trapped in there, the smell of fuel. The sirens." Tears sting my eyes, recalling the two young people clambering over to me after the accident. The girl held her hand behind my head, supporting me. Her boyfriend struggled to wrench the door open without jostling me. They stayed until paramedics arrived, the young woman answering calls on my cellphone. Tears course down my cheeks. "God, people are good."

Jack can only nod. Emotion has hit him, too. He tightens his grip on my hand. "Thank God for the air bag. If it hadn't been for the seat belt and the air bag," he says, and stops. I know what he means. I would've been tossed out the windshield.

"The bruises are well worth it."

"Detective Yarrow wants to talk with you. Are you up for it?"

"Of course." I try for a smile, making my cheek hurt. "Not missing anything, then? Limbs still attached? No surgery while I wasn't paying attention?"

"No, but your face is banged up," Dirck says. "Not a pretty sight."

"It's not really that bad." I refocus and see Donna standing at the end of my hospital bed. She says, "A scratch or two. A scrape on your cheek and a few stitches, that's it." Her face is pinched, with frown marks etched between her brows.

"Stitches? That bad? Please don't give me a mirror."

"You look like you went a few rounds with Sugar Ray, kid," Dirck says. "If all you got was a couple of black eyes, you're damn lucky. The big worry is head trauma when the car flips like that. It's the coup-contrecoup thing, where the impact and velocity sends your brain sloshing forward and back and you just end up with Jell-O in your skull. That can be real bad. It's veg time, maybe worse."

"Thanks, Dirck. Nice of you to cheer me up."

"That's okay. I picked up a lot doing *Doctors on Call.* Too bad that series didn't catch on like *ER.* I coulda ended up like George Clooney."

"Coulda, shoulda, Dirck." I turn to Jack, feeling his hand on my shoulder. "Tell me the truth. Are my dancing days over?"

"Not with me." His face breaks into a smile and I melt in the dark caramel of his eyes. "And I owe you a dinner."

"That's right. I haven't eaten. Ready when you are," I whisper.

"So, you guys are an item, I hear," Dirck says, a folksy cheeriness in his voice. "That's really great. Glad to hear it. Megsie could use some happiness in her life. I don't know what I'd do without Pru."

"She must be missing you, Dirck," I murmur. "Are you heading back to her soon?"

"Can't say, kid. Until Chelsea turns up and this business with Elaine is cleared up, all bets are off, you know that. I can't jump ship now."

I glance at Donna. Her mouth is a straight line. I turn my head slightly and see Doug sitting in an armchair just behind her, glaring at Dirck.

"Hey, the gang's all here," I say, smiling in spite of the pain.

"Mind if we join you?" Detective Yarrow hovers just outside the doorway, Detective McCauley behind her in the hallway. "How are you feeling? We were hoping we could have a few words with you, if you're up to it."

"Okay. That's fine. Jack said you were here. Just let me sit up a bit." Jack reaches for the remote control on the bed while Donna leans over to rearrange pillows behind my head.

"You'd probably like us to clear out, right?" Doug asks.

"If you wouldn't mind waiting outside for a few minutes," she says, "we'd appreciate it."

"No, hang on, here," Dirck says, crossing his arms. "I'd like to stick around a minute and hear what you've found out. Elaine was shot and killed. Now Meg gets shot—in the same neighborhood!"

"Somehow I don't think this is going to affect the real-estate market in Holmby Hills, Dirck. Or are you worried you'll be next?"

"Very funny, Meg. I'm not thinking of myself here. Although, now that you mention it, since I'm staying at Donna's, who can say?"

"No one. So maybe you should stay in a hotel, to be on the safe side—"

"That's not the point. At least with me around, Donna's got some protection."

"Okay, okay, you two!" Donna says, then turns to Detective Yarrow. "Since we're all somehow involved, can you tell us what you think is going on? Do you have any idea who's behind this?"

"Not yet. That's why we want to ask Meg if she saw anyone last night."

"No, I didn't. In fact, the road down to the park was empty. No other cars. I don't remember seeing anyone when I turned the corner."

"Man, that's something!" Dirck exclaims. "No one? Nothing? I gotta figure there's some trigger-happy kid out there playing at being a sniper. You know, they put stuff like that in a movie and some young punk is gonna play it out for real, am I right?"

"Anything's possible, but right now there's nothing to substantiate that theory," Detective Yarrow says, giving Dirck a frosty look. "You know, we can always come back later if you'd all like to visit here for a while."

"No, wait. I don't mean any offense, Detective, but we gotta ask ourselves, who's next? Why? We need to get to the bottom of this." Dirck is playing Columbo again. "If there's no sniper out there, you gotta look to motive. Elaine's dead, her kid's missing. What about Elaine's husband, Chelsea's father? Whatshisname, Horne? You tracked him down yet?"

I roll my eyes and look to Jack. "Welcome to my so-called former life." He smiles and squeezes my hand.

"Yeah? Scoff if you like," Dirck says, turning to me. "I'm making a good point here. Maybe this guy has a vendetta, like he got a bum deal and he's getting even."

"Easy, Dirck," Doug says, reaching for his arm. "We don't need this now. It's not the time."

"But, easy question," Dirck says, turning back to Detective Yarrow. "What about this guy, Horne? Did you haul him in yet and ask about his wife and kid?"

Detective Yarrow gives a measured nod. "He came to us. He and Elaine divorced years ago and he's not Chelsea's father."

"You kidding me? She said he was."

"He claims you are. And Chelsea knew it because she came to him and asked."

In the shocked silence that follows Detective Yarrow's revelation, hideous thoughts ricochet through my brain at sonic speed. *What? How can this be? Not possible!*

As if in answer, the terrible hush in the hospital room is shattered by a triumphant roar. "Of course!" Dirck booms. "Shoulda figured she's my girl! The voice . . . the talent!"

I look at Dirck, who's beaming with pride. A small voice inside me responds: *But when Chelsea was born, we were still married.*

"You're too damn full of yourself, Dirck," Doug says. "Shut up. You're not thinking straight."

My gaze shifts to Doug, his eyes locking on mine. He shifts forward in the chair, his hands gripping the armrests as though he's about to spring to his feet. My inner voice informs me that of course Dougie was aware that something was going on between Dirck and Elaine. *Why didn't he tell me?*

"Elaine shoulda said something to me. I coulda been a real father to Chelsea. It's my right!"

"You were married, remember?" Doug's voice is quiet but emphatic. "Now shut up."

All eyes seem to shift to me, but my attention is still focused on Doug. *Is this why he despises Dirck?—the reason he warned me not to pursue getting involved with Elaine and Chelsea? He had to know!*

"Okay, okay, big deal. Meggie, I'm sorry it had to come out like this, but it was a long time ago. A coupla quickies, okay? Who knew there was a kid involved? There's no need to get upset now."

I look at Dirck. "No? You don't remember?"

Bewilderment clouds his eyes. "What? What? We were going through a bad patch. You know, like any married couple."

It's just as well Dirck doesn't remember. But I look back at Doug, who surely does. *Why didn't you say something at the time? You could have spared me such a lot of heartache.* During the filming of the last episodes of *Holiday*, Dirck had reluctantly agreed we should try in vitro. Dougie had finessed my work schedule to accommodate the procedure. I didn't get pregnant. But Doug was privy to everything and had to have known about Dirck and Elaine. *Why the hell didn't he tell me?*

"Look, what does it matter now?" Dirck says. "Wow, you know, it just hit me. My girl tracked me down in New York. That's how she came to be in my acting class. And if it hadn't been for what I taught her, she wouldn't be where she is now."

"She's missing!" Donna says. "We can't find her, remember?"

"You're right," he says, turning to Detective Yarrow. "My daughter is missing. What're you doing about it? You've got to find her!"

"Get him the hell out of here," Doug says. "That's enough."

"Mr. Heyward, let's take this outside, please. We can talk out in the hallway." Detective Yarrow glances at me, her plump face chalky, her eyes suffused with regret. "Detective McCauley, take him into the hall, please."

"Megs, I hate to leave you like this. Maybe we need to talk," Dirck says.

"Out!" Jack says, his voice a guttural explosion. "Now!"

"Okay. You're the boss."

I close my eyes in the silence that follows, but there's no escaping the horror. Donna lays her hand on my shoulder, fingers spread wide and firm, as though to restrain me should I try to rise up and scream.

I hear feet treading on linoleum, then Dirck's voice in the hallway. "Oh my God, Pru! Hey, don't anyone say anything to Pru, okay? That'd be a disaster!"

My hand shrinks inside Jack's firm grip. He's heard everything, the whole works. My face burns, imagining what's going through his mind. My second husband a fugitive felon, the first a clueless philanderer! If only I could fly out the window and sail into oblivion. Where's a speeding bullet when you really need it?

"Meggie." Doug's voice is soft and pleading. "Hear me out, please."

"Too late! Don't come near me!" I cry. "Don't even try. I trusted you!"

I turn my face into the pillow, squeezing my eyes tightly closed, aching to die, to disappear. If only I could get my brain to shut down. Donna lifts her hand from my shoulder and I feel her move away, knowing she's taking Doug with her. I hear the soft whoosh of the door closing.

Tears boil under my eyelids. In an instant, Jack gently lifts me from the pillow into his arms, cradling me. Before I can draw another breath, his mouth is on mine, kissing me tenderly, holding me close as though I might actually take flight.

"It's okay, Meg," he whispers, his lips brushing my ear. "It's okay now."

Tears course down my cheeks. I look away, not trusting myself to meet his eyes. "I'm so sorry you heard all that."

"It's okay, darling. You're safe with me. Trust me."

"Then don't let me think. Or say any more." He brushes my hair from my cheek, his lips on mine, taking me to another place of sweet oblivion.

"I hope I'm not hurting you," he says, planting soft kisses on my eyelids and cheeks. His tone is light. "Hey in there, want to look at me?"

I open my eyes. "I'm here. All yours." His gaze brims with love. Trust. Jack makes me believe I'm safe, that everything will be okay. He hands me a tissue, then takes another to gently mop my tears.

Shame and humiliation don't begin to describe how I feel. I wish I'd never found out! But what happened all those years ago is not something I care to talk about. More than enough sordid details of my life have been exposed for one night.

I shift gears to the present. "So, enough about me. What about you? How did it go with Immigration?"

Jack looks at me in surprise. "Seriously? You really want to know?"

I nod. "I really do."

"Not well. There was no official hold, so the passengers were released. By the time I arrived, they were gone. We lost them."

"I'm so sorry."

"I'm even sorrier. If I'd been with you this wouldn't have happened. Someone tried to take your life less than an hour after you dropped me off. Why? Did you have any sense of being followed?"

"None. There was no one behind me when I made the turn. There was no one in the street."

"You drove straight to Donna's? Did you make any stop on the way?"

"No. The only thing I recall is pulling to the curb when I got a text message. I thought it might be you, but it was someone else."

"You mind telling me about it?" His voice is casual, but I know he's picked up on my hesitation. "I'm sorry, darling, but we need to talk about this."

"I know. You remember I mentioned there was a call girl the bartender introduced to Chelsea? She was doing research for the pilot episode, which is about the murder of girls working for an escort agency. Jinx goes undercover to investigate, and I thought maybe Chelsea took her research too far. I asked the bartender to text me the girl's name and phone number, that's all."

"And he did."

"Yes." Jack gives me a look, waiting for me to come clean. "Okay, I called the number and left a message. I didn't say my name, just asked her to call my phone number. That's all."

"Did she call back?"

"Not before the crash. I haven't checked since. I don't even know where my cellphone is."

Jack reaches into a plastic bag hanging on the back of my hospital bed and fishes out my phone. "You said the young couple answered your cellphone?"

"Yes, in fact you spoke to the girl. So did Donna." He hands me the phone and I quickly check messages. "Nothing here from that number, and the battery is getting low. I'll have to get Donna to bring me the charger." I start to turn the cellphone off when I catch Jack's eye. "What?"

"Would you mind if I took the number and name?"

Again he picks up on my hesitancy. "No, of course not. Please, take down whatever you want."

Now is not the time to give Jack reason to doubt me. I hand him the cellphone, wondering if we'll ever manage to get past the cat-and-mouse games that have defined our relationship from the beginning. I look away while he takes down the information, my nonchalance not very convincing.

"Thank you, Miss Barnes," he says, handing back my cellphone. "I see you have quite a few admirers. I took the liberty of recording their numbers."

"What?" Then I see his laughing eyes and grin. "There's only one admirer I care about. Call me anytime." I lean over and give him a kiss. "So, you're not going to chastise me for following up with a call to that girl?"

Jack is silent a moment, regarding me solemnly. I've opened myself to the very chastisement I'd hoped to avoid. I watch his shirt expand, contract, waiting for the rebuke. I'm ready for it, but I am not about to exacerbate the situation by mentioning that I also have the license plate number of the red convertible that delivered Chelsea to our first meeting. He'll only wonder how I came up with that information, too.

"Let's just say it might have been better to hand the number over to Detective Yarrow." He gives me a tight smile. "You're a taxpayer. Use the resources."

I let that slide, not wanting to get into how meager my tax contribution currently is. "You know, it was just an instinct. Nothing more."

"You could've been killed."

"There's no connection. No one knew what I was going to do or where I would be last night any more than I did."

Jack sits back, crossing his arms over his chest. I try to read his thoughts, knowing his brain is churning with what I've told him. I'm also feeling tired, a wave of drowsiness settling over me.

"You need to rest now, Meg. Don't think about this anymore."

My eyes close, wetness forming under my eyelids, dampening my lashes. "Sorry, Jack. Maybe I'm not thinking straight, but I just don't want what I've told you to cause problems between us. I'm not trying to play detective, I promise, but—"

He takes my hand and I feel his warm breath on my cheek. "Please, darling. Sleep now. I'll be right here with you. I'm not going anywhere."

I drift off, a pall of gloom descending on me. I hover in a shadowy place, too warm, then too cold, my skin uncomfortably prickly, my limbs heavy, immobile. I try to lift myself up, but I hang in a fearful place, on the verge of falling. I see light but can't reach it. I want to cry out, but my lips are frozen. Then my mouth seems to melt, my lips feeling cool moisture. I open my eyes to pale light and a face peering down at me.

"Hi, there. I'm Jean, your night nurse. How are you feeling?" She swabs my lips again.

"Okay, thanks, Jean." With a sense of relief, I get my bearings. I look down at the saline lock taped to my hand and the clamp on my index finger taking my temperature.

The nurse moves aside and I see Jack in the bright light of the hallway, talking to Detective Yarrow, still wearing what appears to be her official ensemble. Idly I wonder if she has a closet full of mismatched navy jackets and black trousers, or if this particular outfit is on continuous recycle. Detective McCauley isn't much of a fashion plate, either, but at least his khakis and navy windbreaker look like some sort of uniform. I lean on my elbow, trying to sit up, but fall back in the bed, groaning. Jack hurries to my bedside as the nurse adjusts the pillows.

"Thanks, Jean. I hurt. My shoulders and chest ache. I think somebody sat on me."

"It was the seat belt, I'm afraid," she says. "You'll be even sorer tomorrow."

"Need some help?" Jack asks. "How're you feeling?"

I groan again, making a face for his benefit. He smiles and brushes a strand of hair off my forehead. "I see they're back. Any news?"

"No, but when you're feeling up to it, they'd like to talk with you again—without a roomful of onlookers. Should I have them return in the morning?"

I smile. "How about now? They don't have to wait."

Jack glances at the nurse. "It's up to her," she says. "I'd keep it to a couple of minutes. She'll drift off soon, anyway."

"Besides, I'll feel worse tomorrow. And I'll be no prettier."

"You're beautiful." He leans down, kissing my forehead. "If you don't mind, the sooner they can talk to you, the better. They'd appreciate it."

"Sure. Let's do it."

I sip from the straw in a cup the nurse holds for me. By the time she's eased pillows under my arms and behind my head, Jack has returned with the two detectives.

Christine Yarrow looks at me with sheep's eyes, her embarrassment apparent. I know she's feeling bad and I may as well deal with her mortification sooner than later.

"Well, you sure put your foot in it, didn't you? You must be a hoot with family at Thanksgiving dinners."

She blinks, surprised, until she sees me smile. "Miss Barnes, Meg . . . I am so sorry. I did not put it together and I should have, but he just—"

"What? Got under your skin? A narcissistic sociopath like Dirck? He enrages me, too, so please don't feel bad. What's Horne like? Does he have a first name?"

"Alec. He's English, teaches humanities at a junior college. Nice, unassuming man. Says they were married for ten minutes. He barely knew Chelsea since the time she was a toddler, but she looked him up and he spilled the beans. Again, I'm so sorry. I shouldn't have said what I did."

"That's okay. It's done. Anyway, it's interesting that Chelsea sought him out. If she confronted Elaine with the truth, it would explain their falling out two years ago. That must be when she headed to New York to look up Dirck."

"Your instincts are on track. Horne acknowledged that Elaine blew up at him when she heard what he'd told Chelsea."

"In any case, Alec Horne doesn't sound like a sniper."

"No, but a sniper may be what we are dealing with—and please don't credit your ex-husband with that theory. We're still checking everything out. Jack says you might have something you want to tell me."

I look at Jack. "What did you say to them?"

"I passed along everything, Meg. I can't withhold information they need to investigate." His look is steady, trusting me to understand. "They also need to hear about it firsthand from you."

"Okay, I accept that." I shift my gaze to Detective Yarrow. "Elaine and I spoke with Chelsea's boyfriend the other night. He's Jeremy Sloan, a bartender working at Gilligan's over in Westwood." I go on to explain the call-girl connection and suggest my theory that perhaps Chelsea took the research into her role too far. "The plot was tied in with an escort service. It's just a hunch I had that maybe she got in over her head with the wrong people, I don't know."

"Thanks, we'll check it out. So you're saying you had drinks with Elaine Horne the night she was killed? *Before* dinner? When exactly was this?"

"Happy hour, around four thirty or five o'clock. This was a couple of hours after I saw her at Chelsea's house and a few hours before she turned up at Donna's."

"Did this boyfriend have any idea where Chelsea might be?"

"No, but I got in touch with him again and he sent a text with the call girl's name and number. Jack's already given you that information. On my way home, I called the number and left a message for her. She didn't get back to me."

"Maybe that wasn't such a good idea, calling her. Did you leave your name and address?"

"No, just my number."

"Any reason why you're just telling us all this now?"

"Sorry, I just forgot to mention it yesterday."

"You forgot?"

"It didn't come up. It only occurred to me later that I hadn't told you. Anyway, Donna called and I had to hurry back home. Elaine stayed at the bar a while longer and then showed up unexpectedly for dinner later."

"That sort of accounts for the missing hours. Anything else you might have overlooked?"

"That's it for now. Would you mind letting me know what you find out? Because I really don't want to get either the bartender or the call girl in trouble."

"Right. We'll keep that in mind."

"No, I mean it," I say, my voice rising. "I'm not accusing either of them of anything, so I'd hate for this to get blown out of proportion. I don't know that she's actually a call girl or with an escort service, you know? I only have Jeremy's word on that."

"One more thing. Was Elaine aware of your hunch? Maybe you can tell us more about your actual conversation."

"Elaine wasn't pleased to find me at Gilligan's. She was already suspicious, so I didn't mention that I was there to talk with Jeremy, although I'm sure she figured that was the case. I sort of remember what we said." My words jumble; I'm beginning to fade. As half-remembered observations come to mind, I relate them, but it becomes a struggle to speak.

When I open my eyes again, sun is streaming through the window of my narrow corner room. Jack emerges from the bathroom. Patting his face dry with a hand towel, he steps into a radiant beam of sunlight, looking like a movie star entering a floodlit soundstage. He's freshly shaved, and his spanking white shirt, loose at the collar, is blinding. So is his wide grin. He tosses the towel on a chair and heads for the lump of toxic debris on the hospital bed that happens to be me.

"Hey, there, sunshine, good morning. How're you feeling?"

I shrink back into the tangle of bedding as he advances. "No! Stop! Stay away until I've been hosed down and fumigated."

"You look just fine to me." Jack laughs, but in a show of chivalry, he stops at the foot of the bed. He reaches under the mound of blankets and grasps my bare feet. "I'm glad you got some sleep."

"But *you* didn't! How do you manage to look so good after being up all night?"

"Trade secret. Known only to agents in the Bureau." He wiggles my toes back and forth, which is somehow sexy and all I happen to be up for at the moment. "Besides, my carry-on bag with a clean shirt was still in the car."

"That only explains the window dressing," I say, hoping he'll continue romancing my toes.

"Okay, you want a serious answer? Just sitting here watching you sleep peacefully is all the rest I need. That was a serious incident. I'm worried about you."

"I know. I was lucky and I'm very grateful. What about Detective Yarrow? Is she coming back to interview me further?"

"She didn't say. You know, your instincts are remarkable. And you're very observant."

"Tricks of the acting trade. But I think I fell asleep in the middle of talking. I don't even remember what I said."

"You did well, and if you think of something else, give me a call." He tucks my feet back under the blankets.

"Wait! You're not leaving, are you?"

"I'm afraid I have to. Besides, if your toes are all the bare skin I'm allowed—"

"Deal breaker. Sorry, but I'm thinking of you. As much as I would love to do all the things we like doing, it's not happening. Not until I'm dainty fresh and completely adorable—stop!" I hold up my hands as Jack advances toward me, a comical gleam in his eye.

"Do you have any idea what it took for me not to climb into bed with you last night?"

"I'm guessing tubes, blinking monitors, open wounds seeping fluid and a whole lot of public exposure."

"True." He smiles. "There was a lot of foot traffic through here, but I didn't object to the rest of it." Still minding his manners, he strokes my blanket-covered feet and keeps his distance. "But we deserve some time together. This wasn't how I thought our evening would turn out."

"As John Lennon said, 'Life happens when you're making other plans,' and I'm afraid it's the case. When will I see you again?"

"That's what cellphones are for. I think they'll probably spring you later today, so let me know. If I can, I'll be around to pick you up. How's that?"

"Perfect." I sit up enough to reach across to take one of his hands in mine and squeeze it. "Keep me posted, okay?"

"I will." He puts on his jacket and unspools the tie he's retrieved from his pocket. "Whatever happens, promise you'll let me know. I don't care what it is, Meg, call me before dealing with it on your own. No more following up on your Jinx-like hunches, okay?" His face is serious. I know he requires assurance.

"I promise. Besides, I'm not up to dealing with much of anything right now."

"All you have to do is take it easy. I'll see you later." He picks up his bag and adds, "If you'd like, I'll take you someplace quiet for dinner."

"Quiet and dark!" I laugh. "No restaurant will have me. I'd put everybody off their food."

"Just leave it to me." He smiles and closes the door quietly.

My cheeriness dissipates the moment Jack leaves. For one thing, I hurt. Every square inch of me is sore and achy. I don't have the courage to ask for a mirror. Another item of concern is how I'm going to pay for what I know will be a gigantic hospital bill. With luck, my SAG-AFTRA insurance will cover most of it. I recall barely meeting the eligibility minimum last year, earning just enough to continue getting basic medical coverage. I certainly didn't earn enough to actually live on. I have no savings. And I no longer have a car. A weight settles in my chest. If I do get out of the hospital today—and I can't afford to stay longer!—I'll be spending my time sorting out insurance and making the dreaded call to my agent that auditions are out of the question until further notice.

More than that, Jack and I don't need an additional obstacle in what is still a fairly new romance. We're still trying to bridge a trust gap. It would not help matters if he thought that I was continuing to "play detective." But there's a red sports car out there somewhere and a license plate number only I know. Some secretive part of me refuses to tip my hand about everything. Where's the fun in that?

14

I close my eyes and drift off again, awakening to find a nurse, tall and caramel-skinned, hovering over me. "Good morning, I'm Mirella," she says in a Caribbean-flavored accent. "Just give me a minute here while I finish up. I see you haven't touched your breakfast. How're you feeling?"

She shoves aside the bed table, on top of which is a breakfast tray that must have been delivered while I was sleeping. The metal lid and cling-wrapped containers look so unappealing I quickly glance away.

"I'm not feeling too bad, all things considered. When can I go home?"

"You'll probably be on your way as soon as the doctor has seen you. Everything's looking good." She helps me swing my legs free of the blankets and stand from the bed.

On my way to the bathroom, I'm stiff but far steadier on my feet than I thought I'd be. I flick on the light and, without thinking, glance in the mirror.

I gasp, not so much in horror as in surprise. My face is pale in the harsh light, and my hair is matted, but the few stitches on my forehead are not of Frankenstein caliber. My eye is discolored and my cheek scraped raw, but I'm already plotting how to cover the damage with makeup if the need arises. I carefully wash my face, brush my teeth and run dampened fingers through my hair to give it some curl.

The gloom that descended on me lifts and I start counting my blessings, one of which is that I'm alive. The second is that Jack is still in my corner and romance appears to be on the bubble. I will also heal, pay my bills and somehow afford to replace my Volvo. I climb back into bed and reach for a cup of cold coffee just as Donna appears at the door.

"Stop! Don't drink that!" Donna sweeps into the room carrying a hamper. She's wearing a colorful sundress with a cotton sweater and beams at me with visiting-hour cheeriness. She sets a red-plaid vintage thermos and a carton of half-and-half on my tray. "Good morning! I've brought you fresh-brewed French Roast and enough breakfast for all of us. I picked up Doug on the way over here."

"Dougie's here? Where?"

"Just outside in the hallway," she says, speaking quietly. "Look, we're both really upset about what happened. It had to be awful for you. I am so sorry."

"I'm fine now. I'd just as soon forget about it."

"But Doug is very distressed. He really needs to talk with you."

"What's between Doug and me happened a long time ago. It's not something I care to dredge up."

"Nothing needs to be said." She gives me a fixed look, her voice firm. "But don't shun him. He's really hurting."

I give myself a moment, knowing I could never shut him out of my life. Whatever happened, he means too much to me. "I know. I understand."

She flashes a relieved smile, then hurries out to the hallway. Moments later, Doug follows Donna into the room, a bouquet of flowers in his hand.

"I see you're ready for your close-up," he says, his voice gruff with emotion.

"I wish I'd used a stunt double."

"Woulda helped." Dougie hands me the flowers. "I seem to recall you like daisies."

"I love them, and they don't get enough respect. Thank you."

I hold the bundle of daisies in front of my face, looking at Dougie through the opaque cello-wrap. "Did I see you wince when you saw me?"

"If I did, shame on me. How do you feel?"

"Like I spent the night in a cement mixer and lived to tell the tale. Otherwise, fine."

"It could've been a lot worse," Donna says, still radiating cheerfulness. She takes the bouquet from me and deposits the daisies in my water jug. "You'll feel much better after eating something."

She busies herself spreading a pale yellow cloth on my bed-side tray and unpacking the overflowing hamper. My mouth waters as she sets a carafe of orange juice, a bowl of fresh mixed berries, a pot of homemade peach preserves and a basket of muffins and croissants on the table. She pours coffee for Dougie and me, tipping just the right amount of cream into my cup.

I take a greedy sip and sigh deeply. "Thank you, Donna. Just what I needed."

Doug settles himself in the armchair wedged next to the bed. Coffee cup in hand, he gives me an appraising look. "You still wonder why I worry about you?"

"There's no need," I say firmly. "Any word about Chelsea?"

"Not a peep."

"How about Ed Ackerman? He's got to be going nuts with a pilot starting production next week and no leading lady."

"You're right. He's already got a replacement on tap. You'll probably be recruited to teach her hat tricks, if you're up to it."

"That's not what I want to hear. Besides, my hat is still on the run, remember?"

"A hat's a hat and actresses are thick on the ground out here, if you hadn't noticed. Ackerman's got to take care of business. There's nothing solid to indicate the girl didn't go missing of her own volition. He's gotta move on. We start shooting next Monday."

"We've got a week, which means there's still time. Technically, she's only been missing three days."

"What about Elaine?" Donna asks. "I wonder if she has people back in Indiana to arrange for her funeral? We should offer to help."

"I assume her body is still with the medical examiner," Doug says. "You know, the police are still trying to account for a couple of hours before she came to your place for dinner."

"Actually, I saw her," I blurt out. "We had happy hour together."

"I forgot about that," Donna says, handing me a glass of freshly squeezed orange juice. "You didn't mention it to the detective?"

"I told her last night."

Dougie leans forward. "Happy hour? You two weren't exactly best buddies."

"No, but we happened to run into each other and had a glass of wine together."

"You mean, of all the gin joints, you just happened to frequent the same one? How did that happen?" Dougie sighs, realizing he's treading on slippery ground. "Never mind, none of my business."

I nod in agreement. There's no point in addling him further by mentioning that the gin joint's bartender is Chelsea's boyfriend. He'd only ask me how I know that and chastise me for sleuthing around as "Jinx" again.

"Okay, you two. Time to eat." Donna hands me a plate and passes the breadbasket. I take a buttery croissant. A smattering of crispy flakes falls onto my chest as I bite into it. Dougie takes a bran muffin, but it's not sufficient distraction to shift him from the subject of Chelsea.

"I know what I said sounded harsh. It doesn't mean we're not concerned about her. But without any clue where she might have gone and no report from any hospital—to tell you the truth, I don't know what to think." His voice trails off and I catch him staring at the bran muffin on his plate as though it could provide an answer.

I polish off my croissant and reach for a blueberry muffin. "The peach preserves are delicious, Donna. Am I tasting a hint of ginger?"

She smiles. "Glad you like it."

Doug is still staring at his muffin, lost in thought, when a portly man breezes into the room, announcing himself as Dr. Wardour. "I followed my nose," he says. "That smells like great coffee."

"I'll pour you some," Donna says.

"Thanks, but I better take a look at my patient, here, if you don't mind."

Doug, carrying his plate with the muffin in one hand, coffee in the other, goes into the hallway without a word.

Donna follows, taking her coffee cup with her. "Meg, I've brought you a change of clothes," she says, her hint none too subtle. "We can leave whenever."

"I don't see any reason to keep you here," Dr. Wardour says after examining me. Following my assurances that I will take it easy, I get my discharge papers.

Donna packs up her hamper while I put on the fresh tee shirt and jeans she's brought. Doug, having finally finished his muffin, heads out to bring Donna's Mercedes around to the entrance. I text Jack to let him know Doug and Donna are taking me home. Dressed in street clothes and feeling remarkably good, I'm still asked to ride in a wheelchair to the hospital entrance. I take the hamper from Donna and put it in my lap as an attendant wheels me to the elevator.

Doug pulls into the pickup crescent and pops the trunk lid. Donna stows her hamper and climbs into the back seat. I sit next to Doug, holding my bouquet of daisies and a plastic bag with the clothing I wore yesterday.

"Home, Jeeves," Donna sings from the back seat.

"Sure thing, ma'am," Doug says, steering Donna's 1972 baby-blue Mercedes onto the street. With light mid-morning traffic, we manage to arrive at Doug's house in less than a quarter of an hour.

"Meg, you want to come in for a minute? I've got something to show you."

"If you two don't mind, I have to get back," Donna says, climbing behind the wheel of her Mercedes. "See you later!"

We wave her off, then I follow Doug around the side of the house to the garage. He punches the remote button on a key ring and the garage door grinds open. Then he hands the set of keys to me. "She's all yours," he says. "I started her up this morning and she purred like a happy kitten."

I peer into the gloom of the two-car garage and realize Dougie has just given me the keys to his wife Edie's prize possession: her 1983 Oldsmobile 98 Regency in custom canary yellow with a white top and whitewall tires.

My mouth falls open, but I manage to say, "Dougie, no. You can't."

"I can. What else am I gonna do with it? Besides, Edie would be proud to have you driving it." He turns and heads into the house. "Go on. Take it. I don't want to see it when I open those garage doors again."

I stare in wonder at the Olds. Once seen, the 98 Regency is not easily forgotten. It's certainly not the ideal vehicle to provide shelter for a homeless person, and I speak with some authority. If I'd attempted to reside in the luxurious environs of Holmby Park in this conspicuous boat on wheels, I would have been rousted in short order.

Edie loved her car. She herself was an unprepossessing, somewhat plump housewife, married to a successful film director who had enjoyed an especially good year when he bestowed the Olds 98 on the occasion of her thirty-ninth birth-day. It was the car she wanted. She was not a woman who desired furs and diamonds: an Olds 98 was all the bling she coveted.

By the time I pile my gear in the roomy passenger seat and back the Olds out of the garage, Doug is already taking Ridley for a walk. I pass them a block from the house and park at the curb. Doug stops and gives the car a long look, his eyes bright with a sheen of moisture.

"I'll sign her over and get the papers to you. Everything else you need to know should be in the glove compartment."

"I'll take good care of it." I wrap my arms around his thin shoulders, feeling the roughness of his safari jacket against my cheek. "Thanks so much."

"While we're at it," Doug says quietly, "are we still okay with each other? No hard feelings that I didn't tell you about the two of them way back when?"

"If you had, we probably wouldn't have stayed friends, Doug. There are some things you just can't tell someone."

He nods, looking relieved. "That's how I saw it, too, at the time. I didn't know about the kid, but I kinda suspected. Don't think I didn't consider saying something. I wouldn't want to see you hurt for the world."

"So let's forget it." I give him another hug.

He doesn't reply and I know he can't. His chest heaves against mine and I hold him even closer. Then he stands back, watching as I climb into the driver's seat. Perhaps he's picturing Edie, a trademark bright kerchief tied jauntily around her pulled-back hair, cruising into the studio lot to meet him for lunch.

I haven't checked the odometer, but if ever there were a "Sunday best" car, it would be Edie's Olds 98, which never traveled the open road, never saw a freeway. She used it exclusively to tool around town for lunch, do errands and attend daily morning mass at Good Shepherd. If Doug has any misgivings about me taking good care of Edie's car, he doesn't betray them.

I wave as Doug and Ridley get on with their walk. As I turn the corner, I see Donna up ahead, her Mercedes idling at the curb. She gives me a thumbs-up and pulls out, driving ahead of me the short distance to her house. I realize she and Dougie have worked it out, showing caution in putting me behind the wheel of a car after what happened last night. I'm not surprised when Donna takes a back route that avoids the corner where I was shot. By the time I drive up to the garage, she's already carrying the hamper into the kitchen.

I park my '83 Olds next to her '72 Mercedes, the two old birds both looking game in their dotage. I roll the window down and sit back, looking around the plush crème interior with its wood-grain trim, breathing the lingering scent of Edie's sweet floral fragrance. Cotton rugs cover the floor mats on both the driver and passenger sides, reminding me how fastidious Edie was. I make a mental note to launder the cotton rugs and dust the interior at least once a week. Checking out the contents of the glove compartment, I find a tin of throat lozenges and a tube of Fire & Ice lipstick wedged in with service statements.

Perhaps it's the sight of these prosaic items that reminds me of everything I stashed in my Volvo. I realize I have to find my car and retrieve the contents from my own glove compartment.

I start to roll up the window when I hear Dirck's voice. "So how many gallons to the mile on that baby?"

I turn to see him dropping rubbish into a bin. At least he's making himself useful. Without responding, I continue rolling up the window.

It's true that when Edie took possession of her Olds 98, gasoline was a buck-and-a-quarter a gallon, but I'm just grateful to have wheels, even whitewalls, however much gas the car guzzles. Besides, in the time it's taken me to drive Edie's Olds home, I've fallen in love with it. I climb out and gently close the door to find Dirck standing at my shoulder.

"I heard Dougie palmed Edie's car off on you. I told Donna maybe she should install a gas pump in the driveway to save you both trips to a filling station." He laughs. I ignore him.

"You think it'll pass a smog test?" He laughs again. "You better hope those pimpmobile tires hold up."

"Shut up, Dirck! It's a damn fine car and I'm lucky to have it."

"Hey, lighten up! Welcome home."

"Thanks." I push past him and enter the back door to the kitchen. I can smell fresh coffee. I want some even if it means sharing space with Dirck.

"I would've come along this morning, but I slept in. Man, I was zonked after last night. Hospitals really do me in. How're you feeling?"

"Fine."

"Hey, if you're pouring, I could go for a cup, too." He leans against the counter, standing inches from me. "It's, like, weird we hardly ever get to talk."

"Why?" I take another mug from the cupboard and fill it. "We didn't talk for nearly a decade." I hand him the mug and pick up mine.

"You know, maybe lack of communication was our big problem. I'm sure as hell willing to take some of the blame for what happened back then. I hope you're not still upset over this thing."

"Thing?" I stare at him, my hand shaking with the urge to toss scalding coffee on his manly-man outfit, but I don't want to mess up Donna's pristine kitchen. "My God, you never disappoint."

"Oops," he says. "Looks like you're still steamed. You can't let something like this eat you up, Meg. Let it go, girl."

"Yup, you're right." Carefully gripping my coffee mug tightly in both hands, I head for the stairs.

"If you're looking for Donna, she's out in the garden."

"Thanks." I change course and walk down the hallway to the French doors in the den, Dirck at my heels.

"There's no reason we can't be friends. I mean, like, cordial conversation, you know? Pru would enjoy meeting Jack, and there's no reason we couldn't all be on good terms."

I quicken my pace. The idea of a couples' night with Dirck and Pru is so distasteful that—but then I stop and turn to Dirck, the full implication of what he's said sinking in. "How would Jack and Pru ever even meet?"

"I'm glad you brought it up. I was thinking of bringing Pru and Priscilla out to LA for a while. It would be great for all of us to get together."

"I wouldn't make plans just yet. If Chelsea doesn't turn up soon, she'll be replaced. You won't have any need to be here."

I open the French doors and step outside, a fresh breeze fanning my sense of relief. No Chelsea, no Dirck. He could be heading back to New York very soon. But I regret the thought instantly when I realize it would mean something awful has happened to Chelsea.

"Wait, that's my daughter you're talking about," Dirck wails. "They can't do that!"

Despite the fact that he's the most irritating man on the planet, it's never taken much for me to feel sorry for Dirck. Seeing his anxious face induces the sort of reaction I have to guard against because it generally leads me to do things I regret.

But then I hear him say, "I mean, of course I feel bad for her. She's my daughter, after all, but this is a real blow. I was kinda hoping I'd have time to test the waters. If I could teach and do some voice work, we could move out here. With a kid, it would be nice to have more space and a backyard."

I steel myself. Now is not the time to either toss scalding coffee on him or go soft and end up with the entire Heyward family in the guest house. "I'm really sorry, Dirck, but that's the way it is. Ed Ackerman already has someone in mind."

"You know who? Maybe I could—"

I spot Donna coming out of her orchid pavilion carrying a plant with creamy white blossoms that I've learned is a Phalaenopsis. "For you," she says. "Welcome home! I'll put it in your room."

"Thank you! It's beautiful. I'll take it up. I'm going there anyway to get some papers. I just came back to get the towing receipt from you so I can check on the Volvo."

Donna shakes her head. "The police told me they were impounding it as part of a criminal investigation. They hauled it off on a flatbed truck to a crime lab somewhere. They're not going to let you near it."

"My car?" I stare at her, somehow not comprehending. "But it's my car."

"You can kiss that baby goodbye," Dirck says. "She's junkyard scrap once they're through with her."

"Dirck, please!" Donna glares at him, then takes my arm. "Let's go inside."

The two of us walk across the lawn to the den. "I'm really sorry," she says under her breath, "but he's getting on my nerves."

"It's his job in life."

"He excels at it." She closes the French doors firmly and we watch Dirck amble off to the pool house. "I can't kick him out until Chelsea's found. I know that, but—"

"For her sake, let's hope it's soon." I sink onto the Chesterfield sofa, the energy draining out of me as my head rests against the cool, nut-brown leather.

Donna plops down next to me, dropping her hand on my knee. "You know, it meant a lot to Doug to give you Edie's car, but we both thought twice about letting you drive it home. You've been through a terrible trauma. And the fact remains, someone out there tried to kill you. First Elaine, then you—"

"And didn't succeed with me. I know what you're thinking. It's on my mind, too. Why? And whoever it is, will someone try again? It just makes no sense."

"No, and that's the scary part. So, as much as I love having you here, I think it might be better for you to stay with Jack for a while. He thinks so, too."

I sit up, alarmed. "You discussed this with him behind my back? Thanks for planning my life."

"His idea, thank you very much. It's for your own safety. Besides," she says, batting her eyelids with mock innocence, "it means I'll have Dirck all to myself."

I burst out laughing. "Lucky you!"

"My secret plan. Little does he know I have a lot of furniture rearranging in mind for him."

Moving in with Jack is what I hoped might eventually happen, but under more romantic circumstances. "So, when does this transfer take place?"

"As soon as the armored car arrives—my God, you're being silly!" Her exasperation is evident and she gives my knee a quick shove. "Could you possibly look on the bright side? It's not like you're being sent off to do hard time!"

"I'll miss your cooking."

"I know," she says matter-of-factly. "Anyway, the doctor told me to make sure you rest. Why don't you take a bath and I'll bring up some tea. You really ought to nap for a while."

"Again, planning my life."

"Someone has to." She gets up and heads for the kitchen. "Go upstairs and take a bath."

Given my marching orders, I'm soon lying back in a tub brimming with hot water and aromatic salts, a cup of lemon-ginger tea in hand. My thoughts center on Jack, specifically on how I can manage to pack some essential clothing and grooming items without looking like I'm moving in. I don't want to arrive at his apartment with a suitcase! I'm estimating how much stuff I can stow in my shoulder bag when Jack calls.

"Hi, sunshine. How're you feeling?"

"Right now, pretty good. I'm up to my chin in bubble bath."

"Wish I were there." There's a smile in his voice, with a shade of huskiness as he adds, "But tonight's soon enough. How about dinner?"

"I'd love it. Want me to pick you up? I've got new wheels."

"So I heard." I detect a brief hesitation before he says, "Actually, I was thinking it would be nice to have some time together to make up for Two Bunch Palms. How would you like to stay out at the beach with me for a while?"

I smile, happy to play along. "Sounds good. I'd like that."

"Great. Then why don't you rest up today and I'll drop by later. Maybe you can follow me out to the marina."

"Really? You think that's necessary?"

"If you don't mind. Just a precaution."

"Okay, I understand. But you know I'm not going to just hide myself away."

"Stay in today and let's talk tonight," he says, a growing urgency in his voice. "I have to go, darling, I'm sorry. I'm about to meet with someone. Just promise you'll stay in, okay?"

"Of course." I stretch my foot to the old-fashioned silver chain attached to the rubber plug in the drain and cross it twice around my big toe. "See you later."

"Good. Get some rest. Love you."

"Love you, too. Bye."

I yank the plug and listen to the gurgle of draining bathwater, knowing I've probably just lied to a man who has said "love you" to me for the first time. Does "love you" mean "I love you"? I don't think so. I've said "love you" to Donna and any number of other people in the same way I'd say "Ciao." The difference is that Jack and I have never spoken the word "love" to each other in any context.

By the time I can make myself move, the tub is drained and I'm shivering. But I know what I have to do.

I climb out of the tub, wrap myself in a terry-cloth robe and dig my cellphone out of the plastic bag. It's drained of juice. I plug it in to recharge and sit next to the wall socket to call Detective Yarrow. She's unavailable. I'm put through to Detective McCauley, who answers his phone in a leaden voice. He perks up considerably when I mention my name.

"You okay? How ya feeling?"

"I'm fine, thanks for asking. I've got some information to pass along. I'm sure it won't amount to much, but thought you should know that when Chelsea met me in the park, she was dropped off by a guy in a red convertible."

"You know who it was?"

"No, but it wasn't Jeremy Sloan. He doesn't drive a red convertible."

"You know that for a fact?"

"I asked him." Then hastily add, "But that's all I did. I just want to assure you that I didn't try to check this out on my own."

"Good. I don't suppose you might have a license number for the vehicle you saw?"

"Actually, I do." I reach into the plastic bag for my wallet and find the scrap of paper. "You ready?" I unfold it and read the numbers.

"Thanks. Lucky thing you wrote that down. Any particular reason for doing that? Something suspicious about the car?"

"No, not really. Nice car. Just happened to see the license number."

"And then wrote it down and kept the piece of paper."

There's a silence I know better than to fill. I've opened another can of worms. If I mention Corky and the filming, I'll risk putting him through a visit from the police for no good reason. In light of my visit to his house yesterday, I'd like to avoid giving his family any more cause to be apprehensive about me.

"Okay, we'll look into it." McCauley sighs. "Is there anything else you may have forgotten to mention?"

"That should do it." Remorse is already lapping at my brain. I stare at the rug, envisioning some guy I've never met being grilled in an interrogation room because I pointed a finger at him. I know what that feels like and hate myself for making this call.

"You know, there really wasn't anything suspicious, now that I think of it. Chelsea looked happy. There was nothing wrong. Could we just put this down to my overactive imagination and forget I called you?"

"On a recorded line? I don't think so."

"Damn."

"Recorded line."

"Okay, sorry. But I'd really like to drop this."

"Why wouldn't you want to report a license number that could lead to finding this young woman? There seems to be a pattern here with you."

"I don't like the idea of getting people in trouble with the police, like Lisa and the bartender and now this guy, whoever he is. Just go easy, okay?"

"Sure. Whatever you say."

"By the way, were you able to track down Lisa?"

There's a pause before he asks, "You'll be at this number?"

"It's my cellphone. Call anytime. And let me know what happens, okay?"

Before I say anything more to incriminate myself or anyone else, I politely end the conversation. McCauley has left no doubt in my mind that calls made cannot be unmade. *What have I done to Jeremy and Lisa—and some guy in a red convertible?*

Fatigue washes over me. I lie down on my bed, listening to the gentle sounds of chirping birds outside my window and the faint swish of cars passing on the street below. My mind, in its sluggish state, mulls over the events of the past few days. Slowly things become clear to me and, whatever the consequences, I have to follow my instincts.

Eventually, Donna taps on my door and enters. "How're you feeling?"

"Good. Just resting. Thanks for the tea."

"You're very welcome." She picks up the tray on my bedside table. "I'm just going out to do some errands. I'll be back in an hour or two."

"Take your time."

I wait until I hear her pad down the stairs, then get up and dress. I throw on jeans and a tee shirt, then stand by the window until her car heads down the driveway. I grab my keys and cellphone and hurry out.

Minutes later, I tap the code to open the gates and walk out onto the street. I glance to my right and see that the memorial to Elaine is still in place, the yellow tape around the red cones fluttering in the soft breeze. Walking quickly, my eyes alert to movement around me, I cross the park and angle toward the curve in the road off the boulevard.

After replaying the dark, blurry loop in my head again and again, I need to check out the scene myself in daylight. Maybe I can figure out what actually happened to me last night. There's debris on the embankment where my car flipped, and sparkles of chipped glass in the roadway, but no memorial to me, thank God.

If my sturdy Volvo took a bullet for me in a last act of vehicular bravery, it's just one more reason to cherish her. How ironic that she should meet her end on the fringes of Holmby Park. A lump settles in my throat as though I'm grieving a death in the family. After all the nights spent parked at the curb, curled up on her soft, comforting upholstery, I'll miss her terribly.

I cross the roadway and see a man with a dog up ahead. It's Doug and Ridley, both standing stock-still, watching me approach them.

"You're out for a long walk. How's Ridley holding up?"

"Pretty good. We took a rest in the park and had a hotdog. What are you up to?"

"Same as you. Find anything?"

"Just trying to get the lay of the land. I ran into Detective Yarrow out here earlier. She said she'd probably be getting in touch with you."

"I already spoke to Detective McCauley."

I start walking slowly along the edge of the road, picturing my turn off the boulevard and glass shattering into my lap. "I'm kind of sorry I've mentioned anything to them. My gut feeling is that none of it will lead anywhere, except to cause a few people trouble they don't need."

"Spilling everything to Yarrow and McCauley is the wise bet. It's not for you to figure things out." Doug and Ridley follow in my wake, both huffing on the incline up to the corner. "In fact, I'm not sure it's a good idea for you to even be out walking around here."

"You really think the killer is still lurking in the vicinity?" I step back onto the curb as an orange transit bus hurtles past. "I'm guessing whoever it was had to be hovering right around here."

I spot the black tread marks in the road where I swerved, then follow an oily path up the ivy-covered embankment to where my Volvo flipped. I shudder and look down at the ground, gazing blindly at a crosshatch pattern in the hard-packed earth.

"You're right. But if you're looking for spent shells, Detective Yarrow already found them."

"Really?" I look up at Doug, whose expression is grim. "Then there's no reason to think it couldn't have been a crazy sniper, some jerk randomly—"

"You know better than that. There's nothing random about this. And Elaine wasn't the target."

"No." I shake my head slowly, giving voice to my own growing suspicion. "I am. Someone took down my stunt double by mistake."

15

As if to prove his point that I shouldn't make an easy target of myself by being out on my own, Doug and Ridley escort me back to Donna's house. The logic of having these two wheezing along beside me as protection makes little sense, but the gesture is sweet. By the time we reach the gates, dog and master are winded.

"You're sure you don't want to come in? I know Donna would love to see you."

"Thanks anyway. I don't need another run-in with Dirck. We'll just take a breather in the park and head home."

I punch in the code and wave to Doug as he and Ridley cross the street to settle on the nearest bench. As I make my way up the driveway, I'm pleased to see that Donna is still out, but not happy to spot Dirck bounding out the front door. He glares at me, arms braced across his chest. My first thought is that Donna has deputized him to keep me from wandering off the plantation. He's wearing his tough-guy black leather jacket and a scowl that looks like he means business. Leave it to Dirck to dress in an appropriate costume for confrontation.

"There you are! Where have you been?"

"Just walking around the yard. I thought I might have a swim." With luck, he hasn't seen me enter through the gates.

"I was looking all over for you. I got some news."

"Chelsea?" I stop at the edge of the portico, my body tensing. "She's been found?"

"No, but I might have a lead. I had a Skype session with an actor in New York, who informed me Jerry Schlitz and Chelsea hooked up out here. He says they were really hot and heavy, you believe it? I had no idea he'd made a move on her!" Dirck grinds his hands together, cracking his knuckles. "The thought of that creep all over my daughter—man, if he had anything to do with her going missing—"

"Easy, Dirck. He's as concerned as we are. He has no idea where she is."

"How do you know that? You talked to him?"

"Of course. You were the one who told me about Jeremy. I've already checked him out."

"When?"

"Elaine and I saw him the other night."

"You and Elaine?" Dirck gapes at me, arms spread wide in his gimme-a-break pose. "You kidding me? The police know this?"

"Of course. I already told them." I speak in a calm tone, taking guilty pleasure in knowing every word I utter is a dagger nicking his flesh.

"I don't believe this!" he thunders. "Why the hell am I always the last to know?"

"Really?" I look at him complacently, waiting for his brain to process the connection. "The last to know?"

"What? What?" He glowers. "You going to hold that Elaine thing over my head forever? I said I was sorry."

"Actually, it's the call-girl thing. I figured it was worth seeing Jeremy after you told me how you coached Chelsea to prepare for the role."

As slow dawning breaks into full-blown panic, Dirck gasps. "I never told her to—wait! Now you're blaming this on me? Like it's my fault?"

"I'm only suggesting she may have gone gung ho with her research."

"You told the police that, too? How's that going to make me look? My daughter, a call girl! You ever think of that?" He runs down the steps, brushing past me on the way to his car. "I wouldn't put it past that creep to pimp her out!"

"Where are you going?"

"Where the hell you think? Jerry's the one who set her up. I'd like to hear about it firsthand!"

I race after him, yanking the passenger door open as he turns the key in the ignition. "Don't go off half-cocked, Dirck. Let the police deal with it."

"Like they're doing such a great job!" He slams his door shut and throws the car in gear. I slide into the front seat and pull the door closed just as he starts backing up. "What're you doing?"

"Coming with. I know where the place is and I don't want you getting in trouble." I plug in my seat belt as Dirck burns rubber tearing down the driveway. "Easy! You're going to plow into the gates."

Tires squeal as he slams on the brakes; I smell smoking carbon. Why couldn't I resist igniting his famously short fuse? I should know better!

The gates slowly open while Dirck drums his hands on the steering wheel. "What the hell was she doing with a half-assed actor like him? Where's the future? He woulda just dragged her down. I mean, this guy stiffed me! He didn't pay me for his acting classes. What kind of person does that?"

"I know, I know, awful. But don't do something you'll regret, okay?"

"Sure," he says, squealing out onto the road without looking in either direction. "You know, it'll be kinda fun to confront this guy. He's sort of a pretty-boy wimp. What she sees in him, I'll never know!"

We all have our own ideas of fun. Trapped in a rental compact with my former husband is not my idea of pleasure. Besides, he's a native New Yorker and drives like a New Yorker, which only works if you are driving in New York City and consider navigating through traffic an elaborate amusement-park ride.

I learned to drive on a farm tractor and view driving as an occupational skill, not a game of bumper cars. It took me three years of marriage before I could convince Dirck not to drive with one foot on the accelerator, the other on the brake pedal. He also likes to gesticulate, sometimes with both hands, fluctuating speed according to his rate of speech. Donna, too, is a terrible driver. The devil in me would like to see them take a road trip together.

These are my thoughts as I grip my seat in terror while Dirck drifts across lanes without signaling. If purgatory is eternity with people you can't abide, I've encountered my special hell on earth. Driving on meds with a concussion and two broken arms, I could do a better job of getting us to Gilligan's.

When traffic on Wilshire Boulevard comes to a standstill, I take a deep breath. Despite the hellish ride, I'm still glad I came along. I have a few more questions to put to Jeremy that I'd prefer to ask in person. If he's lying, I'll have a better chance of detecting it. For that matter, I also have a few things to clear up with Dirck.

"Do you mind if I ask you a question? Did Chelsea call you that night after she finished working with me?"

"She may have. Why?"

"When we talked the next morning, you knew all about Donna's house and that I was living there. You even asked if you could stay. It must've been Chelsea who told you about it."

"Yeah, I guess so. She was pretty impressed."

"How impressed?"

"She told me I shoulda stuck with you and not gone off with Pru."

"What? That's very funny. She knew it wasn't even my house!"

"Fine, laugh if you want. I shouldn't have told you. But she went on and on about the place."

"You must have spoken to her immediately after she left. Was she in the park? Did she mention waiting for a ride?"

"No, or I would have told the detective. Chelsea was walking and talking, but I don't know where. Last thing we did was confirm our Skype session the next day."

That means that Chelsea had time to make at least two phone calls before she disappeared: one to Jeremy and the other to Dirck.

Amid a blast of honking horns, Dirck squeezes through traffic and hangs a right from a left-hand lane. He whips up a residential street and asks, "Are we anywhere near this joint?"

"We're two blocks away. Start looking for a parking spot."

He finds one in a space marked LOADING ZONE up the street from the restaurant. He pulls in and parks, looking pl-eased with himself. "What the hell if I get a ticket. It's a rental."

I grit my teeth and release the seat belt. If a parking ticket is the worst that comes of this outing, I'll be grateful. As we head toward Gilligan's, I caution Dirck to control his temper. "If he sees that you're angry, he'll clam up. Besides, if Chelsea digs this guy, it's her business, not yours."

"Yeah? Maybe you should stay in the car and mind your own business."

"Yeah? Maybe too late," I say, walking up to the door of Gilligan's.

I step inside, greeted by a gust of chilled air and dead silence. We've arrived during that hushed, morgue-like lull between lunch and cocktail hour to find a completely empty restaurant. There are no customers and no one staffing the reception area.

While I look around, Dirck strides inside, his footsteps echoing on the terra-cotta tile floor. He raps his knuckles on the bar. "Hellooooo, anyone home?"

A male voice I recognize as Jeremy's calls from the patio, "We're closed until four o'clock."

"The barn door's still open, buddy."

"Sorry, but—" He appears in the archway, the words scarcely leaving his mouth before the sound of Dirck's inimical voice strikes home. He blinks twice, then blurts, "What're you doing here?"

"So, how's about a beer, Jerry? I mean, why tip a stranger, eh?"

Jeremy's eyelids drop to half-mast as though he's sizing up a full-moon bar-crawler. "Hey, Dirck. No trouble, okay?"

"Given what you owe me, how about one on the house?"

"It doesn't work that way here. I could get in trouble, you know?"

"Take it easy, Jer." Dirck laughs. "We just dropped by to visit. And you can mail me the check for the classes, now that I know how to find you."

Before things get rough, I step deeper into the bar area so Jeremy can see me. "Hey, it's not quite happy hour yet, is it?"

The moment my voice registers, Jeremy's face contorts into a rapid succession of expressions that, sadly, I doubt he has the acting chops to duplicate on camera. "Wow, you two both here together? Sorry, but now's not such a good time. We're closed."

He glances back toward the patio and I hear, "Is that her? Why is she here?" It's a kittenish voice I recognize instantly.

"Lisa? Is that you?" I call out. "Could I talk to you a minute?"

"Haven't you done enough?" A busty babe with cascading strawberry-pink hair, dressed in shorts and a low-cut tank top, sidles up next to Jeremy. Teetering on platform wedges, she glares at me through bruised eyes. One cheek is swollen. Her lip is cut. "Why can't you just leave me alone!" she cries plaintively.

"I'm so sorry! Lisa, please tell me what happened." I start to move toward her, but she holds up her hand.

"All's I did is try to help your friend. You got me in trouble." Tears roll down her puffy face, trailing black mascara.

"With who? The police?"

"You gave 'em my number. Why'd you do that?" she wails.

"My fault, Lisa," Jeremy says, glaring at me. "I shouldn't have trusted you. They came here, too, asking questions. I could've lost my job! Why the hell did you go to the police? We didn't do anything."

"I'll tell you why, you sleazeball," Dirck booms. "My daughter is missing. I'm guessing you pimped her out like she's some hooker! I want to know where she is."

"Chelsea? Your daughter?" Jeremy's face buckles in horror. "She never said she was your daughter. I swear. Sir."

"Where is she?"

"I don't know," Jeremy says. "I wish I did."

"But you set her up, you scumbag. Is she with some pimp, thanks to you?"

"No!" Lisa cries. "Nothing like that!"

"Of course not," I say in as soothing a tone as I can muster. "Chelsea told me how much you helped her. She really appreciated it. In fact, she was looking forward to seeing you when she finished working with me that night. But something happened. You were going to pick her up, right? She'd left her car somewhere?"

"Yeah, at Ernie's place. I had a . . . an appointment, so Ernie dropped her off. Then we were going to pick her up for dinner after, but she was, like, a no-show. Gone. No call, nothing."

"So her car's at Ernie's?"

"No, when we got back later, it was gone."

"Ernie? Ernie?" Dirck bellows. "So who's this Ernie? Your pimp?"

"He's not a pimp! He's my . . . my manager!" She turns and totters at surprising speed back out to the patio. I move to follow her, but Jeremy blocks my way.

"Just leave her alone. Let her go."

"Yeah? Is she your girlfriend, too?" Dirck yells. "Are you two-timing my daughter with some hooker?"

"Shut up, Dirck," I say, "that's enough." I run past him out of the bar and back onto the street, hoping to catch up to Lisa.

Even in her platform wedges, she's somehow managed to sprint out the back way, through the patio shrubbery. I spot her racing toward Wilshire. She stops and waves. A red convertible turns the corner and pulls to the curb. The driver leans over and pushes the door open. Lisa hops in and the car takes off before she's pulled the door closed. I stand for a moment, watching the convertible speed through a yellow traffic light and disappear up the boulevard.

As I turn back toward Gilligan's, I look up the street and see a tow truck ratcheting Dirck's rental compact up on its back wheels. Streams of thought race through my brain as unflattering windows open on ancient scenes of marital strife. Hasn't this all happened before in another time and place? Do I really have to play all this back? I glance up at the street sign that reads TOW AWAY ZONE: LOADING ONLY and try to calculate the cost of retrieving an impounded car.

I see a long night stretching ahead and consider calling Jack. However, that would mean explaining why I set out on a misguided venture with my ex-husband when I'd promised to remain at home. None of this bodes well for a romantic evening at the beach.

By the time I reach Gilligan's, Dirck's blue rental car is already on its costly journey to an out-of-the-way barbed-wire enclosure somewhere. I try to come up with a gentle way of imparting this news to Dirck.

However, when I enter Gilligan's, happy hour is in its first flush of arrivals and Dirck is ensconced on a stool, drinking a frosty mug of beer. Jeremy has his hand on Dirck's shoulder and the two are deep in conversation across the bar. They look up as I approach. I've apparently interrupted some sort of misty-eyed male bonding.

"Hey," Dirck says, "I wondered where you'd run off to. Listen, Jer and I have a lot to go over. You think you could take a cab home?"

"Not a bad idea. Oh, by the way, your car was towed."

"Oh, man!" Dirck says, clapping his hand to his head. "Towed? I can't park up the street for ten minutes? What kinda fascists run this damn city?"

"Bummer," Jeremy says, with feeling. "Hey, man, hang out for a while and I'll help you get it back."

"You okay with that?" Dirck asks me. "Just go on home and I'll check out the neighborhood until Jerry's off work."

"Fine by me." I smile and wiggle my fingers in farewell. "See you around, guys."

I walk toward Wilshire Boulevard and look down the street toward the Federal Building, where Jack is toiling away. For one fleeting moment, I again consider surprising him, but quickly dismiss the idea. My surprise visit would entail way too much explanation.

Instead, I stroll to the corner, my eye on a city bus worming its way through rush-hour traffic. Even if I could afford a taxi, Los Angeles isn't a town where you can stick out your hand and hail a cab—and, lucky me, a ready-made option is lumbering up to the curb. The door wheezes open and I board.

The bus is crowded, but I manage to find a seat in the back. I check messages on my cellphone, then decide to take another look at the video I shot the night Elaine died. The image on the screen is small, but I'm still able to glimpse the water geyser, the approach of the fire truck and the darkened park beyond. Again I see the headlights of a car swing around the north side of the park, coming from Sunset Boulevard; a bicyclist cuts across the road in front of it. A squad car, lights flashing, races down the boulevard. Detective Yarrow's face pops up, looking at me over Detective McCauley's shoulder.

It occurs to me that perhaps I should forward the video to her, although the car is clearly coming toward the park area, not leaving it. There's hardly anything suspicious as far as I can see. On the other hand, I've promised Jack I'll fully disclose any leads I have, so I may as well comply. I pull up Detective Yarrow's email address, attach the video and press Send. If she has the tools to pick out the car's license number, more power to her.

I don't have to ride too many stops up the Wilshire corridor before I alight near Holmby Park, but it gives me time to reflect. Reporting phone numbers and license plates to the police may be the prudent thing to do, but discretion is advised. I hurt Lisa. I almost cost Jeremy his job. I gave the guy in the red convertible an excuse to vent his anger on a strawberry blonde with little ability to defend herself. Now I've sent video that just may get some anonymous motorist a surprise visit from a detective.

Conclusion: Nothing against the police, but they have their own way of dealing with things. I can operate with a bit more finesse on my own.

I walk down the residential street, pausing at the scene of my near demise. The embankment is healing, with crushed ivy and ferns quickly rejuvenating to cover the Volvo's tire tracks. There's already little sign of the trauma to the pavement. I stand at the corner, looking around, glancing at the crosshatch pattern in the hard-packed earth at my feet and trying to imagine how someone could have so nearly taken my life—and then wondering why.

I skirt Holmby Park and head toward Donna's house, figuring that I'll have just enough time to shower and dress before Jack picks me up. I mentally pack my shoulder bag with essentials that include my outmoded laptop and a few changes of clothing. Just as I'm tapping in the code to open the gates, my cellphone rings. I glance at the caller ID and answer.

"Hi, Corky. How's it going?"

"Okay, good," he says, then whispers, "Can I talk to you?"

"Sure, what's on your mind?"

"Can you hang on? I need to go outside."

I hear the strain in his voice and deduce he's bumped up against yet another artistic concern he needs to share. I welcome the break in working out my own dilemmas to help sort out his. By the time the gates have opened and closed, Corky is back on the line, still whispering.

"Hi, hey, any chance we could hook up tomorrow? I mean, you know, meet?"

"What's up?"

"I need to talk to you. Like, just you and me, all right?"

I hear the quiet urgency in his voice. "Is everything okay with you? I hope I didn't upset your family yesterday."

"No, it's not you. I mean, it is, but that's what I need to talk to you about."

"Want me to come by?"

"No! Sorry, no, that wouldn't work. I'm going to get my mom to drop me off at the La Brea Tar Pits in the morning so I can shoot some stuff. Can you meet me there?"

"Sure. How about just outside the Page Museum. What time?"

"Like, ten o'clock?"

"You got it. See you then."

I would like to think that Corky hasn't developed the sort of agonizing adolescent crush on me that could take the better part of tomorrow morning to resolve. On the other hand, he could have been so embarrassed by the hand-holding heart-to-heart we engaged in yesterday that he's hoping to let me down easily by telling me I'm way too old for him. Either way, tomorrow morning is beginning to look awkward. It occurs to me that I could ask Donna to pack up some ginger snaps or fudge to bring to our rendez-vous. Food helps.

I turn my key in the door and slip inside, hoping Donna is in the kitchen and won't hear me enter. Unfortunately, as luck would have it, she and Doug are sitting in the living room, enjoying wine and canapés. Donna is wearing one of her more exotic caftans. Doug is sporting his regulation safari-jacket-and-jeans ensemble. Oddly, they raise their glasses as I enter, although neither of their faces looks particularly convivial.

"Nice of you to show up," Donna says pointedly. "I thought you were staying in today."

"I was, but Dirck asked me to accompany him to a meeting. I obliged, but the meeting went on longer than we anticipated, so I came home for fear I would worry you. Could I have a glass of wine, please?"

Both eye me suspiciously, but Doug pours me a glass of exquisite Montrachet from the bucket on the table. Where else but in Holmby Hills does the house pour come from a renowned chateau? I take the glass and greedily imbibe. "Cheers!"

"Cheers, yourself," Donna says. "I put out some nibbles in case you and Jack want to join us. He called to say he's on his way."

"Perfect." I glance at the assortment of "nibbles" on the coffee table: it looks more like a high-end smorgasbord stocked with smoked salmon, an assortment of meats, crudités, cheeses and crackers. I'm torn between diving in and running upstairs to pack.

"I'll be as quick as I can."

I race up the stairs, glass in hand, my mind a jumble again. Food and wine will do that to you. But it's also occurred to me that I've left Dirck in the company of Jeremy, who just may come up with some forgotten clue to Chelsea's whereabouts. If that's the case, and Dirck storms off in vigilante mode to rescue his daughter, it could spell disaster.

T he face," Dirck moans. "Why'd they have to mess with my face?"

Indeed, he's not a pretty sight. We're back in a hospital again, this time in an emergency room cubicle where Dirck, minus his leather jacket, lies on a gurney, hooked up to drips and monitors.

"Hey, squeeze in," Dirck bellows as we push the drapes aside to enter.

He's holding court, his baritone rumbling magnificently despite broken ribs. Even with a black eye, significant bruising and an arm in a sling, he's in high spirits. With a nod to Detective Yarrow, hovering at the rear with Jack and Donna, he says, "I was just filling her in on what went on. I got jumped, you believe it? Never happened to me in New York, but I come out to Lotusland and get the crap kicked out of me. But if you think I look bad, you should see the other guys!"

He does a series of cartoon *whop! pow! kazowie!* sounds that make everyone laugh, including Detective McCauley and a young intern standing at the head of the gurney. "No one sucker punches me and gets away with it!"

I roll my eyes, joining in the laughter. "You're a one-man SWAT team, fella!"

"Who did this to you?" Donna asks. "Was it a robbery?"

"Yeah, they got my wallet. But, hell, I would've given it to them. They didn't need to beat me up. I just went for a breather while I was waiting for Jerry, this former acting student of mine, to clock out and help me get my car out of the pound. Then this car pulls up behind me. Two guys jump out and start beating me. At least I didn't lose teeth. It's crazy! Broad daylight! I gotta think these goons are tied into Chelsea, somehow. Who's behind this?

That's what I want to know. I mean, we're gettin' picked off one by one, right, Megsie?"

Dirck is so animated I begin to wonder if his meds need to be dialed back, but I remind myself this is nothing more than his natural reaction to being the center of attention. He really can't get enough of it.

"Don't let us interrupt anything, here," Doug says to Mc-Cauley.

"That's okay. We're just finishing up." He glances at me. "We'd like to get a word with Miss Barnes, of course. Maybe outside?"

"Sure, anytime." I move toward Jack and Detective Yarrow, preparing to leave.

"Hey, guys, that's it for me already?" Dirck sounds disappointed as half his audience starts to walk out of the cubicle. "If there's anything else you need, you know how to find me."

"You've been a big help, Mr. Heyward," McCauley says, edging around Donna. "Just take it easy now."

"Hey, I was wondering," Dirck says, catching McCauley's sleeve. "Any chance you could work some magic with that impound place? You know, all things considered, maybe they could waive the fees on my car?"

"Yeah, sure. I'll have to get back to you on that," McCauley mutters.

"Hey, wait! You can't all go. You just got here," Dirck says, sounding even more plaintive.

"We can stay a little while," Donna says. "I think they're going to keep you for the night."

Jack turns to me, speaking quietly. "I'll just go to the waiting room until you're finished."

"No, please stay with me."

The two of us follow McCauley down a corridor to an L-shaped space fitted with several molded plastic chairs and a water cooler. I've had no time to fill Jack in on what happened, and I know he's wondering what I was doing in Westwood when I'd said I'd be home. He arrived at Donna's just as the sun was going down and had barely walked in the door when the call came about Dirck. Within minutes, we were all in separate cars traveling in convoy to the emergency room at UCLA Medical Center.

Jack remains standing as I settle into one of the chairs across from McCauley. "You and Detective Yarrow wouldn't be here if you didn't think this was connected to Chelsea and her mother, right?"

"It was Heyward who called us, which was the right thing for him to do. Do you think there's a connection?"

"You mean as far as 'picking us off'? I assume Dirck is stringing Chelsea's disappearance to Elaine's murder and the attacks on both of us, but I don't know that it's all connected. This might be a separate incident."

"You want to expand on that?"

I glance at Jack before seizing the opportunity to explain myself. "I went along with Dirck this afternoon to make sure he didn't do something stupid to Jeremy, Chelsea's boyfriend. But Lisa was there, the gal with the escort service that I told you about. Someone had beaten her up and I'm guessing it was in retaliation for attracting a police investigation. She said as much, blaming me for getting her in trouble. I suspect that's why Dirck was attacked."

"But why not you?"

I shrug, "Just lucky, I guess." McCauley raises his eyebrows. "I mean it. I ran outside to follow Lisa and saw the guy in the red convertible swing around and pick her up. They didn't see me. When I went back inside and told Dirck his car had been towed, he suggested I go home on my own. I was long gone by the time Dirck was attacked."

"It was the same red convertible you saw before?"

I nod. "Exactly, and I already gave you the license plate number. I think the driver's name is Ernie. After seeing him pick up Lisa today, he's obviously involved with her line of work, probably her so-called 'manager.' You checked him out, right? Interviewed him? It's probably why the girl was beaten up, don't you think?"

"Excuse me a minute." McCauley shifts in his chair and takes a moment to check messages on his phone. He glances up at Jack, standing in the doorway, and then looks back at me. "So, nothing more you want to add?"

"Wait a minute, you've talked to this driver already. Ernie something? He and Lisa were supposed to pick up Chelsea that night, but she didn't call. Did he say why he dropped her off at the park in the first place? What about Chelsea's car? Who took it? Why?"

"That's a lot of questions."

"I gave you a lot of information, remember? Where does it lead? Are we any closer to finding out what happened to Chelsea?"

"We can't really say for now. We're piecing things together." McCauley stands. "Thank you for your help. You know how to reach us if anything else comes up."

"Could I see Detective Yarrow?"

"Looks like she's already gone, but I'll let her know you want to get in touch. Any particular message?"

"No. Thanks anyway."

Without another word, I walk out of the cubicle, reaching for Jack's hand as I go. Halfway down the corridor, I turn to him, seething. "This is infuriating! You wonder why I don't want to tell them anything? It's a one-way street with these people. Why should I trust the authorities when they don't trust me?"

Jack squeezes my hand and guides me out through the double doors to the waiting room before speaking. "You know, it's possible you might have been told something if I hadn't been present."

"You're with the FBI. I should think they'd be happy to have you there."

"Think again. No one's brought us in on this." He puts his arm around my shoulder. "C'mon, let's get out of here."

"I'd like nothing better. You know, if I'd kept all this to myself, at least Lisa wouldn't have been beaten up. Or Dirck."

"Do you want to say goodbye to him?"

"No need. I'll see him again soon enough."

We walk down another long corridor to the parking structure and take an elevator. Jack's dark BMW is parked next to my bright Olds 98.

"Isn't she lovely!" I exclaim, taking in the gleaming burst of sunshine parked amidst a monotonous lineup of white, black, and gray cars.

"I'm not likely to lose you in traffic," Jacks says with a smile. He holds the door while I slide in behind the wheel, then leans in to give me a quick kiss. "You know the way. I'll be right behind you."

I slide my hand to the back of his neck and pull him closer, breathing in his heady warm-raisin scent that no cologne can match. "Hmmmm, tasty," I whisper, running my tongue along his ear. "Bottle it and we can make a fortune."

"Just for you, baby." He turns his face to mine and we kiss again. "Hungry?"

"Always. But let's not stop anywhere, okay?"

"Leave it to me," he says, gently closing the door.

I back out and pull ahead, waiting for Jack before driving down the parking ramp. I punch up KJAZ and am rewarded with John Coltrane's "Blue Train," the haunting tones carrying me through Westwood to the San Diego Freeway. I remain in the slow lane, wrapped in music and thoughts of Jack, visible in my rearview mirror. Enjoying the oddly intimate connection, I watch him flick on his turn signal a moment after I turn on mine. Heading toward the marina, I roll down the window and fill my lungs with cleansing ocean air.

The first time Jack took me home to his condo, he pressed a switch just inside the door of the darkened entryway and immediately the entire apartment sprang to life with music and soft lighting. At the far end of the living room, a matte-finish steel grill silently rose to reveal a balcony invitingly lit, with a glimpse of moon and stars in the night sky. I joked then that he should arrange for the hot switch to activate a robotic device that would pour a glass of wine before flipping steaks on the kitchen grill.

The effect of this transformation never ceases to delight me. This time, as though he just dropped in from next door to serenade us, we're greeted by the soothing sounds of Chet Baker singing "Time After Time." I hum along with Chet as Jack opens a bottle of pinot grigio and pours wine into two chilled glasses. He hands me one and touches his glass to mine.

"Cheers. I'm happy you're here."

"Cheers, yourself." I smile. "I'm happy to be here, too."

And I am. I look around the comfortable, clutter-free space and feel at home. The only furniture is a glass-and-chrome coffee table, a couch covered in pale linen and a black leather Eames chair. Pictures lean against pale, bare walls on a floor covered in wheat-colored carpet. Hidden from view inside a built-in cabinet made of smooth wood the color of sand is an array of electronic equipment and some books.

One of my Furniture Dreams would be hard to conjure up in such an environment. The absence of mementos of a life lived with someone else is perhaps another reason I feel so at ease here. But the primary reason for my contentment brushes my cheek with a kiss and puts an arm around my shoulders. I smile and so does he.

He takes my glass and I follow him into the bedroom, another uncluttered oasis, with a balcony providing a view of the starlit sky. A full moon illuminates the room, highlighting a white linen coverlet and a bank of pillows and providing all the light we need.

Jack wraps his arms around me, stroking my body. He slips my tee shirt over my head and pulls the thin straps of my teddy down, kissing and fondling my breasts. My hand slides between his legs, feeling his hunger as I slowly coax the zipper down. He moans softly as my fingers caress him. He eases me onto the bed, kneeling down, then pulling back my jeans, his kisses forming a path the length of my body. We know the terrain of each other's bodies and how to tantalize and give pleasure. The sex is sensational enough, unhurried and passionate, but the real wonder is that we somehow found each other in the first place.

We lie in each other's arms, sharing a pillow and listening to Chet Baker croon "I Fall in Love Too Easily," the plaintive tenor voicing lyrics entirely too apt. Lord knows, I've been "fooled in the past."

I turn my head to see Jack's face limned in the moonlight, shadows playing off his deep-set eyes under the strong ridge of his forehead. There's no question that he's a handsome man, with a lean face and a cleft in his chin attesting to it. But I also see a furrowed brow and the hint of sadness in his eyes. He lost his wife after a long illness, a chapter or more of his life story that he still hasn't fully shared with me.

Jack is a private person, keeping his thoughts to himself even, as I've experienced, while sharing a post-coital pillow and glass of wine. That is why I am surprised to hear him say, "Not me," as we listen to the refrain.

"That's not me at all," he says again, with more emphasis. "I don't fall in love too easily or too fast." He turns to face me. "It happens slowly and it's for keeps."

I stroke his cheek, looking into his eyes. "That's the only way I would want it."

I take my time, my fingers, and then my mouth, caressing his body. His hand on my breast slides south, exciting me again. I ride a wave of euphoria that seems to penetrate to my very soul.

Do I even dare think that maybe this time I've found love that will last? I don't need to jump aboard a fast-moving train again; this one is not going to leave the station without me. We can take our time.

Later, wrapped in a soft robe, I perch on a stool at the kitchen counter, wine glass in hand. I've set a table for two on the balcony and lit candles. Designer pizza, the fancy kind with smoked salmon, caviar and dill cream, has already been delivered to Jack's door by a gourmet shop down the street. Barefoot, wearing jeans and a shirt, he busily assembles an endive salad with Gorgonzola and walnuts.

He looks up and smiles as we both hear the distant chime of my cellphone. "Any idea where you left it?" he laughs.

I race back into the bedroom to retrieve my phone from my jeans pocket. I see it's Donna on the line and go out on the balcony to take her call.

"I was worried when you didn't come back. Are you all right?"

"Sorry, I should've called earlier. How's Dirck?"

"Fine, staying overnight in the hospital. I think he's working up a reality show. He says his life is, to quote him, 'the stuff of great theater.' He even persuaded Doug to shoot video of him on his cellphone so he could send it to Pru."

"That poor woman!"

"That's what I thought. Did Jack take you for dinner?"

"We're just about to eat. How're you doing?"

"Better, now that I know you're okay. Actually, Dougie is here having some supper. He brought Ridley with him, too."

"I may stop by in the morning to pick up some things. Is there anything you need me to get on the way?"

"No, nothing. Enjoy your dinner."

I end the call and then turn the ringer to vibrate. A warm sensation of well-being washes over me. I close my eyes and breathe in the tangy musk of the marshland, knowing I'm in the only place I want to be.

When I open my eyes, I see Jack watching me. "Okay?"

I smile. "More than okay. But I'm famished!"

We make short work of the pizza and salad, but linger over the last of the pinot grigio. Looking out on the water, my chin cupped in my hands, my mind fastens on the events that have unfolded since Chelsea's disappearance.

"You know, it's been four days already and there's still no word from her. I can't stop thinking that somewhere, right now, she desperately needs help. How could she just vanish like this?"

"Thanks to you, the police have some leads. Leave it to them now."

"They're useless! How could they not find her? And Elaine's murder . . . my God."

"Easy, Meg. There's nothing more you can do."

Jack picks up the empty platter and salad bowl, carrying them to the kitchen. I know better than to pursue this line of conversation and spoil our evening together. Another thing I've learned about Jack is that his thinking process is as orderly as his cutlery drawer; everything is in its place, handy when needed and out of sight when not in use. Idle speculation and rumination are of no consequence to him tonight. This is our time. I pick up our empty plates and follow him to the kitchen.

"If I can remember how to use your fancy espresso machine, I'll make some cappuccinos."

"Good idea," he says, with enough enthusiasm to let me know he's glad I've changed gears.

Minutes later, coffee cups in hand, we're back on the balcony, looking out over the moonlit marshland, when I hear a ping, signaling a text message. I pull my cellphone from the pocket of my robe and see a message from Corky Shaw that reads: *better take a look.*

I open the link he's sent and my stomach rolls over as a YouTube video pops up on screen with Dirck's image, his face battered, his arm in a sling. "My God, Jack, he's posted about himself in the hospital!"

Jack glances at the video playing on my cellphone screen, then goes into the living-room cabinet that houses his computer equipment. While he pulls up the YouTube video, my eyes fix on the horrifying images playing out on the small screen. "He's crazy," I murmur over and over. "He's crazy!"

I join Jack in the living room and we watch the video together on the large monitor. "Donna mentioned that he'd asked Doug to record him on his cellphone so he could send it to Pru, but I think he's taken it a step further. What is he thinking?"

Without comment, Jack replays the video, watching intently. Dirck, sitting up in a hospital bed, appears in close-up, a "selfie" recorded with his cellphone at arm's length. He speaks slowly, emphatically, in Jeep Wrangler mode.

"I don't blame you for not recognizing me. I'm Dirck Heyward, a victim of street crime, and this is the ugly truth of what it looks like. Most of you know me as Brick Storm, star of the '80s series *Aces High*, set in Vegas, or Trick Patterson in the crime drama *Precinct Hell*, or even—" Thirty seconds go by in which Dirck plows through his guest-star series credits before he says, "But this isn't about me."

"Like hell," I mutter, as Dirck launches into his account of Elaine's murder. He's obviously switched arms, because we have another angle on his face. I can only imagine how many takes he's scrapped before settling on the one he's uploaded.

"Many of you may have seen me interviewed the night of her death, talking about my dear friend, who tragically died of a gunshot wound. What most of you couldn't know, and what I am revealing now publicly for the first time, is that famed stuntwoman Elaine Farris was the mother of my beautiful daughter, actress Chelsea Horne. My grief over Elaine's death has sadly been overshadowed by the mysterious disappearance of my daughter, who is set to begin production on the new series *Jinx*, on which I have been working as her acting coach—"

"I'm sorry, Jack. I can't watch this thing all the way through again. Why did he do such a stupid thing?"

It's a question neither of us can answer, but both of us are aware of the ramifications of having this information out on the Internet. Wherever she is, this revelation must be agonizing for Chelsea—and might possibly put her in even greater jeopardy.

While Jack takes a call from his office, I stand on the balcony, sipping coffee and looking out on the fog-shrouded wetlands. The dense early-morning marine layer hugs the inlet, blanketing the marshland in a chill, moist stillness. A sudden hoarse scream pierces the quiet, startling me.

"Look up there," Jack whispers, coming up behind me. "A red-tailed hawk circling for prey—and there's another one over there."

Above us, two hawks soar through the lead-gray sky, one of them swooping down, emitting a rasping screech. The second one circles around, displaying its crimson tail feathers as it glides overhead on widespread wings. Another hoarse scream and the first hawk dives into the marsh, disappearing in the tall reeds.

"It's a smorgasbord out there," Jack says. "Frogs, rabbits, rats, you name it."

"A cruel, cruel world," I remark. "Everything is someone's else's meal."

"Yes." He nods. "Fortunately it's murder and mayhem I don't have to deal with."

There's an edge to his voice, and I wonder if it has to do with the phone call. "Is everything all right?"

"From the Bureau's standpoint, yes. It looks like we'll be closing in on the sex trafficking ring finally, but it also means I have to go back up to Seattle this morning." He rests his arms on the railing and looks out on the wetlands. "The timing is rotten. I don't want to leave you."

"I'll be fine. Are you worried about what Dirck might've unleashed?"

"It can't be good, whatever it is. I don't want you hurt." He reaches for my hand, pressing it to his lips.

"Dirck may have brought more harm to himself by attracting all that attention. You notice I wasn't even mentioned, which is just as well. I wouldn't much like having TMZ looking too closely at the dates of our marriage and her birth." I lean into him, feeling the warmth of his body, but also the tension. "I wish he'd kept his mouth shut for once, but he's put the focus on finding Chelsea, which is where it should be."

Jack makes no comment. I'm sure he's thinking about the shooting incident involving me, which thankfully Dirck did not mention. After a moment, he says, "I'd like you to stay here. I think it's the most secure place for you right now. I'll probably be back tomorrow."

"I understand. I'll stay here tonight, but I promised to meet Corky this morning. I don't want to disappoint him." I wrap my arms around Jack and press my face against his shoulder. "Don't worry. Just do what you have to do in Seattle and I'll be here waiting for you when you get back. Are you ready to go?"

"In a few minutes."

"Good." I give his ribs a squeeze and look up at him with a smile. "We can leave together."

A quarter of an hour later, I wave to Jack before pulling out ahead of him onto the narrow beach road. The fog is already lifting. The distant hum of rush hour traffic replaces the cawing sounds of predatory birds circling the wetlands. But there's also a primal survival-of-the-fittest ethos at work in traffic on the San Diego Freeway, which I avoid by pulling off onto surface streets.

With KJAZ playing softly, I also avoid references to Dirck's YouTube video on talk radio. Flipping through the morning television shows earlier, I was relieved at the newscasters' restraint. The only brief clip I saw broadcast from his video was prefaced by, "A father's plea for the safe return of his daughter—" But the news is still breaking, and since it involves a young blond actress and a new television series, the story can only grow. I have no doubt Dirck will stay on top of it.

I arrive at Donna's, gratified to see that there are no news crews parked on the street outside the gates. I suspect that will change once Dirck announces he's leaving the hospital. Perhaps it's just as well that I'm staying at Jack's place.

I'm about to mount the steps to the front door when I glimpse Doug's car parked near the orchid pavilion. He's either stayed late or dropped in very early. I'm betting he spent the night. My suspicions are confirmed when I walk into the kitchen. With Ridley curled on the floor between them, Doug and Donna are seated in the breakfast nook, looking cozily connubial. His feet are bare, his shirttails loose. She's wearing a housecoat, not entirely buttoned. The morning papers are open on the table and there's a lingering smell of coffee and bacon. They both look as though they've swallowed canaries, not pancakes.

"Morning!" they sing out in cheerful voices.

Clearly I'm not the only one in post-eros bliss. I ruffle Ridley's ears and he looks up at me as if to say, *Who knew? But if they're happy, I'm happy*. He rests his snout back on his paws with a sigh.

"You want some coffee?" Donna asks. "Help yourself to a pecan caramel roll. There's orange juice in the pitcher."

"Just coffee, thank you." I take a cup from the dish drainer and pour from the vacuum carafe on the table. "Jack says hello."

"Everything okay?" Dougie asks.

"Fine, fine. I think I'll just take my coffee and go upstairs." Honestly, I feel like I'm intruding. "I have to make some calls and check email."

"Good idea," Doug says. "You'll probably want to give Ed Ackerman a call. He said he's been trying to reach you. I already got an earful."

I stop in my tracks. "I didn't even think of him!" I take my cellphone from my shoulder bag and see I've left it on vibrate and have a screen full of messages.

Donna pulls her iPad out from under the newspapers and flips it open. "Dirck's posted another video. He's blaming the producers and the network for keeping Chelsea's disappearance under wraps, which is silly. And it's been picked up by some of the news outlets."

Doug snorts and says, "After talking to Dirck in the hospital this morning, Ed's blowing a gasket, comparing him to Julian Assange. You can imagine Dirck's version of all this. This ain't sitting pretty with Ed or the network. He seems to think you're the one who can put a lid on the SOB."

"So Ed thinks I have some control over a guy I divorced nearly a decade ago? A taste of celebrity is a banquet to Dirck. He's not going to give this up."

"I couldn't agree more. Any ideas?"

"Tell Ed the only way to shut Dirck up is to offer him a TV series of his own. Who knows? Maybe it's worth it!"

"If this media attention helps find Chelsea, I'm all for it," Donna says. "I don't know why Dirck's not pressuring the police more in these videos."

"He's doing that, too, but he's getting more mileage out of the network angle," Doug says.

"Okay, okay. Got it." I swill the rest of my coffee and leave the cup in the sink. "Let me see what I can do."

I hurry out to the garden, punch up Jeremy Sloan's number on my cellphone and anxiously stab the call button. I pace across the damp lawn toward the pool house, counting the rings. Just as I begin to fear I'll hear a voicemail greeting, his sleepy voice grunts, "Yeah?"

"Jeremy, hi. Sounds like I woke you up. Sorry, it's Meg. Listen, gotta ask you something—why did Dirck get beaten up? They didn't touch you, right? Just give it to me straight."

"Whoa, hey, you musta knocked back more than one Red Bull this morning—"

"Jeremy, I'm serious. Tell me, why did Dirck get beaten up?"

"Hang on, I wasn't even around. They went after Dirck because he dissed Lisa, called her a hooker. They don't like that."

"Wrong terminology? He got beat up over semantics?"

"She was very unhappy. Look, talking to you just gets me in trouble. I told the cops everything I know and I don't know much. I just pour drinks, okay? Chelsea's my girl and I want to find her more than anyone, but I don't know where to look. I already asked Lisa and she says they've got nothing to do with her going missing."

Jeremy may be dumber than a bowl of Froot Loops, but the belligerence in his voice warns me to dip my spoon carefully. "Sorry, didn't mean to cause you any hassle. You're absolutely positive this guy in the red convertible—"

"Ernie. His name is Ernie something. I barely know him, but he doesn't like being called a pimp. So, yeah, he's got a short temper, but the guy was trying to be helpful to Chelsea, just like Lisa was. People get a little starstruck when it's the movies, you know? They want to be a part of something."

But what I've got by the time we hang up is nothing. If there's anything linking the various incidents of the last few days, I'm not seeing it. I stand at the edge of the pool, staring into its turquoise depths, my thoughts free-floating. There's not so much as a ripple on the surface, nothing on the smooth concrete bottom, and nothing comes to mind to connect a disappearance, two shootings and a street crime. A cloud passes overhead, shadowing the water but offering no pattern, no clues. Perhaps there's no connection, but neither can I accept coincidence. How can it all be random?

I punch up Dirck's number on my cellphone, still warm in my hand. He answers on the first ring but says, "Hey, hang on, hang on—" I listen as he resumes a conversation with someone in his hospital room. By the gist of it, he's speaking with a reporter.

I break in, shouting, "Dirck! Dirck, could I talk to you, please?"

"Almost done, hang on," he bellows, then goes back to his other conversation.

Cellphone pressed to my ear, I walk the length of the pool and back, hearing Dirck call Chelsea "a chip off the old block." Eventually he comes back on the line with me and says, "You heard all of that? Spreading the word is the only way to find Chelsea. Leads are already coming in, with sightings all over the place. It's working, Meg!"

"Still, I'm not sure you should be saying some of these things to the media, especially talking publicly about what happened to Elaine—"

"Stop right there. Chelsea's my kid. This is family stuff you wouldn't understand, okay? Pru's okay with this, so I don't care who else gets bent out of shape, I want to find my kid and get justice for Elaine. That's my mission."

"I think it's what we all want, but this video—"

"You're just jealous because I went out front with this. For once, you're out of the loop and you can't deal with it. I'll tell you something, Meg, you sit in your ivory tower thinking you can pull all the strings. Well, you don't have a clue what it's like for the rest of us who have to struggle and fight for what's right."

"Dirck, for God's sake, where is all this coming from? I'm talking about exposing information on YouTube that could be detrimental to Chelsea. Sometimes you say things that get you into trouble. Just use some restraint."

"What I do is none of your business anymore. If your buddy Halliburton or Ed Ackerman put you up to making this call, tell 'em to butt out. This is family I'm fighting for and I've got the bruises to show for it."

"Okay, okay, I won't say another word. I hope you're feeling better."

"Yeah, thanks. Look, I gotta take another call. It's Anderson Cooper."

I sometimes wonder if Dirck isn't the nightmare version of Clark Kent, longing for glory that comes only with the Superman suit he's been denied. Who can ever make it right for him? Certainly not me, and I have to stop trying.

Seeing the time on my cellphone screen, I hurry back into the house. I stop first in the pantry to scoop cookies into a plastic bag, throw a couple bottles of water in my bag, and then run upstairs to my room to grab some forgotten toiletry items before racing off to meet Corky. A part of me is looking forward to spending time with him, if only to take my mind off everything else. Besides, the park area around the Rancho La Brea Tar Pits is one of my favorite places in Los Angeles.

Located in the Miracle Mile district of museums on Wilshire Boulevard, the tar pits are dark pools of dense oil pushed up by pockets of methane gas that have seeped to the surface for tens of thousands of years. The excavated fossils of prehistoric animals, both predators and prey, that were trapped in the tar are on display in the George C. Page Museum, where I've arranged to meet Corky.

I find metered parking on Sixth Street and walk into the park, struck again by how much it's changed since I first started coming here. I remember a time when I could walk along wooden planks overlooking an excavation pit where volunteers wielded small brushes and instruments in search of fossil fragments. Now, access is more restricted, perhaps just as well. Very recently, one of the tar pits was the site of a murder investigation, with a police diver plumbing the depths in search of human remains.

I spot Corky lying on his back in the grass alongside a footpath, focusing his camera on a cloud formation. I can't resist sneaking up and peering into his lens. "Ready when you are, Mr. DeMille."

Corky sits up, grinning. "I saw your shadow. Knew it was you." He shades his eyes and looks at me more closely. "Wow, what'd you do to your face?"

"Just a little accident." I plop down on the grass next to him and exhume the plastic bag of homemade ginger snaps from my shoulder bag. I hand him one and take one myself. "Expect to find chocolate chips in there. Donna can't resist dumping them into every cookie batter she makes, no matter what the recipe calls for. How're you doing?"

"Good, okay." He nods slowly, as though reconsidering his response, then takes a bite of cookie. He looks down at the grass, chewing slowly. "You're right. Chocolate chips."

"Told ya." I laugh. "Not bad, though."

He nods some more, clearly needing to get something off his chest and working up the courage to do so. Then, in a rush of words, he blurts, "I hope you know I really appreciate all you've done for me. It really means a lot. I sometimes can't believe someone like you would even give me the time of day." His face reddens and he looks away. "I just wanted you to know how I feel. You're, like, totally awesome."

"Thank you. That's very kind of you to say." I wonder if this is presaging a fraught disclosure of just how enamored of me he is. After all, I'm dealing with a boy/man who has tender feelings for Ida Lupino and sees in me her reincarnation.

I proceed with caution. "Corky, you're very talented and it's a pleasure to work with you. Really, I'm learning such a lot from you. But I hope there's not any sort of misunderstanding between us. Is this why you wanted to see me this morning?"

"Well, I've been wanting to tell you that, but there's more." He looks around, growing more uncomfortable. "Could we walk?"

"Of course." I hand him another cookie and we get to our feet. "Let's find someplace in the shade." We start to amble down a footpath behind the museum. "What else is on your mind?"

"My family. That's the real problem."

I feel my own face reddening. "Look, I'm sorry. I hope nothing I've done caused trouble for you at home. If I can undo any damage, please let me know."

"I don't think you can. Besides, I don't think it's your fault. I never thought so. My mother feels the same way. But my dad and uncle, that's another story."

"I was afraid of that. I got the feeling that maybe your mom and Uncle Joe jumped to conclusions. I'm sure they got the impression that something must be going on between us. I'm sorry about that."

Corky gives me a startled look. "When? Why would he think that?"

"No reason, I guess." I backtrack fast, trying to get a handle on what we're talking about. "Your Uncle Joe didn't seem too happy when I arrived. Then later, after we were watching that video you shot in the park, he seemed really upset. I think your mother was okay, but not your uncle."

"Yeah, I know. He and my dad really didn't want you at the house, but my mom said it was okay for you to come. She doesn't blame you."

"For what, exactly? I think we're talking at cross-purposes, here. I need to know what's come up that they don't want me visiting. After all, I've been to your house several times before. We've been filming in your garage."

"But that's before my uncle knew where you lived. See, we didn't always live in the house we're in now. In fact, my parents only rented it about two years ago. We used to live—actually, we had a nice house not too far from where you live, but we lost it. We had to move."

"You lost your house?" I feel myself growing very still and realize I've stopped walking, almost stopped breathing. "How?"

"My uncle invested in a big property development deal and got my dad to buy in, too. Then it all went bust."

"A development up on Mulholland? The one my former husband Paul was involved with?"

"Yeah, 'fraid so."

"I see." My scalp tightens and I feel lightheaded. Whatever I may have thought Corky was going to confide, nothing could be worse than hearing this. I move toward a park bench and sit, the impact of what he's said sinking in. Some of Paul's investors included a few of my well-heeled friends, who lost small fortunes. That was bad enough. But his slick Ponzi scheme, involving overinflated mortgages in a volatile housing market, cost many more people their life savings and, indeed, their homes—something I can never put right. I lost everything, too, including friends, reputation and all that I owned. The real suffering is knowing how much ruin he caused others—including, it appears, the Shaw family.

"I'm so sorry, Corky. I don't know what to say."

He sits down next to me, silent for a long moment before saying, "I know."

"I'm sure there's more. You better tell me the rest of it."

"It kind of wrecked things for us. My mom had a little money set aside after my grandmother died, but otherwise we lost everything. It was worse for Uncle Joe. He'd pulled money out of his printing company, which wasn't doing that well anyway, and lost the business. Even my Aunt Linda left him."

"What about your parents? How're they doing?"

"Sort of okay. My dad still has a job. But it didn't help that my mom told him not to invest and my uncle roped him in anyway. Uncle Joe is my dad's younger brother and was always talking big, so it turned into a real mess."

"You know, when I read your script, I knew where you got your story from. It was pretty obvious to me, but I should've figured out that there was even more behind it. That's why you wanted me to play Gloria."

"Yeah. My mom said writing the script was my way of working things out. The real trouble started when I sent it to you and you said you'd take the role. My parents were shocked. I still can't believe it!"

"Why not? It's a good script." I manage a smile. "Besides, maybe I needed to work some things out, too."

"Okay, good. I feel better." He reaches for the bag of cookies I've left on the bench. "I had to let you know where things stood. I was really embarrassed that my dad and uncle were so rude to you."

"Don't be. I hardly blame them. It must be difficult for them to see me around and be reminded of all they lost because of Paul. But they don't think I had any involvement in the fraud, do they? They know I was cleared, right?"

"That's what my mom told them, but—" Corky kicks at the grass.

"I ended up losing everything, too. Absolutely everything I ever earned and owned was taken from me. Do they know that?"

"Sort of. I mean, it said in the newspapers that you went bankrupt. And, of course, you didn't go to jail. I think at first they were okay with me knowing you. They went along with it, but then at the park—"

"With your Uncle Joe? What happened then?"

"He saw where you lived."

My mouth drops open as realization hits. "He thinks that house is mine? It isn't! I'm only staying there with a friend. Is that why you and your mother drove by that day?"

He nods. "She wanted to see for herself. On the one hand, she's really glad for all you've done for me, but it's hard for them to see how you're living when they lost everything because—"

"I understand." I flash on the images Corky recorded of us that afternoon in the park when Chelsea arrived, followed by the montage of us walking, talking and sitting down at the picnic table. Worse, I recall the final images of myself posing with the top hat on my head, laughing and waving into the camera as the gates opened to Donna's house. "Your uncle must have been livid. I am so sorry."

"I hope you don't mind that I told you."

"No, of course not. I'm glad you did. I don't know if it would help, but maybe I could talk to your family and explain."

"Can't happen!" He shakes his head vehemently. "My mom promised my dad I wouldn't see you anymore. I wanted to let you know that."

"So your mother doesn't know you planned to meet me this morning?"

He shakes his head, looking miserable. "She just dropped me off. I told her I'd take the bus home when I finished shooting here."

"Maybe I could talk to your Uncle Joe. Where does he live?"

"We don't know." Corky shrugs. "He won't say. He won't let my mom drive him home, just to the bus stop."

"He doesn't have a car?"

"Sometimes he borrows ours, but otherwise he takes the bus. Or bikes."

"When you see him next time, would you tell him I'd just like to talk with him? You can even give him my phone number. I want him to at least hear the truth."

I shake my head, feeling sick. How many other people like Corky Shaw's family were devastated by my former husband's scam? Paul Stevens—only one of his many aliases—was a con-man. Even if I'd had a reason to look into his background, I couldn't have known he'd served time in prison—and that was only the beginning of the secrets he kept from me. I'm aware that there will always be people who will wonder what I knew, when I knew it.

Jack, of course. Surprisingly, even me. While I played no active role in Paul's business dealings, there were red flags I overlooked. I should have had suspicions, but did I want to know the truth? I loved Paul with abandon and chose to trust, not question. The terrible guilt I feel for the consequences of turning a blind eye haunts me and, I fear, will always shadow my relationship with Jack.

"You want to walk some more?" Corky asks, breaking into my thoughts. He slings a canvas bag onto his shoulder and stands up. "I should probably catch a bus."

"You're through filming?"

"I didn't really have any to do."

I hand him the plastic bag containing the rest of the cookies. "C'mon, let me drive you back. I can drop you at the bus stop near your house. Your mom won't know."

18

"I feel like we should be in a parade or something," Corky says, climbing into the front seat of the Olds 98. He regards the vintage seat belt a moment, a relic manufactured before he was born, then plugs it in. "Maybe I could use your car in a film someday?"

"Sure thing."

I start the engine and we're both quiet, realizing there probably won't be a next time if his parents forbid him to associate with me. This turn of events is more troubling than I care to admit. I like Corky. It's hurtful to no longer be considered a suitable mentor to him for reasons entirely beyond my control.

"What'd you think of the video I sent you last night about Chelsea?"

"Disturbing." I swing down a residential street and onto Wilshire Boulevard, the La Brea Tar Pits visible on my right. "I'm sorry Dirck posted it. How did you happen to see it?"

"I've got Chelsea Horne on Google Alert. She is really hot. I don't think my uncle thinks much of her, though. He calls her a spoiled brat."

"What would give him that idea?" My hands tighten on the steering wheel. "Wait, when did he say this to you? Last night?"

"Yeah. When he called, I'd just come across the YouTube video."

"And when you mentioned Chelsea, he said, 'She's a spoiled brat.' Interesting. Did he ask about me at all?"

"He asked if I was going to film any reshoots with you. But then I told him I wasn't supposed to see you anymore."

"Did he say any more about Chelsea?"

"Um, he didn't like it that I thought she was hot. And he got really mad when I told him about the YouTube video and what your husband was saying."

"Former husband. Technically speaking, my former, former husband."

"I know. Chelsea's father. Anyway, Uncle Joe told me to forget about her."

"I see." What I'm hearing opens up troubling concerns, but I don't want to risk pressing Corky too hard. I keep my suspicions to myself as I pull into the left turn lane on Fairfax Avenue and smile at him. "Well, you're absolutely right and your Uncle Joe is wrong. She is definitely hot."

"Yeah." He grins. "I hope I haven't given you a really bad impression of my family. They're nice people, but this has been a bad time for them. They'll come around."

"You're right. Things will get better. So, Uncle Joe works as a printer? Do you know where?"

"No. He got a job with someone who used to work for him, but I don't know his name or where the place is. They do printing but sell boxes and supplies wholesale. With all these big chains taking business away, it's really tough."

"Is there any chance you have some of that video in your camera that I could see again?"

"Oh, yeah, hang on." He slides a laptop out of his canvas bag. "Got it all here."

"Great. After all those cookies, I could go for a cup of coffee. How about if I pull up to that donut shop for a minute and we can take a look."

At a speed Edie would have found alarming, I swing her yellow Olds into a run-down mini-mall and park. Corky sits at a metal table in the shade while I go inside to buy a container of coffee and a Coke. By the time I return, he's pulled up the video he shot of Chelsea in the park. After watching it again, I ask to see some of the other video from that day.

"It was nice of your uncle to help you out. Where'd you go after we saw you?"

"We drove around the neighborhood, then passed by where we used to live. I figured he'd feel better about my project if he could be a part of it and see what I do. That's why I gave him the role of the bookie."

"Good thinking." We watch the video as the camera sweeps along a leafy residential street in a Westwood neighborhood, then stops at a two-story traditional house with an attached glass arboretum. "Charming! So this was your former house?"

"This was Uncle Joe's. We lived three blocks away. He hadn't been back there since he and my aunt had to move out."

Remembering how hard it was for me to drive by my own house after new owners had moved in, I ask, "How did he take seeing it again?"

Corky's hand hovers over the keyboard a moment, then he abruptly shuts off the video. "It probably wasn't such a good thing to go by there, but it was his idea. He sorta broke down and started saying things and blaming people for robbing him. But nothing was going good for him anyway. That's what my mom says." Corky flips the lid down on his computer. "Maybe it's better not to go into this. I hear stuff my parents say and I shouldn't talk about it. You'll think even less of my family."

"Please, I understand. I don't mean to pry. Why don't you finish your Coke and I'll drop you off? We don't need to say another word about this."

"Good, because I want us to be friends." He slurps his cola, looking relieved. "Maybe we can still email?"

"Of course. Whatever you're comfortable with." There are still more questions I want to ask, but I don't want Corky to pick up on the suspicions forming in my mind.

Parked in the hot sun, the Olds is an oven. "My God, we could bake cookies in here," I say, rolling down the windows. Corky laughs. "Why don't you tell me about your next film project?"

I drive leisurely, taking a longer route than necessary to give him time to talk about his new script. As we approach his neighborhood, he directs me to the bus stop. I drive up to the curb just as a bus is pulling out. "Sorry I can't take you all the way home. Is that bus up there the one your uncle takes?"

"No, it's another number." He starts to open the door. "Thanks again for understanding."

I reach over and touch his arm. "Listen to me, you have a great family, and I am very sorry for all you're going through. I wish none of it had happened to any of us. I hope your Uncle Joe calls me so I can talk with him."

"Me, too. Maybe it will help."

"By the way, yesterday you said that Chelsea had already left when you filmed me going into Donna's house. Did you think Chelsea and I had finished work and she'd gone home?"

"Yeah, why? You were alone."

"Right. You and Joe didn't see her, of course, because she'd already gone through the gates. Then after you finished filming that afternoon, Joe took you home and caught the bus here?"

"Not exactly." Corky blows his cheeks out and shakes his head. "Uncle Joe dropped me at the house and then drove off again. My mom was furious because she needed the car and he didn't bring it back until late."

"And there was no way to reach him? He doesn't have a cell-phone?"

"No, when he calls it's from a payphone. So that was the end of letting him use our car anymore. My dad was even angry with me, like it was my fault."

"That's what families are like." I smile sympathetically. "But you and I are still friends, so keep in touch."

He beams. "Thanks for saying that."

Corky climbs out of the car just as another bus pulls in front of me. "Maybe your Uncle Joe will be on that bus," I say offhand-edly.

"Could be. That's his route." He rolls his eyes and gives me a look. "But I sure hope not. That's all I need." He shuts the door and waves as he walks away.

I wave back and wait for the bus to pull out, then follow it. My hands are tight on the steering wheel, processing everything I've heard about Uncle Joe. I go through a rough timetable in my head. After filming me entering the gates to Donna's house, Joe and Corky probably drove a mile or so into the residential streets of Westwood. Allowing for more filming in addition to dropping Corky off and driving back again during rush hour traffic, could his uncle have been in Holmby Park by the time Chelsea left after our session together? Indeed, possible. Then what happened?

While following the bus from one stop to the next, I play out various scenarios in my head. Was Joe Shaw angry enough that he came back to try and see me? Did he try to enter the grounds? Did he run into Chelsea as he was deciding what to do? She had time to make two phone calls, so . . . could he have offered her a lift? Followed her? Why? Did he even speak to her? If so, what did he want?

Occupying my mind with these questions helps me put off asking myself why in the world I am following a bus. Do I really expect to see Joe Shaw on a street corner? Sidewalks in Los Angeles are mostly devoid of pedestrian traffic anyway, and I hardly expect to encounter him out for a stroll.

The futility of this exercise is compounded by the cost of the fuel I'm using to stalk a city bus. I've already exceeded my limited budget with the purchase of the coffee and cola. That thought leads me to think of the life Joe must be leading if he, too, has gone through bankruptcy and lost everything. Unlike me, he doesn't have a car to live in. Can he afford a room somewhere? As the bus lumbers ahead, I try to put myself in Joe's place. After all, I have some familiarity with what he's experiencing.

I travel past used-car lots, industrial sites, big-box stores, derelict streets where every shop window has an iron grill, and still other neighborhoods just on the verge of gentrification. The proliferation of nail salons seems to cross all demographics; I begin to count them, then realize it would be more useful to keep my eye out for print shops.

Throughout what seems like a senseless hour-long journey, I have the odd sensation that Joe Shaw is somewhere in the vicinity just ahead. I realize I am now obsessed, unable to stop and turn around. I also know that even if my suspicions about Joe prove to be true, I can't help but feel sorry for him.

Eventually the bus pulls to the curb and stops. The last of the passengers get off. A moment later, its bulk shudders and sags as the motor is turned off. Stopped two car lengths behind, I drive up close to the curb and turn off the ignition. I sit back, looking around, then see the bus driver, a heavyset woman with thin, bleached hair, step onto the sidewalk. She swings her arms above and across her body, exercising, but her eyes are on me. I climb out of the Olds and walk toward her.

"You must like the smell of exhaust," she says as I approach. "Most people are trying to dodge around me."

I smile. "You saw me back there?"

"Hard to miss in that showboat you're driving. My brother had one of those." She's got a friendly face and a voice to match. "You lost?"

I nod. "I'm not too familiar with the area."

"Didn't think so!" Her laugh is hearty. Then recognition dawns. "Don't I know you from *Holiday*? You're Jinx Fogarty. I just saw you on *The Today Show* not long ago."

"Hi, I'm Meg. Nice to meet you." I shake her hand.

"Lucille," she says, peering into my face. "Looks like you tangled with an alley cat and the cat won."

"No, just a minor car accident. Anyway, I wondered if this was the end of the line."

"Nope, but this is as far as I go on my schedule. What can I do you for, my dear?"

"A guy I know takes this bus route. His name's Joe Shaw. He's tall, sort of stocky. Dark eyes."

"Tall, stocky, dark eyes? Name's Joe? You kidding me?" She laughs, rocking back on her heels. "You're asking if I know this guy from the route?" She laughs again. "Sorry, Jinx, that describes half the guys riding the bus. The other half are *short* and stocky with dark eyes."

I laugh along with her. "Anyway, it was worth asking."

"That's okay. Wish I could help. I been driving this route a good five years." She starts walking to the corner, still swinging her arms. I keep in step with her. "Sorry, gotta stretch my legs. Anything else about this guy? Maybe a beard?"

"No, clean-shaven." I look across at the bus and notice a metal frame attached to the front. "Is that for bikes?"

"Yeah. Not all buses have racks. Your guy travels with a bike?"

"Maybe, at least sometimes."

"Okay, not a lot of people use the rack, but there's a guy, kind of tall, that I sometimes pick up maybe seven, eight stops back. It's just down from a towing place. There's a body shop on the corner. He's a mean son-of-a-gun, sits up front, never takes his eyes off his bike because you can't lock 'em to the rack. He's always afraid it's gonna get stolen. Don't know his name. Never says a word."

"Sounds about right."

"And this is a guy you want to find? You could sure do better!" She tips her head toward the bus. "You can follow me, if you want. I go around the block and head back in maybe fifteen minutes after I get some coffee."

"That's okay. I can probably find it. Thanks!"

"Hey, you mind saying it? You know—"

"Awfully good of you, my dear!"

"All in a day's work!" she says, laughing, as I sprint to my car.

Ace Towing would be hard to miss, located where the last remaining dilapidated turn-of-the-century mansions are either being torn down or moved to more gentrified neighborhoods. I remember seeing the junkyard as I passed by, an urban wasteland locked within a thick grid of metal pipe and steel fencing topped with rolls of razor wire. I drive by slowly, seeing that the entrance to the enclosure is through a narrow L-shaped wire cage, presumably another deterrent to anyone bent on theft.

I make a turn at the corner, cruise down the street and find an alley behind the towing lot. I make another turn and travel down a broken, bulging cement strip past padlocked, wood-frame, two-story garage units from an era when the help lived above the family car. At the corner, I turn again and see the body shop on the corner. I park in a shaded space, leaving the motor running, feeling entirely too conspicuous in Edie's blast-from-the-past Olds Regency.

I glance toward the back end of the junkyard and see the frame of a Volvo hunkered in the dirt, separated from her chassis, and feel a pang of longing. If only I had my old plain-wrap Volvo back!

But as conspicuous as my car is, I'm reluctant to step out onto the street, where I'd stick out like a sore thumb. The midday sun is still scorching the pavement. People aren't out walking around for their health in this quasi-industrial area. I sit back and take stock, the Olds idling while I decide what to do. I could wait to see if Joe turns up at the bus stop on the corner. I could also scout the area for a print shop where he might be working. What are the chances that the tall, stocky man with dark eyes and a bike, who catches a bus on this street corner, is Joe Shaw? My prickling scalp tells me the odds are good.

But if Joe is out there, I'd just as soon surprise him rather than let him spot me first. I rummage through Edie's glove compartment again and find a bright bandana. Sliding my hand under the seats, I come across an old gob hat. I flip the rim down into a tight, unstylish cloche and pull it onto my head, which at least conceals my ginger hair. With the addition of my Ray-Bans and the jaunty bandana, it's the best I can do to disguise myself.

It's not the sort of neighborhood that Edie's Olds 98 is accustomed to visiting. With no alarm system, and an old-fashioned, non-electronic key, the Regency would be easy to hotwire. I lock the door and walk away, hoping there's some residual benefit to all those early-morning trips Edie and her car made to attend mass at Good Shepherd.

A bus pulls up just as I reach the corner and toots twice. Lucille waves; so much for my attempt at masking my identity with a hat and a kerchief. I wave back.

I look up and down the street and see a couple of fast-food joints, a liquor store, a nail salon and a shop with a window advertising tropical fish, but no print shop. With my sandals starting to burn into the soles of my feet, I decide to check out Ace Towing, where at least there's the shade of an awning.

A surly-looking woman wearing oversized coveralls with the name "Mort" stitched above a zippered pocket sits in a cubicle behind a scratched Plexiglas window. I take in the myriad stained and curling signs tacked around the booth, all of them demanding payment in cash for exorbitant towing and storage fees.

The woman addresses me without looking up. "Yeah? Whaddya want?"

Her bark could penetrate lead, but I respond with a smile in my voice. "Hi, how're you doing? I was wondering if Joe Shaw—"

Still not looking up, she says, "Night watchman. He doesn't start his shift until nine o'clock. You can go around to the alley and see if he's in. Number eight."

"Number eight?" I repeat dumbly.

"Yeah, eight. You from the print shop?"

I nod. "Yeah, the print shop. He wasn't there, so—"

She shakes her head. "Sometimes he takes a late lunch. You want me to call him?"

"No need. I'll come back later. He knows me."

"Maybe you better talk to Mort." She nods in the direction of the junkyard.

A potbellied man wearing coveralls with "Mort" stitched above the pocket emerges from a shed and ambles toward me. Hands in pocket, looking affable, he sizes me up as I approach. He gives me a genial nod and asks, "Looking for Joe?"

"Yes, hi. You're Mort, too?"

"We're all Mort. Makes it easier. We get the jumpsuits cheap."

I offer up an appreciative chuckle. "Look, I'm really early. I'll come back later. Besides, Joe knows how to reach me."

Mort looks a little less affable. "We're not too formal around here, but maybe I could tell him who's calling. You know, if you're a bill collector, he kinda likes to know in advance."

I break out my widest smile. "C'mon, a bill collector? Gimme a break. Joe and I go way back." I start moving toward the wire-enclosed entrance. "I'll just head back down to the print shop."

"It's up the street, not down," Mort says.

"Right, depends which way you're coming," I laugh. "Nice meeting you, Mort."

I hurry back out of the yard. The woman in the booth glances up as I pass through the metal turnstile. It's a quick look, but gives me time enough to see that her left eye is bruised and her lips suck in where teeth are missing. A flicker of acknowledgment flashes in her eyes and I realize she's seeing a kindred spirit in my battered face. My God, what have I walked into?

Back on the street, I take a deep breath, knowing it's time to let someone know where I am. Jack is out of town. Donna is my best bet until I see if my hunch pays off. I head back toward my car, checking messages on my phone as I decide what to do next. I'm not even sure where I am.

I return down the street toward the alley, looking for some indication of "number eight." Then I see that the two-story garage units are marked numerically. I walk down the crumbling cement drive until I reach a sagging wood-frame building with a pad-locked double door on the ground floor and a small grimy window up above.

I move closer to the building and start to call Donna, then decide to text instead. I tap out a message, cc'ing Jack: *Looking for Corky's uncle, Joe Shaw . . . I'm in an alley behind Ace Towing . . .* I stop, trying to remember the cross street as my eyes fall on the padlock. It's new. The hasp is old and rusty. The observation barely registers as I hear a sound behind me and turn.

Just as Joe's gun slams my wrist, I clamp my thumb down on Send. My cellphone crashes to the cement, shattering. For good measure, Joe steps on it, grinding my phone beneath his shoe.

19

My eyes lock on Joe's, but I see the tremor in his hand holding the gun.

My own hand is shaking from the blow to my wrist. I rub it gently, trying to ease the pain. "I'm afraid we got off to a bad start, Joe. After talking with Corky this morning, I wanted to speak with you. I think you may have a misimpression about me."

"Well, doesn't that just make all the difference," he says, the sarcasm delivered in icy tones. His lips spread in a semblance of a smile, but his eyes are hard. "I'm going to give you a key and you are going to unlock the padlock. You'll open the door and we will enter. Keep in mind that a gun will be aimed at your head the entire time, understand?"

"Of course. I presume it's the same gun that failed to kill me the first time. Or the second."

A convulsive tremor jerks his upper body. I flinch in response and see the gun waver in his hand. His eyes are frozen in hatred and he's breathing through his mouth, almost panting. "Third time lucky."

I see no resemblance to the courtly man in the suit and fedora who charmed me with his old-world manners. His voice is a hoarse croak, his agitation palpable, signaling just how tightly he's wound.

He could shoot me now, but he's too close. His hand trembles with the weight of the gun, the indecision. I can smell his sweat, the fear. He's fighting for control just as I am.

With that flash of awareness, a chill sweeps over me, freeing my mind. Remaining motionless, I relax my weight against the rough wood of the garage door, weighing my chances. He's tall, muscular. I'm braced solidly, my weight on one foot. All it would take is a swift kick and a lurch to the side when he hands me the key—

Then his other hand opens and he flips the key onto the cement drive. He steps back, giving himself distance from me. "No stupid moves. Pick it up."

"Wait, could I have a word with you first?"

He responds by waving the gun. I make a show of rubbing my wrist, wincing, stalling for time. I look across the alley to the back end of the towing lot, hoping to see movement, perhaps one of the Morts. I strain to hear voices, but there's only the distant sound of traffic on the boulevard.

He waves the gun again. I move to pick up the key, turning my body at an angle and reaching to the side in case he intends to strike my head with the butt of the gun.

My eyes fall on the smashed cellphone, wondering if my message was received. Failing to reach me, would Donna try to call Corky, knowing I'd arranged to meet him? Would she ask about Joe Shaw? Would Jack try to track down Ace Towing? Would either of them even sense the urgency . . . or just wonder if the Olds 98 broke down and I had to have my car towed? What I do know is that once I'm in the garage, I've lost any advantage I may have.

What would Jinx do—that is, if she didn't have a posse of seasoned writers plotting her every move? I could pretend to faint. I could take my chances screaming. I could just hold my ground and not move. What would Joe do then?

"You're wasting time." He waves the gun toward the garage. "If you want to see your little friend, I suggest you open the door."

There's my reason. *Chelsea.* I pick up the key, flimsy and almost weightless in my hand, and move toward the padlocked door. If Chelsea is inside, I can't take any more chances until I see how she is. The key slides in easily, but I have to yank on the rusting hasp to open the door.

Dust motes dance in the light filtering into the cool darkness. The space is almost completely taken up by an old, light-blue Corolla hatchback.

"So you do have a car, after all."

"Not mine." He prods my back with the gun. "Keep moving, off to the left."

It has to be Chelsea's car. I skirt the Corolla on the driver's side, almost tripping against a bike leaning against the wall. I reach out to catch myself, my hand brushing against a wheel. I glance down and see the tread, recalling the crosshatched marks in the dirt near where somebody shot at me. Who would think twice about a guy on a bike in a park? A guy on a bike probably killed Elaine, then sped silently across darkened Holmby Park to make his getaway. I figure it was Joe.

"Keep moving. Stop at the stairs in the back."

I hear the garage door pulled closed behind me. Wedged between the car and the wall of the garage, I edge forward, my eyes adjusting to the dark. Pale light filters down on a spiral staircase in the back. I grip the metal and wait. The garage was built at a time when cars were smaller than Chelsea's hatchback. There would barely be enough room to stand back and open the doors. I try to imagine the logistics of holding someone hostage while maneuvering a car into this space.

"Okay, up the stairs, one step at a time."

Daylight sifts through the dust-caked window. Chest-high to the floor, I pause on the steps and look around. Obviously the living space is not up to code, but there's a cot in one corner with a rag rug on the wood floor next to it. A molded white plastic unit in another corner appears to be a shower. A curtain hangs open on a suspended metal ring around a toilet and sink. Next to the cot is a small microwave on top of a miniature refrigerator. But where's Chelsea?

I feel the gun barrel tap against my shin. "Move!"

Rounding the top of the stairs, I grasp a metal post for support. Out of the corner of my eye, I see Joe mounting the stairs, one hand on the railing, the other holding the gun. I grip the post tightly, shifting my weight in preparation for a sharp kick to Joe's head. He stops, his gun aimed at my head.

"Move, I said!"

I take a few steps deeper into the room and see a rubber air mattress against the wall to the side of the stairs. A gray army blanket covers a bulky form, matted blond hair spilling across the mattress onto the floor.

"Oh my God, no!" In three strides, I reach the mattress and sink to my knees, my hand touching a shoulder. "What have you done?"

"She's not dead. I'm not dragging a corpse out of here."

I gently pull the blanket off her face. Her eyes are closed, her lips parted. I brush my fingers across her forehead and her eyes pop open, blinking at me rapidly. "Chelsea? Are you okay?" She blinks again and I realize she's signaling me.

I look up at Joe, who's sitting on the cot, holding the gun. "I think she's unconscious. What'd you do to her?"

"Nothing. She won't eat."

"Is that what makes her a spoiled brat? Maybe she doesn't like the accommodations."

He doesn't answer. I glance toward the cobwebbed rafters, pulling the neck of my tee shirt over my nose to shut out the putrid air. I breathe in the scent of my own body and look at Joe again. He's sweating, his pallor more apparent in the gloom. I realize he's panting for air again. Is it stress or illness? I shift my body and lean against the pole, pulling my tee shirt down.

"How long have you been living like this? You look like you need a doctor."

"Can't afford one," he pants. "Don't need one anymore."

I lower my voice, seeking a soothing register. "I'm so very sorry, Joe. I know how that is."

"Like hell!"

"Yeah, it's exactly like hell." I speak slowly, keeping my voice as neutral as possible. "I really do know what it's like. For me, it was sleeping in my car, waking up to every sound in the night. I had nowhere to turn. Nothing left to hang on to. I felt humiliated. Angry. Wanting only to hide. Like you, I was robbed. For me, it was by my own husband. Trust me, Joe, I've walked in your shoes. Thanks to a friend with a big heart and a nice house, I'm off the streets."

Without warning, he grabs a heavy work shoe off the floor and hurls it at me, striking me in the shoulder. "Don't make me laugh! You were in on it! Your kind never suffers."

I wince, choosing my words carefully. "Joe, I can't tell you how sorry I am about everything you and everyone else lost. The man responsible for that is in prison now. You want me to pay for what's happened. But I had no part in what Paul did to you and so many others. If I could put things right, I would."

"Liar! You drive fancy cars. Spend your days hanging out with kids, playing around. It's all a game to you. You have no idea the pain!"

"This is not a game." I nod toward Chelsea. "Does she know what happened? What you did the other night?"

He looks away. "It was a mistake, right?" I wait for a response, leaving the question hanging before answering it myself. "That's what I figured. It was just a mistake made in the dark of the night. You're not a bad man, Joe. You're not someone who would do this. I don't think you even had a plan."

His eyes narrow. "You don't know anything."

"You're right. I'm just guessing that you came back after dropping Corky off. I think you mistook Chelsea for me in the twilight. You didn't know she had come up to the house with me. Once she saw you with a gun, you had no choice. Maybe you thought I'd figure out how to come and find her, but I didn't. This is about getting at me, not anyone else. You've got me here now. You can let her go."

The gun wavers in his hand. His lips move, but there's barely a sound. He speaks again and I hear, "Too late."

"Not too late," I say firmly. "Don't let it end like this. You've already taken one life. Let her live. Her life's just beginning."

I watch his shoulders slump. He stares into the middle distance, as though trying to make up his mind. I know better than to say anything. A minute passes, maybe two, then he shifts his gaze, regarding me with detachment. When he speaks, his voice is stronger. "Your keys. Give them to me."

"My car keys? You're taking my car?"

"Just moving it. We don't want anyone seeing it, do we?" His smile is almost friendly. "I won't be gone long."

I take the keys out of the front pocket of my shoulder bag and slide them across the floor. "You'll let her go?"

His smile fades. He stands and looms over me, unbuckling his belt with his free hand. I shrink back, tensing for whatever he might have in mind. He walks behind me to the spiral stairs. "Don't move!" he barks. Leaning down, he slings the belt around my chest, securing my arms, and yanks me tightly against the metal support pole before fastening the buckle. He lashes my hands together with a flexible tie, locking them tightly palm-to-palm.

"That should hold you until I get back."

I close my eyes, my head falling forward, waiting for a blow to my head I'm certain is coming. Instead, I hear him going down the stairs, the pole jarring against my back with each heavy footfall. The garage doors creak open, then slam shut. I hear a soft rustling sound next to me.

"Welcome to summer camp," Chelsea says, struggling to sit up. "But I don't need visitors. I need to get the hell out of here!"

"Sorry, I know. I'm hoping someone picks up the text message I sent. How are you doing?"

"You kidding? Food's terrible. He microwaves burritos. I'm vegetarian. Curfew's around the clock." Words spill out of her in a rush, but she looks wan, emaciated. Her eyes are dark holes in a pale face, her lips parched. She shakes off the blanket. Not surprisingly, she's wearing the same tee shirt and jeans I last saw her in. Her feet are bound, her wrists secured. She holds up her hands to show me the thin, flexible band locking them together.

"It's a bitch if you need to scratch. Trust me, after four days I itch."

"Thank God you're alive. It's been five days already. Did he hurt you?"

"Five days? Time flies when you're having fun." Her eyes well and tears roll down her cheeks. "I fought like hell when he got me here. Lot of good it did me." She turns her head into the light, revealing a bruised cheek and greenish swelling around her left eye. "Why the hell did you come on your own? He's crazy! He's not going to just let us go, whatever you say."

I swing my legs over to my shoulder bag, hooking the strap with the toe of my sandal, and slide it toward Chelsea. "Check inside. See what you find. I think there's a nail clipper somewhere."

She grabs the bag with her bare feet and pulls it toward her. "He's barely here. But when he is, he rants. Nonstop. He's crazy!"

"I'm so sorry. There was no reason for him to take you."

I expand my chest against the belt, leaning as far as I can from the pole, then contracting, trying to wiggle my arms loose. I glance at Chelsea, who's rummaging in the bag. "Has he hurt you otherwise?"

"No, not like that. It's like he forgets I'm even here. When he goes out, he ties a dirty rag around my mouth. I crawl to the toilet and back. Stare at the walls. I never hear a sound from outside." A water bottle rolls out of the bag. She clamps it between her knees, twisting the cap loose with her fingers. "God, I was stupid!"

"What happened?" I inch the belt up my body, at the same time forcing my hands against the plastic strip. "Tell me what he did."

"I was trying to call this guy Ernie, who'd dropped me off. I was going to grab a bite to eat with him and his girlfriend, Lisa, before they took me back to my car. Then I hear a sound in the bushes behind me and it's that guy holding a gun, calling me a bitch and a lying thief."

"Until he realized you weren't me."

"Right. But that didn't matter." Chelsea bends over the plastic bottle, seizing it with her teeth and lifting it to tip water into her mouth. I watch her struggle, her chest heaving with every swallow, water spilling down her chin. She lets the near-empty bottle fall into her lap, then digs back into the bag.

"He held the gun on me, forcing me to get into his car and making me drive it here. I kept looking for a chance to run a red light, crash into something, but—hang on, found it!" She pulls out the nail clippers and twists her fingers to pry them open.

"So he locked you up here, then left—"

"With my car keys, yeah. Like an idiot, I'd told him where the car was parked. I kept hoping Ernie would see him taking it, but—anyway, an hour or so later, I hear him driving into the garage. He brought me a burrito." She begins nipping away at the black plastic tie. "Still, I feel sorry for him."

I don't respond, knowing Chelsea isn't aware that Joe killed her mother. I expand and contract my chest, shrugging my shoulders to work my way out of the belt.

"Joe's a night watchman at the towing yard. I suspect that's where he's moving my car. I figure we have ten minutes, tops. How are you doing, Chelsea?"

"Close, close," she mumbles, then lifts a hand with the cut strap dangling from her wrist. "Let me get my feet undone, then I'll free you." She shifts on the air mattress, pulling my Jinx hat, scuffed and flattened, from under the blanket. "Sorry, no time to practice." She flicks it across the floor to me.

"Bad girl. You shouldn't have taken it in the first place." I grunt, exerting as much strength as I can muster to loosen the belt around my arms. "I bet you were wearing it when you walked out of the gates, right?"

"You think this is a bad karma thing because of your dumb hat?" She cuts through the strap binding her feet, giving me a triumphant look.

"Yeah, because it made him think you were me—wait, he's back!"

We both freeze at the sound of the garage door creaking open. I barely breathe listening to the scrape as the door is closed again. There's a shuffling sound, then the clatter of something metal. The car door is unlatched and a moment later, the engine is started.

I dart a look to Chelsea, who mouths, "He's leaving!"

I shake my head and whisper, "No, the garage doors are closed."

The realization of what he's doing hits both of us as exhaust fumes rise quickly up the stairs in the small space. Chelsea's eyes widen in panic. She moves next to me, reaching behind my back with the nail clippers.

"Cut, but leave them in place," I whisper. I feel the strip go slack and hold the ends closed with my hand. She tugs the belt up my chest, freeing my arms, but leaves the leather draped around my shoulders.

We freeze again at the sound of a heavy thud against the wall, then a footfall on the stairs. Chelsea dives back to the air mattress, her movements fluid and silent as she pulls the gray blanket over her body. My head falls forward, my palms holding the loose end of the flexible strip in place around my wrists.

Each footstep is slow, followed by a metallic thud. The room is darker now as sunlight fades from the grubby window. I pray Joe doesn't look too closely at my hands bound to the support pole. His arm brushes against my back as he nears the top of the steps and heaves a metal container onto the floor.

My eyes flick sideways and I see that it's a red fuel canister. I also see the muzzle of the gun in his hand just inches from my cheek as he moves past me. In the instant it takes me to flash on seizing the gun, the moment passes. My heart thuds with the adrenalin rush. I try to slow my breathing as the exhaust fumes begin to make me lightheaded.

I watch Joe out of the corner of my eye. He stops next to the cot, panting, and looks at me. "No mistakes this time."

"Please, Joe," I whisper. "Don't do this."

"It's done."

He sets the canister on the floor and grunts with the effort of kneeling down next to it. He pulls a lighter out of his pocket, then lays his gun down as he tips the canister onto its side and starts to twist the cap.

I try to isolate the movement of my hand from my upper arm, still wrapped in the belt, as my fingers inch toward the black disk on the floor near my hip. My action is so quick I barely realize the disk has left my hand until I see it slam into Joe's throat, knocking him backward. I scrabble across the floor, pitching my body against his, my elbow cutting up under his chin as I grab the gun.

"The window!" I shout.

Chelsea grabs the work shoe and hurls it through the window. Glass shatters as she dashes around me, pitching herself onto Joe, kicking and pounding him with her fists. He rolls sideways, his hands clawing at his neck, gasping for breath. Chelsea rocks back on her haunches and I hand her the gun.

I turn to the window, fill my lungs, then bunch the bandana to my nose and fly down the steps, my feet barely touching the treads. The car door is open. My eyes stinging, my lungs bursting, I reach across the steering wheel to the ignition.

With the engine turned off, I struggle toward the garage door. It's latched, the padlock hanging open. I fall against the rough wood, my fingers feeling pudgy and disconnected as I groggily reach for the padlock.

In the distance I hear sirens, or perhaps it's just a painful ringing in my ears. The doors give way and I fall to the ground.

20

It turns out Lucille, the bus driver, is the unlikely guardian angel responsible for our dramatic rescue. It's against the rules for city transit drivers to tweet behind the wheel, although Lucille claims she sent the message at a bus stop, her feet firmly on the pavement—but her tweet saved our hides:

#JinxFogarty fans: just spotted her @AceTowing on Crenshaw in her yellow Olds. Hey Joe she's looking 4 u. Ur in trouble now!

In under 140 characters, with a fortuitous hashtag, Lucille's tweet ricocheted to the right quarters, including Corky, his mother and, oddly enough, Detective Yarrow. Donna, alerted by my text, got in touch with Corky, then the police. But Lucille's tweet had given Christine Yarrow a good start tracking me down.

Jack was in the passenger lounge of Seattle-Tacoma International Airport when he received my text. He called Donna, then Detective Yarrow. By the time he boarded his flight, the two were in direct communication and he knew I was safe. As I lay strapped to a gurney, breathing through an oxygen mask, she pressed her cellphone to my ear. Through a woozy fog, I heard Jack's husky whisper.

"Thank God you're okay. I'm so sorry I'm not there with you. How are you feeling?"

"Okay, but please . . . hurry back."

"I'll be there as soon as I can. We're about to take off. I love you, darling."

Tears streamed down my cheeks. "I love you, too."

"It's what I wanted to hear, Meg. Love you. Bye, see you soon."

It's what I wanted to hear, as well, and this time there was no mistaking what Jack meant. Christine Yarrow pocketed her cellphone, then wiped away my tears.

"I'm glad you're safe. We all are." She smiled and patted my arm. "But I'd rather you stick to playing Jinx onscreen than endangering yourself like this again."

"I will," I said, because I knew it was what she wanted to hear. But then I looked over at Chelsea, strapped to another gurney, an oxygen mask on her face. I'd owed it to her. Had it not been for me, she wouldn't have been kidnapped and her mother would still be alive.

After being treated by paramedics, Chelsea and I were transported to a hospital for an overnight stay. For Chelsea, learning that her kidnapper had also killed her mother only compounded the harrowing ordeal. I broke the news to her myself, knowing it couldn't be kept from her for long. I explained as gently as I could what had happened.

"Her visit was a surprise. You couldn't have known about it. Unfortunately, I think Joe mistook her for me that night. I'm so sorry. Dirck was there, too. We'd had dinner together at Donna's house beforehand, all of us concerned because you were missing."

"So stupid, it's all so stupid," Chelsea sobbed. I held her close, comforting her. "Mom was upset that Dirck was working as my coach and said terrible things to get me to drop him. If it's all come out, then you probably know that he's my father. Did she tell you that?"

"No, but I found out. Obviously, it was a surprise to Dirck, too."

"After all my mother did for me, I should've left well enough alone. She didn't want me to know, but once I did, she couldn't stop me from looking him up. It really hurt her. I never let on to him who I was, but I didn't tell her that."

Joe Shaw died from cardiac arrest before an ambulance arrived. For the Shaw family, learning of Joe's crimes was a shocking blow. I felt especially sorry for Corky's father, who blamed himself for not recognizing how deeply troubled and ill his younger brother was.

By the time Jack got to the hospital, I was sitting up in bed, nursing a sore wrist and a bad headache. "I know," I said when I saw his anxious face. "We have to stop meeting like this."

"Promise me that, will you?" He hurried to my bedside and kissed me tenderly. "I'm glad to see you."

"Alive, you mean. I'm sorry, Jack. But I had to find Chelsea."

"I know, I understand, but you worry me."

"I worry myself sometimes, but I can't help it. I'm glad you're back. Is your case wrapped up?"

"Essentially, yes, it's up to the prosecutors now. Unfortunately, breaking up one ring won't be the end of it."

"No, of course not. You know, when you go off on a case I worry about you, too."

"It's my job, it's what I'm trained to do. But Meg, if anything happened to you, I couldn't—" His voice trailed off. He sat on the edge of the bed holding my hand, his pain evident. "I lost someone I cared for very much. I can't lose you. How do I keep you safe?"

Don't go away, don't leave me. The words were already forming on my lips, but it wasn't the right answer. "Trust me, Jack. I'll trust you. We're who we are and we'll always have secrets we don't share. It's too late to change that. But trust in each other will help keep us safe."

Two days later, we held a small memorial gathering for Elaine, with Doug rounding up some of her old colleagues to attend. Donna and I put together food and drinks for everyone, and Doug cut together a reel of some of Elaine's stunt work. Dirck, of course, was present, but subdued. He wasn't asked to offer remembrances.

Whatever transpired between Dirck and his daughter was private, although the two appeared to be on cordial terms. After the memorial, they hugged farewell on Donna's doorstep before Chelsea climbed into Jeremy's Mustang and waved goodbye. Any doubts I'd had about Jeremy's suitability as a boyfriend vanished when I saw how lovingly he cared for her.

The following morning, we took Dirck to the airport in the Olds 98. While waiting for him to finish packing up, Doug sat in the front passenger seat, running his hand across the dashboard. It was a gentle touch, a caress Edie would have cherished. I think she'd also appreciate that I'd laundered the floor mats and gave the interior a good dusting, just as she would have done.

I told Doug and Donna that I could haul Dirck to the airport myself, but they insisted on accompanying me—perhaps all of us indulging in the perverse pleasure of knowing that Dirck was finally on his way home to New York and didn't want to leave.

For one thing, Pru announced she has another bun in the oven. As much as he adores little Priscilla, the idea of having another child fills Dirck with panic. But more importantly, his newly discovered adult daughter and former student decided she no longer needed him as an acting coach. He had not taken the rejection well.

On the way to the airport, in the back seat with Donna, he said, "It's like a King Lear thing, you know? 'How sharper than a serpent's tooth it is to have a thankless child.' I mean, after all I did for her!"

"It's not as though you raised Chelsea," Donna reminded him. "She didn't really owe you anything."

"I gave her free acting classes! I encouraged her. She probably wouldn't have gotten the role of Jinx without me. It's not as though I didn't have the inside track. Nobody knew that role like I did."

"Ahem," I said, as a gentle reminder.

"You know what I mean, Meg. I was there the whole time, observing everything you did. Besides, when she came to study with me she knew I was her father and never came clean about it. That I can't forgive!"

We rode in silence, letting the recriminations fester inside Dirck without comment. His rancor had been building since Ed Ackerman informed him he no longer had a job on the series.

"And another thing," Dirck said. "Don't take this the wrong way, Meg, but I'd hate to think you had anything to do with getting me dumped. Just because you got yourself a plum role out of this is no reason to shut me out."

"Whoa," Doug said, turning in his seat to look at Dirck. "Don't blame Meg. It was Ed Ackerman's decision. The whole show's been revamped. After news broke about how Meg tracked down Joe Shaw and rescued Chelsea, the network demanded that she join the cast. It's promotion you can't buy. Jimmy Kimmel, Jimmy Fallon, Ellen DeGeneres—even Jon Stewart jumped on board. Who the hell would turn their back on that kind of publicity?"

"I was part of all that, too, you know, and paid a price. My shoulder will never be the same. Story of my life," Dirck muttered.

I pulled up at the curb in front of the departure terminal and popped the trunk.

"You've got the lunch I packed?" Donna asked. "I made smoked salmon sandwiches on the whole-grain bread you like."

"Got it," Dirck said, patting the outside pocket of his carry-on bag. "Thanks a lot, Donna. It makes flying coach tolerable. I'm going to miss your cooking." He leaned over and gave her a hug. "Maybe one day I'll bring the family out so you can meet them."

"You do that," Donna said, less heartily than is her customary nature.

Doug and I got out of the car to help Dirck with his bags.

I gave him a hug, then reached into my pocket for a small blue velvet box. One of the few mementos I had left from our marriage was a locket Dirck's mother wore until the day she died. She bequeathed the heart-shaped pendant to me. Dirck was her only child and I'd always meant to give him the gold case that contained his baby photo and strands of silky hair.

I pressed the box into his hand. "For Pru," I whispered.

Dirck glanced at the familiar velvet box, smiled and gave me a kiss on the cheek. "Thanks, Meg. No hard feelings, okay? If you and Chelsea fly in to do *The Today Show* next week, let's get together."

"Absolutely. I'd like nothing better."

Dirck walked toward the terminal, his gait reminiscent of John Wayne.

"Liar," Doug said, under his breath.

"Hey, it's a long flight home. Let him leave with a smile on his face."

At the revolving doors, Dirck turned to wave one last time. We waved back.

Now, nearly a week after Dirck's departure, Chelsea and I stand in the pool house, pumped up and ready for our debut. We've been practicing together daily, feeling more and more like the team we've become.

The irony is certainly not lost on me that the two of us will be costarring in the newly-newly retitled series, *Jinxed*, as a mother-and-daughter detective team. After hectic negotiations, a new pilot script has been approved and we start filming in ten days. Needless to say, hat tricks figure prominently.

I peep out through the drapes drawn across the French doors, concealing us from the partygoers. Donna has indeed served up "Hollywood on a Plate," dispensing top hats as party favors to every guest. Ed Ackerman has sprung big time for a gala press party, sparing no expense for this night under the stars. Potted palms line the pool, and a Disneyland of twinkling lights illuminates the trees and walkway leading up to the patio, where a platform draped in rhinestone-studded black velvet has been erected.

I stand back, catching an unexpected glimpse of myself mirrored in the darkened window, not displeased by what I see reflected. I'm wearing a fitted swallowtail jacket that once belonged to Marlene Dietrich, a perfect stand-in for the iconic jacket I once wore as Jinx. Culled from Donna's costume archive, the only thing that betrays its vintage is the smell of cedar from the closet and a lingering whiff of Dietrich's Jean Patou.

My eyes travel to Chelsea standing next to me, wearing a cropped tuxedo jacket from Donna's collection, hers once worn by Judy Garland in concert. Our outfits don't match, and that's the point. We're mother and daughter, not twins. Besides, Chelsea is wearing shorts and I'm wearing leggings with my ensemble. I don't do shorts. Period.

Dougie pokes his head around the door. "You girls ready?"

"Now or never," I say.

Chelsea gives me a sly look. "You think you can handle this?"

I wink. "Eat my dust, kid."

Dougie swings the door wide as a loud thump of music blares. A follow spot picks up the two of us as we strut up the steps to the platform. We turn our backs to the audience, strike a pose and raise our arms—but only I have a black disk in my hand. I snap the brim, flip the top hat into the air as I turn around and catch it on my head, the spotlight full on my face. The applause is thunderous!

I toss the hat in the air again and twirl in a blaze of hot white light, but before I can catch the hat, Chelsea steps in and flips it onto her head. The gasp from the audience turns into laughter and applause.

Chelsea does some break-dance moves, flicking the hat from hand to hand, then twirls, tosses the hat, and I catch it on my shoulder. I let it roll down my arm to my fingertips, then flip it in the air, catch it on my head and wink.

Doing a cocky walk, I sling the hat in the air, twirl twice and prepare to catch the hat as I've done before. Suddenly Chelsea bumps my hip and catches the hat on her head. Again the audience roars at the playful rivalry. I extend my hand with a flourish to acknowledge her feat. Chelsea grins triumphantly and twirls away, her turn to showboat. I dance on the fringe of her limelight, waiting to step back in.

In a swift move of my own, I slide behind her, pluck the hat from her head and toss it high. She skirts around me, her long arm slicing up to take back the hat. She falters and the hat skitters out of her fingers, tumbling down. I kick my leg up, catching the hat on the tip of my shoe, then kick again and trap the rim between the palms of my hands.

More laughter as Chelsea dips her head under the hat, reclaiming it as she swings away. The music hits a crescendo of drum rolls, begging for a grand finale. She steps back, slings the hat high, twirls, catches it in her fingertips and holds it aloft for a beat.

She gives me another sly look, tosses the hat high, does a back flip and catches it on her head—the signature Jinx move I am way past doing. I bow and blow her a kiss, signaling the passing of the torch.

She tosses the hat high and I dive under it, catching it, then casting it in a double-spin throw with the hat landing on my head, cocked over my right brow. We shoot our arms in the air, striking a pose, and then both bow, drinking in the applause.

I'm winded but exhilarated. I look out on the crowd, spotting Lucille, the bus driver, standing front and center, clapping her hands and whistling. Beside her is Detective Christine Yarrow. I salute Corky and wave to his parents, who are all standing just to the left of the stage with many of the cast and crew of *Jinxed*.

Waiters are busily passing out champagne and top hats to everyone as the follow spot beams across the crowd. Chelsea and I take one last bow, wave to the crowd and hurry down the steps.

I give Chelsea a hug. "You know, you're not bad. You could do this for a living. Think about it."

She laughs. "I already heard we were taking this baby on the road!"

I turn and give Ed Ackerman a hug, then look around for Jack.

He's easy to spot, standing off by himself near the orchid pavilion, smiling and watching me. The milling crowd passes between us, yet I know he's there, waiting for me. I savor the moment as we regard one another across the distance, a glimpse at a time, trusting we'll always be there for each other.

Not too easily and not too fast—there's no need to rush when it's for keeps. For now, I'm still bunking at Donna's house, but with Dougie spending more time there I've begun to feel extraneous. I can only imagine how her dolls feel. My bathrobe now occupies a hook in Jack's townhouse, but I haven't yet claimed any drawer space. A part of me would feel more comfortable in an interim place I can call my own. At least now I'm earning enough to afford it. If I'm being overly cautious, it's not because I'm in doubt about Jack. I'm still in recovery mode, finding my way back to self-sufficiency.

I cock my top hat over my eye and take two flutes of champagne from a passing waiter before sauntering over. I look into Jack's warm brown eyes, lit with specks of amber, feeling the full flush of pheromones doing their job. I hand him a glass of champagne.

"Hey, mister, you look like a guy who could use some company."

"That, and a whole lot more." He taps his glass to mine. "You look pretty good up there, baby. Even better up close."

"All in a day's work." I raise my glass. "To Jinx."

"To Jinx, and may she keep you out of trouble."

"You think so?" I sip champagne and regard Jack, whose expression has turned entirely too serious. "I thought it was the Jinx thing that generally leads me astray," I tease.

"With any luck, she'll keep you too busy for extracurricular sleuthing while I'm away."

It's my turn to look dismayed. "What? Where? You're not going for long, I hope."

"A while, at least, but I can't turn the case down. I've been assigned as the FBI liaison on an international matter. I leave for Paris on Friday."

"Paris? I don't believe it!" I laugh. "Ed Ackerman just asked me to make sure my passport's in order. We're supposed to film a two-part episode in London next month. Looks like it's either croissants or High Tea for us." I lean in and give Jack a kiss. "Take your pick, sweetheart."

"Both!" He puts an arm around me. "It's great news, and a relief."

"I know, especially since I've got an old friend in London who's in a terrible jam and needs me to help her out."

"What? You're serious?"

"Could be." I grin. "You never know."

"That's what I'm afraid of." He wraps both arms around me, pulling me close for a long, lingering kiss that could go on forever.

To invite Kathryn to speak with your book club, e-mail cumberlandpressbooks@gmail.com.

To be notified when Kathryn's books are available for preorder and/or sale, follow her at:

Amazon
https://amazon.com/author/kathrynleighscott.com

BookBub
https://www.bookbub.com/profile/kathryn-leigh-scott

Goodreads
https://www.goodreads.com/KathrynLeighScott

Facebook
https://www.facebook.com/kathrynleighscottauthor

Twitter
https://twitter.com/kathleighscott

Acknowledgments

Deepest appreciation to Cynthia Manson for her wisdom and unflagging support, and to Caitlin Alexander for her encouragement and masterful editorial guidance. These two remarkable women made this book happen—thank you, my friends!

Many thanks to friends and colleagues who offered encouragement with "first reads" and assisted with their professional expertise: Tim Anderson, Cheryl Carrington, Darlene Chan, David Chaparro, Suzanne Childs, Jo-an Jenkins Evans, Nicholas Evans, Bridget Hedison, Harry Hennig, JD Horn, Sunnie Choi Hui, Michelle Kletti, Ben Martin, Robert Masello, Leesa Mayer, Patrick McCray, Laurin Sydney, Heide Wilsher Wickes, Linda Yellin and darling Ansel Faraj, who exposed me to new technology in filmmaking. Mitch, thank you so very much for showing me around Jean Harlow's "white house."

About the Author

Author/actress Kathryn Leigh Scott grew up in Robbinsdale, Minnesota, and now lives in Beverly Hills and New York City. She continues to work as an actress and is writing her next novel.

Please visit her website at kathrynleighscott.com.